MADN

Madame Ian's Freakshow

Book 2

Marina Simcoe

To Maria
Happy Reading!

Marina
Simcoe
♡

To my Baker.
You are my light.

Madness of the Moon

Marina Simcoe

Marina.Simcoe@Yahoo.com

Facebook/Marina Simcoe Author

This book is a work of fiction. Names, characters, places and incidents are a product of the author's imagination. Locales and public names are used for atmospheric purposes. Any resemblance to actual people, living or dead, or to businesses, companies, events, institutions or locales is completely coincidental.

First Edition

Spelling: English (American)

Editing and Proofreading by Cissell Ink

Madness of the Moon is a Contemporary Fantasy Romance. It contains graphic descriptions of intimacy and some violence. Intended for mature readers.

Chapter 1

STELLA

Lero! The impact of recognition came strong and sudden. It hit me like a physical blow in the gut, making me stagger in my high heels.

The man I hadn't seen in fourteen years closed the door of the limo that had brought him to the private dock of the floatplane charter company in Miami. Tall, dark-haired, and even more handsome than I remembered, he headed my way with long, confident strides.

The wild pounding of my heart drowned out the noise of the busy waterfront. My mind spinning, I felt momentarily disoriented. For a few brief moments, I was a fourteen-year-old girl again, lying on the pavement in front of Lero's townhouse, my knee bleeding profusely—the memory so distant, it had largely become a dream over the years.

Until now...

The man of my dreams suddenly barged back into my reality.

Was it really him?

How could it be?

"Are you from the Javier Moreno Agency?" he asked, offering me his hand in greeting.

I took it mechanically. The warmth of his hand pulsed through my veins with the contact.

Dressed in a dark, well-tailored suit, the jacket undone on this sultry August morning, no tie, the top button of his crisp white shirt open, he was a flesh-and-blood version of the vision from my past.

"*Mademoiselle?*" he prompted, tilting his head to the side, a slight concern showing up in his steel-gray eyes.

I blinked, forcing myself to snap out of the stupor.

I was no longer fourteen—I was twice as old—and I had a job to do. By a stroke of fate, he might be the man of my dreams suddenly materializing in front of me, but he was also a client.

I cleared my throat and straightened my back.

"*Oui, je suis avec* Javier Moreno Realty," I said in French. "*Je m'appelle Stella Alarie. Bonjour, Monsieur...*" I feverishly rummaged through my brain for the name Javier had emailed me earlier that morning when he'd asked me to show the island to the potential buyer.

Lero released my hand.

"...*Monsieur Sauveterre.*" I exhaled in relief, finally remembering the name.

The never-forgotten scent reached my nostrils with the breeze from the ocean. Lero's face might've faded in my memory with time, but not his scent—the rich earthy note of moss and expensive wood, with the calming touch of lavender, and just a hint of sweetness.

I could never quite place his scent. If it was a cologne, I had no idea which one it was, and I'd never smelled anything like it either before or after our brief encounter long ago. For me, it had always remained *Lero's scent*. Even if I'd had doubts about who the man standing in front of me was, I could never mistake his scent for anyone else's.

He took a step closer. There was not a hint of recognition in his calm, gray eyes.

I shuffled back, the high heel of my beige sandal nearly catching in the gap between the boards of the dock. His sudden appearance shocked me. His presence proved overwhelming, threatening to take over my senses as I fought to regain control.

"*Enchanté...*" I started, struggling to collect my thoughts.

"If it's the same to you," he said, politely but somewhat detached. "I'm more than happy to speak English."

Dammit.

I must've butchered the grammar or pronunciation in some horrid way. It'd been a while since I'd spoken French. Though, my ability to speak it was one of the reasons I was here this morning. Javier had said the client was from France. Even out of practice, I was confident I could deliver a convincing sales pitch in French if needed. I just didn't expect Javier's client to be...Lero.

"I understand Javier is not joining us this morning?" Lero enquired in English. His own pronunciation was impeccable, the soft purr of his accent smooth like honey.

"No, he isn't." I shook my head. "He had a family emergency but sends his sincere apologies."

That was why I ended up being the one to show one of our agency's most valuable pieces of real estate to *Monsieur Sauveterre*, Javier's newest VIP client. Usually, Javier worked with his top clients himself. He'd wine and dine them, then show them as many exquisite properties as they could handle. Nine times out of ten, he closed the sale, no matter the asking price. The odd time when he didn't, he'd at least charmed the clients into using his agency for a future purchase.

Today, I had to do all the "charming" for him. Except that it was *me* who had fallen under a spell, standing there awkwardly and gawking at the client.

"Shall we, *Mademoiselle* Alarie?" Lero took charge, gesturing at the six-seat floatplane waiting for us by the dock.

"Right, of course," I mumbled, heading to the seaplane. "We're ready, Jose." I nodded to the pilot standing by.

Jose opened the door for us, and Lero promptly grabbed my elbow, helping me climb in. I doubted I could've done it without his help. As per the company's dress code, my clothes were on the dressier side of the business casual—ivory pencil skirt, elegant powder-blue blouse, and high-heeled sandals—not the most practical attire for climbing into a floatplane or visiting an island in the Bahamas with several white-sand beaches as the main selling points.

Thankfully, I'd pulled my hair into a high bun. Otherwise, my thick, auburn mane would be like a wool blanket on my shoulders in the summer heat.

The two seats behind the pilot's and the front passenger's were turned backward, so I promptly took the one in the very last row, as traveling backward would likely make me motion sick.

Instead of sitting next to me, Lero took a seat opposite of mine, facing me.

I was going to spend the next hour in the small cabin of the Cessna 206, face to face with the man I'd thought would forever remain only in my memories.

⟶◉⟵

FOURTEEN YEARS AGO.

My aunt's old bike brought me a new level of freedom in Paris. Dad never gave me any spending money when sending me to live with my Aunt Beatrice each summer, not even for public transit.

"That bitch is rolling in money," he'd say. "Trust me, she can afford to buy you anything you want."

Maybe Aunt Beatrice _could_ afford to buy me things, but she rarely did. Even when giving me a couple of euros for the metro, she'd never failed to mention that the best lesson to learn in life was that of the value of money.

My father and his sister had gotten equal shares of an inheritance when my grandfather passed away. Dad had gambled his share away quickly, whereas my aunt did well with hers—well enough to open the door to high society, where she met her late husband.

"A man of means," she referred to my late uncle in my presence.

"A filthy-rich, old bastard," my father called him.

I never got to meet my uncle. He was more than twice my aunt's age when she met him, and he died years before my annual visits to Paris started. However, I knew he'd left all his money to Aunt Beatrice, making her one of the richest women in Europe.

She moved to France when I was in grade school. She called the country "the land of our ancestors" because that was where my dad's family moved to New York from in the early twentieth century.

As I got older, I learned my father hoped to get to my aunt's money through me. However, when he'd first arranged for me to stay with her in the summer, I believed it was simply to improve my skills in French.

My skills did improve, though I hardly had anyone to speak with while in Paris. There were no kids my age on the street of luxury townhomes where my aunt lived. And even if any children would've wanted to hang out with me, my aunt would've never allowed it.

Aunt Beatrice kept a strict curfew for me and insisted on knowing my whereabouts at all times.

Finding the old bike in my aunt's cluttered attic made my life so much more exciting. Of course, I still had to tell her where I went and when I'd be back—and God help me if I returned even a minute late—but once out of the house, I could pretty much do whatever I wanted. There was no way for Aunt Beatrice to check on me.

I went anywhere the roads and bike paths would take me, exploring as much of the city as was possible with limited freedom and almost no money.

That evening I was running late, speeding along my aunt's street. If I didn't return precisely on time, I'd be grounded the next day, which meant sitting in my aunt's stuffy living room, listening to the news channel that she perpetually had on, and trying not to lose my mind from her complaints about how the world was ending.

A shiny sports car pulled out in front of me, cutting me off. The driver was speeding, as was I. Neither of us stopped in time. I yanked the handlebars to the side, but it was too late. The collision with the car sent me sliding across the pavement, my right leg and elbow taking the brunt of it.

"Mademoiselle!" A strong male voice exclaimed from a distance. Then, the pleasant scent of something that could be a male cologne reached me as I lay on the cobblestone sidewalk.

Someone touched my shoulder.

"I'm okay," I whimpered. The pain of the injuries hadn't fully hit me yet, but tears of fear and self-pity were already burning my eyes.

"Are you American?" the same voice enquired in slightly accented English. "Where are your parents? Don't move yet," he warned, pressing a little harder on my shoulder. "Where does it hurt?"

"My knee..." The burning pain spread along my skin all the way down my leg, now. "My elbow too, but not as much as my knee."

"Nothing else? How about your head? Your back? Chest?"

"No." I shook my head, partially to demonstrate that it was okay, then made another attempt to sit up.

The man—a very handsome man I'd never seen before—was crouching by my side. His hand under my arm, he helped me into a sitting position.

I sucked in air through my teeth, bending my leg to take a better look at my wound. The skin on my right leg was shredded from my knee halfway down my shin. Angry red road rash surrounded the bloody mess in the middle.

"Let me, please." The man produced a crisp white handkerchief from his breast pocket.

Only now, I noticed he was dressed in an elegant evening tuxedo. Clean-shaven, his short, dark hair styled to perfection, the man appeared to be on his way to some formal event.

He pressed his pristine handkerchief below my wound, soaking the blood that trickled down my leg into the starched material.

It didn't hurt any more than before, but I drew in another deep breath, scared he'd touch too close to the broken skin. Tears rolled out of my eyes. Suddenly, I felt so much younger than my fourteen years.

"Ouch," I whimpered when he skimmed over the wound, soaking more blood with the ruined piece of cloth.

"Hurts?" He met my gaze.

Through the cloudy film of my tears, I saw the concern in his eyes, soft gray under the streetlights.

"I need a band-aid," I sobbed in a small voice as my lips quivered.

Sliding his hand under my calf, he leaned over my leg and suddenly dragged his tongue along the entire length of my wound.

I gasped, staring at him in shock.

He licked me!

Who did that? Not grown men, as far as I knew. It couldn't be right, though I couldn't exactly explain why it would be wrong, either.

"Lero! What's going on?" a female voice shrilled in English with an American accent. It was followed by the sound of a car door slamming shut.

A tall, slim brunette in a silver evening gown trotted our way from the sports car that had knocked me off my bike, her heels beating a staccato rhythm on the pavement.

"Lero? Are you ready to go?" She stopped abruptly, as if just noticing me. "Did she ram into my car? It'd better not have left a scratch."

Not paying her much attention, Lero dabbed at the corners of his mouth with a clean corner of his handkerchief, wiping a faint smear of my blood off his face as if he'd just had a fine dessert.

"Please forgive my friend's lack of skills behind the wheel, Mademoiselle," he said to me. "She insists on driving when she obviously shouldn't."

"Is she okay?" The brunette stood over us, her hands on her hips.

"She will be," Lero assured her, then turned back to me. "Hold this." He pressed his handkerchief to my knee, and I mechanically held it there as he lifted my bike then walked it over to the entrance of the closest townhouse.

"I'll keep your bike in my house for the night, but I promise to have it delivered first thing tomorrow morning," he assured me upon his return. "Where are you staying in the city?"

"Um, with my aunt, just down this street." I waved along the narrow road lit by the cast-iron lamp posts with lanterns.

"Allow me to help you to the car." He reached for me.

Instead of helping me up as I'd expected he would, he lifted me in his arms. I gasped, grabbing onto his shoulders.

"Shh. I've got you." His voice sounded soothing and confident, making me trust him completely.

He easily carried me to the brunette's sports car.

"We're not taking her anywhere." She hurried after us.

"That's the least we can do." Ignoring her protests, he opened the passenger's door and effortlessly slid me into the cushy, soft-leather seat.

"We're late as it is." She stomped the stiletto of one of her sandals.

He turned to her.

"Then you should've left earlier and driven more carefully, Mara. Keys?" He stretched a hand to her. "I'll drive."

He took the keys out of her hand, not giving her a chance to protest.

"My father is going to be furious, Lero," she warned as he got into the driver's seat.

"He'll wait." He started the engine.

"Hey! How about me?" Mara took a few steps after the car as we drove off.

"I'll come back for you," he promised through the open window.

"Is she your girlfriend?" I asked, watching the glamorous figure of the brunette grow smaller in the car's side mirror.

"No. Mara is the daughter of my current business partner."

The two weren't necessarily mutually exclusive. However, I liked that the bossy, uncaring woman currently had no place in Lero's heart.

"Where does your aunt live?" he asked.

"Right there. The corner townhouse on the right." I pointed at the large, glowing windows up ahead, suddenly sad about having to leave this intimate place filled with the pleasant smells of expensive leather and Lero's cologne.

Aunt Beatrice's mouth dropped wide open when Lero presented me to her a minute later. She didn't even peep a word of rebuke for my showing up late, quickly sending me upstairs to the guest bedroom where I stayed.

Going to bed that night, I recalled over and over the alluring scent of Lero, the way his gray eyes glimmered softly under the street lanterns, and the new-to-me feelings of thrill and safety when he held me in his arms.

<hr />

NOW

Over the years, the memories and feelings had faded. I'd trained myself to think of them as a product of the impressionable mind of a teenager.

I was a late bloomer. Boys paid little attention to me back then. No man had ever carried me in his arms before Lero. I'd never met anyone as elegant and sophisticated as him. For the fourteen-year-old me, he appeared almost a god. The way he'd treated me—like his equal—raised him even higher in my mind, giving him the starring role in all of my fantasies for years to come.

As he'd promised, he had the bike delivered to my aunt's house the next morning. To my disappointment, Lero didn't bring it over personally, hiring someone to do it for him instead.

I rode my bike past his townhouse every evening after that, hoping to see him again. I'd washed his handkerchief and even mustered the courage to knock on his door once, trying to return it. No one answered the door, and I ended up taking the handkerchief back to New York with me. I still had it tucked in a drawer somewhere in my condo in Miami. Lero's scent had long faded from it, and the silver embroidery of thorn branches surrounding a cursive letter "L" had dulled with time.

Someone else had lived in that townhouse when I'd returned to Paris the next year, and I never saw Lero again.

Until now.

I stared at his shoes as our plane slid along the water's surface before taking off into the air. His brown Italian leather loafers looked expensive, but not nearly as interesting as the man who wore them. Except that I couldn't muster the courage to glance up at him when he was this close.

I needed to get a grip, somehow.

Lero was no longer the man of my teenage dreams. Today, he was the client, the potential buyer of a very expensive property, and I represented Javier's company. This was strictly business, not a trip down memory lane. I had to get my head on straight.

"Would you care for a drink?" I asked over the noise of the plane's engine and opened the cooler placed next to my seat. The charter company stocked it with all kinds of beverages, including alcohol. Some people became more amenable when alcohol was involved, and Javier never failed to have it on hand.

"I can make you a mimosa." I flashed Lero a smile, lifting a small bottle of sparkling wine into his view.

Lero arched an eyebrow at my offer.

"No. Thank you." His deep voice flowed through the cabin like warm butter.

"No *alcohol*? Or no drink at all?"

"Nothing. I'm not thirsty."

"All right."

I stuffed the bottle back into the ice, wishing I could chug it myself. I could definitely use something to calm my nerves around this man. Sadly, as accommodating as Javier was to his clients, he imposed a strict no-drinking-on-the-job rule for his agents. Instead, I got out a fancy glass bottle of water and took a few big gulps.

The small plane had no AC. The two windows the pilot had left open let some fresh air in, but it wasn't enough for me. My face felt hot, and my palms started to sweat.

Lero didn't seem to be affected by the rising late-morning heat as he calmly watched the seascape through the window.

Using the moment, I furtively studied his profile—straight nose, proud chin, the hard edge of his jawline shaded with a five-o'clock shadow despite it being only ten in the morning. I slid my gaze down his throat to the sliver of tanned chest visible in the opening of his shirt.

As if sensing my ogling, he glanced at me. Being caught, I panicked and dropped my stare to his shoes again. The air around us got even hotter. My face must've turned flaming red; it felt as if it had caught on fire.

As much as I'd admired Lero when I was a teenager, my reaction to him now was definitely that of a woman—vivid, more physical, and so much more intense.

It took me a long time to muster the courage to glance up at him. When I finally did, Lero was calmly looking out of the window again. He obviously wasn't sharing my flustered state.

After so many years, Lero had become more of an immaterial idea than an image. Emotions he'd created in me remained strong in my memories even as his features had faded in my mind. When I looked at him now, it all was coming back to me. I remembered the glimmer in his eyes and every line and angle of his face.

Something about his appearance bothered me, now.

Something was...odd.

He looked *exactly* how he did fourteen years ago. The fine lines at the corners of his eyes and mouth had not grown any deeper. The hands he'd rested on his thighs were large and angular—masculine—but not aged. His skin remained just as smooth and youthful as I remembered.

How old was Lero? Right now, he appeared to be around thirty. Which would make him barely sixteen when I first met him.

That was impossible.

He turned abruptly, catching me staring. Again. This time, I was too slow to fake an infatuation with his shoes. He arched a long, dark eyebrow in a silent question, and I scrambled for an answer.

"How old are you, Monsieur Sauveterre?" I blurted out and immediately regretted it.

Smooth, Stella. Very grown-up and professional. I groaned inside.

"Please forgive me." I raised a hand quickly. "It was so rude of me. You really don't need to answer—"

"I'm thirty-one," he replied calmly, then a teasing spark flashed in his eye. "Old enough to own a property in the Bahamas. If that's your concern?"

Maybe he'd sensed my tension after all, and it was his attempt to put me at ease around him. But I couldn't respond.

Thirty-one?

That would mean that when I first met him, he would have been... Seventeen? It couldn't be true. The man who carried me in his arms that evening in Paris was considerably older than a teenager.

On the other hand, would anyone older than a kid lick a stranger's leg?

Maybe I'd missed something about his appearance back then? The fourteen-year-old me could've misjudged his age in Paris. Everyone older than me had appeared grown-up and sophisticated when I was younger. His formal clothes then and his more casual attire now could play a role, too. My memories might not be as clear as I believed. It'd been a long time, after all. Finally, Lero could be lying about his current age, too, making himself younger, for whatever reason.

At this point, I was just confusing myself with my own questions, none of which were relevant to my job. The most important part was that I had an island to sell to this man, and I couldn't mess it up for Javier.

I straightened in my seat and beamed a well-practiced smile at Lero.

"Thirty-one is a perfect age to own one of the most magnificent properties in the Bahamas. Blue Cay, the island that we're flying to right now, comprises two islands connected by a bridge over a shallow strait that fills in with water during the high tide. The combined size of the property is almost two hundred acres."

What I was saying couldn't be new to Lero. He must've already read it in the listing and whatever extra information Javier had been feeding him to entice him to come for a viewing, but I didn't care. Reciting the info I'd memorized from the brochure helped me get my emotions under control. The familiar flow of a sales pitch made me feel calm and collected.

"A natural bird sanctuary, lush vegetation covers the islands and offers hidden coves and picturesque reefs to explore along the shore..."

Lero appeared to be listening with enough interest, only glancing out the window occasionally.

By the time I'd covered the main amenities of the two villas of Blue Cay, the pilot was descending.

Chapter 2

STELLA

Jose docked the floatplane. Lero got out first, while I grabbed a bottle of water from the cooler and stuffed it in my purse, just in case. He'd had no liquids on our way here. The last thing I needed was a dehydrated client passing out during the most important showing of my career to date.

The client was now standing on the float, offering me a hand. He ended up using both hands to help me climb out onto the float; balancing in my high heels made the task harder.

He then easily hopped off the float onto the dock.

"Ready?" He stretched both arms out to me.

I nodded, adjusting my shoulder bag. Reaching over, I grabbed his hands and jumped from the float to the dock. Swaying on my heels, I managed not to fall. He steadied me with his hands on my waist.

"I've got you," he said softly.

A sudden wave of déjà vu rushed over me, as if I were fourteen again, and he held me in his arms for comfort.

Even my leg felt tingly again, just like it had after he'd licked my wound. The following morning, it had fully scabbed over and healed completely with no trace of a scar in just a couple of days. The much smaller scratch on my elbow had hurt for much longer and left a faint scar to this day.

He lingered with his hands on me, and I darted a glance up at his face. His expression pensive, he inhaled through his nose. I held my breath, waiting for a spark of recognition in his eyes. Something. Anything.

There was none.

He exhaled slowly then released me from his hold, stepping back.

What did I expect? Him to remember me? Why would he keep a memory of a random teenage girl his friend had knocked off a bike almost a decade and a half ago? Meeting him might've been one of the defining moments of my adolescence, but it'd obviously been hardly a bleep in his past.

"Well, as you see..." I cleared my throat, focusing on the task at hand. "This part of the reef provides a natural harbor for the dock. You could travel here by boat—"

"No. No boat." He looked around the crescent of coral reef and the system of teak docks where the pilot had moored the floatplane. "This would need to go," Lero muttered under his breath.

Did he want to get rid of the docks? I didn't own an island—or a boat—but even I knew demolishing the docks would be stupid.

"Traveling by boat is the most common mode of transportation between the islands in this area. It's also one of the most efficient ways to order supplies and obtain housekeeping help—"

"No. That wouldn't be necessary," he cut me off firmly.

"All right." I conceded with a polite half-nod.

My job was to point out the benefits not to start arguments. If Lero preferred to rough it with no supplies while cleaning and vacuuming both villas on his own, it was his prerogative as the future owner.

"Would you like to see the amenities?" I asked as he surveyed the docks, the reef, and the shore nearby.

"Amenities?"

"The houses," I clarified, gesturing up the path from the beach. "The main villa and what the previous owners called the manager's cottage?"

"Of course." He nodded. "Please."

As soon as we got off the dock and onto the packed sand path that led to the master's house, it became apparent how absolutely wrong my shoes were for this viewing.

I tottered on my tiptoes for a few paces, trying to prevent all three inches of my heels from sinking into the sand. Quickly, however, my calves began to scream in pain from the strain that manner of walking had put on them. As a result, my speed suffered greatly.

Oh, screw it, I decided. Would taking off these stupid shoes really deter Lero from buying the place?

"Would you give me a moment, please?" I took my strappy sandals off, then quickly ran back and tossed them on the dock. "I hope you prefer we do this viewing in a timely manner over my close adherence to the agency's dress code?" I smiled sweetly, returning to him.

A corner of his mouth twitched up in a barely there smile.

"Absolutely. In fact..." he toed off his loafers and casually shoved them aside. "I'll leave mine here, too. I'd love to walk down to one of the beaches after we're done with the main house."

Walking barefoot side by side with Lero felt more casual, even relaxing, as if we'd come here for a retreat, not business. I made a conscious effort not to look at his feet anymore, though. Staring at his shoes had been safe, but there was something much too intimate about bare feet for me to risk ogling them now.

The moment we walked into the house, I was able to shift my focus from the man at my side to the property I'd come here to sell.

Javier had sent someone to get it ready for today. The space had been freshly cleaned and aired. The glass double-doors in the large living area were open, letting the ocean breeze in and making the white gossamer curtains billow like sails. This must be their only purpose here—to billow dramatically. I couldn't imagine any other use for something so sheer.

A wide tray laden with sliced fruit stood in the middle of the large dining room table, next to a pewter bucket with a bottle of Champagne on ice and a jug of orange juice.

"Would you like a glass of Champagne?" I moved to the table.

Lero had refused a mimosa on the plane, so I didn't offer to make him one now. If he took a glass of Champagne, I would pour one for myself too, I decided—the rules be damned. My heart continued to pound heavily in his presence. I really wished I'd at least added some Baileys to my coffee that morning—anything to calm my nerves.

"No. Thank you." He shook his head.

"How about some fruit?" I gestured at the tray to cover my disappointment at not getting a drink.

"I'm not hungry," he replied somewhat distractedly as I took a strawberry off the fruit platter.

The stone patio outside of the glass doors appeared to catch his attention. He stepped out and inspected the door frame, then the doors, sliding his fingers over the locks and wiggling the handles. By focusing on the mundane things like doors, Lero was clearly missing some of the best features of this place.

I needed to rectify that. Tossing the strawberry into my mouth, I hurried after him.

"The pool here is truly unique." I swept my arm across the stone patio that housed a large infinity pool. "It's heated and flows directly into the master bathroom."

A glass wall to the side reached below the water surface, separating the indoor portion of the pool from the outdoor. One had to dive under it to swim in or out.

For a moment, I allowed my imagination to run wild, envisioning myself swimming in the warm, crystal-clear water of the pool. Along with my new husband, maybe? During our honeymoon that we would somehow spend in this "piece of paradise," as Blue Cay was called in the listing.

Of course, both the husband and the honeymoon were completely imaginary. I had no man in my life, and my bank account would never allow me to own anything even close to a property like this.

"Can I see the bedroom?" Lero's voice snapped me out of my inappropriate daydreaming.

"Of course." I gave him a highly professional smile. "This way, please."

I led him to the carved double-doors off the living area and opened them dramatically as if drawing back curtains before a show.

The marble floor was pleasantly cool under my bare feet when we walked in.

"Most materials for the construction and finishes came either from the States or Europe," I continued in my best professional tone. "The bathroom fixtures are from the United States. The marble is imported from Italy."

"I suppose they were delivered by boat?" he asked, walking around the spacious room. It had a glass door to the patio in addition to the large glass wall in the swimming pool in the bathroom that was visible through the arched doorway.

"I believe so, but I can confirm it with the current owner. Some things could have also been shipped by floatplane, within the weight limit, of course."

He nodded, his expression contemplative.

"If you're considering any upgrades or renovations in the future," I suggested, helpfully, "you might want to keep the docks until the construction is complete."

In my opinion, there was no practical sense whatsoever for demolishing the docks when living on an island. I hoped for an explanation from him, but none came—he didn't owe me one.

"Does the furniture come with the house?" he asked instead, tipping his head at the wrought-iron poster bed topped with a pure-white spread edged with lace.

"Um. Yes." I quickly averted my eyes from the bed, resisting yet another fantasy. Daydreaming on the job was unacceptable, especially since my make-believe husband's appearance dangerously closely resembled Lero's.

He sauntered to another set of double doors that separated a huge walk-in closet from the master bedroom. The closet was enormous, bigger than my entire condo in Miami. White built-in shelving units lined the walls. A long oval island with dresser drawers and a quartz countertop stood in the center.

"This room has no outside wall, has it?" Lero enquired.

I brought up the house plan in my mind. "No. There is a guest bathroom here, and another bedroom over there."

He nodded, crossing his arms over his chest. A slight frown appeared on his face as he slowly walked the perimeter of the room.

"Would you like to see the rest of the house?" I asked.

People never usually paid *that* much attention to a closet, even those with a lot of clothes. There were still so many rooms for him to see in this villa alone, not to mention a whole other house across the bridge on the other side of Blue Cay.

"The listing mentioned that there is a basement?"

"A wine cellar." I nodded, leading the way out of the bedroom and over to the door downstairs. "It's temperature controlled, perfect for storing any wine collection."

I flicked on the light before entering the spacious basement at the bottom of the stairs. My feet sank into the soft hand-woven rug on the floor. The air here felt pleasantly cool against my heated skin. The soft lighting showcased floor-to-ceiling shelves of wine racks made from dark wood. The smell of wood blended with the scent of Lero, who followed closely behind me, so close I could feel the warmth of his body at my left arm.

"No windows," he said softly, looking around the dimly lit space. "Is it fully below the grade then?"

"Yes. The elevation in this part of the island is high enough to allow for that."

"How about the other place? What did you call it? The manager's cottage?"

"There is no basement there."

"That's a pity." He rubbed his chin, seemingly lost in thought for a moment.

Did he need a second wine cellar? How much wine did he need to store? This place was big enough to accommodate a small winery, I believed. But then again, what did I know about the whims of the rich?

"The elevation is lower where the manager's cottage is located," I explained. "Which would increase the risk of moisture accumulating or even a flood in the basement. If you need more space for wine storage—"

"I don't," he said dismissively, heading toward the stairs up to the main floor.

All right, then.

"Would you like to see the other bedrooms?" I hurried after him. "Each has an ocean view and features a small patio with a walkout to the yard or to one of the beaches."

"No. I'm done here." At the top of the stairs, Lero turned right, toward the main entrance of the house. "Let's go to the second one. The manager's cottage."

"Right... But are you sure? There is more to see here. The formal area includes a grand room that boasts cathedral ceilings and a spectacular view..."

"I'll take your word for it." He swiftly walked out the front door to the square stone patio, then jogged down the several wide steps to the path that led toward a beach.

He obviously wasn't interested in seeing the formal areas of the house.

Did people really do that? Who would buy a multi-million-dollar property without seeing all of it first? Especially since he'd already gone through the trouble of getting here?

Or maybe he'd seen enough and was no longer interested in buying it at all? My heart sank in disappointment. Losing Lero as a client would most definitely upset Javier. It wouldn't make me look good, either.

Well, Lero still wanted to see the other house. Maybe not all was lost yet. Rich people had their quirks. My job wasn't to question but to humor them.

Without a word, I followed Lero down the sand path, trying to guess his mood. Overall, he hadn't behaved like a typical buyer.

This was the first time I'd shown an island to someone, but I'd been selling homes for years now. My usual clients stayed inland, though. I used to mostly sell condo units and smaller houses. I'd just recently added some larger suburban homes to my portfolio. People normally viewed the place they considered buying from the perspective of living there. Usually, they looked at a property's potential for them to relax, work, and entertain. Many viewed it as a status symbol as well.

In Lero's case, he appeared to be most interested in door locks, the closet, and the basement—a bizarre combination.

Maybe, if I knew more about his reasons for shopping for an island in the first place, I could present Blue Cay in a better light to him?

Reaching a steeper part of the path, he waited until I caught up with him. He then took my elbow, helping me descend to the beach.

"Are you looking for a full-time residence?" I asked, adding, "Because the owners of high-value properties can obtain a permanent residence permit in the Bahamas. Otherwise, there is a limit on how long foreign nationals can stay in the country."

"Maybe," he replied, his tone non-committal. "I haven't decided yet."

So, he'd first buy an island, then decide? Not that it was any of my business how he spent his money, of course, as long as he bought the damn thing from me.

"The water is receding right now," I observed as we neared the pretty arched bridge over the narrow strait between the two halves of Blue Cay. "When it's completely gone, the two islands become one for a little while each day."

I wondered what it would be like to walk through the sand under the bridge, to see what the water had brought and left behind. What neat things one could find?

"The property is unique..." I started, but let my voice trail off without finishing another sentence from the listing brochure.

The selling pitch words fell flat and inadequate to describe this place accurately. Anyone who had eyes could see for themselves the vivid beauty of turquoise water caressing the yellow-white sand. Anyone could hear the soothing sound of waves rolling softly onto the beach and the calling of birds around the reef.

I inhaled deeply the air rich with sun and ocean spray. Anyone who'd been stuck in a city most of their lives would appreciate the peaceful beauty of the two little islands in the sea, connected by the bridge, like a couple holding hands.

"It's... It just feels wonderful here," I exhaled, turning to Lero. "So quiet. Don't you think?"

"Hhm. Quiet," he echoed as we crossed the bridge. "Can we walk along the beach here?"

The wide strip of soft sand curved around the west island on the north side. At the far end of it, a set of stone steps led from the beach up to the manager's cottage in the distance.

"Of course," I agreed.

Lero stepped off the path. Once on the sand, he rolled his pants up to his knees, then waded into the water.

I expected him to keep moving along the shore toward the house, but he just stood there, facing the sea. The breeze teased his short, dark hair. It wasn't entirely black, I noticed—the sun brought out some dark copper highlights. There was something wistful in his expression as he gazed out to the horizon.

I mentally went through what I'd memorized about the caves and the reefs of Blue Cay.

"Do you like swimming?" I asked. "There're some amazing places for snorkeling around here."

He closed his eyes, his wide chest rising with a long breath. It would appear he was simply enjoying the warmth of sunshine on his face, but the deep crease between his long, black eyebrows betrayed his intense concentration.

"No. I don't swim," he replied, without opening his eyes.

"You can't?" I came a little closer, allowing the gentle waves to lick my feet. The reef kept Blue Cay protected from larger swells on this side.

"I *can* swim. I just don't do it."

"You...don't like it?" I prodded, spurred purely by my undying curiosity about him.

Why spend so much money on a piece of land surrounded by water if he didn't even like swimming? He obviously had no plans to do any boating in the future either, since he was ready to rip the docks out.

The more time I spent with this man, the less I understood him.

"You don't like water?"

"Not particularly."

"Then why are you considering buying an island?" I couldn't hold the question back anymore.

He released a breath, turning my way. "Because I should have done it a long time ago. I never even realized the need for it until about two months ago when...someone I cared about was gone."

"Gone?" I gasped, forgetting all about being professional. Compassion swelled thick in my heart. "I'm so sorry, Lero..."

He flinched. His dark eyebrows moved closer to each other, deepening his frown.

"Lero? How do you know this name, Mademoiselle Alarie?" he asked slowly, trapping me in his inquisitive stare.

The file from Javier stated only *L. Sauveterre* as the client's name, I realized belatedly. I'd been calling him Lero in my mind only because that was what Mara, the woman in Paris, had called him.

Unsure how to reply, I kept quiet.

He waded through the water, closing the distance between us. Grabbing my upper arms, he leaned closer, inhaling the air around me.

"We've met before, haven't we?" His voice came out raspy. Sunlight flicked through his eyes with a flash of red.

I kept watching his face for the spark of recognition. I didn't even know why it was so important to me that he'd remember, but it was. I held my breath, feeling the warmth of his skin on mine. And I waited for him to remember...

He didn't.

"When?" he demanded from me, instead. "How?"

"A long time ago," I said softly.

To be fair, it *had* been a very long time ago, too long for anyone to remember the brief meaningless encounter we'd had. Even the fact that I remembered it was odd.

"In Paris. I was fourteen years old. I fell off my bike in front of your house, you drove me home."

He let out a long breath, his posture relaxed as if a weight dropped from his shoulders. "Of course."

The recognition I'd been waiting for spread across his face, softening his sharp features.

"The girl with a scraped knee. I remember the flavor."

"You licked my leg."

He winced, the expression in his eyes turning guarded. "Disgusting, isn't it?"

Oddly, I'd never felt disgusted or appalled by that, only confused and...a little intrigued. What would compel a man to do something like that?

"Why did you do it?"

His gaze lingered on my face for another moment, his expression softening even further in the sunshine. He slid his hands down my arms to cup my elbows.

"How is your wound?" he asked, instead of answering my question.

"The wound? Oh, it's gone. Completely." I lifted the hem of my skirt to display the perfectly healed skin on my knee. "It didn't even leave a scar. Do you know why?" I glanced up at him.

He stared at my leg, then slowly slid his gaze up my body. His attention was almost tangible, like a glide of a hand, learning and exploring on its way.

For the first time ever, I felt like Lero really *saw* me. All of me. My clothes. My body. My gender. That he might finally sense the pull between us, too.

Awareness crackled between us, reaching deep under my skin.

His chest heaved. His gray eyes darkened to the color of the cloudy sky. He bent his head down, bringing his face so close to mine, my breath hitched. His lips parted, and for one heart-stopping moment, I believed he would kiss me.

I wished for the kiss to happen so badly, I ached inside from anticipation.

A spark of red flashed through his eyes again—sudden and unexplained. His hands flexed on my arms, fingers digging into my skin. Inhaling deeply, as if struggling for oxygen, he let go of me and stepped back.

"Would you mind if I smoke?" he asked in a low, raspy voice.

Reeling from what could've happened and crushed that it hadn't, I couldn't summon either words or gestures to answer.

Not waiting for my reply, he reached into the inner pocket of his jacket and produced a long, black cigarette. His fingers trembled slightly as he lit it then took a long, greedy drag.

Tilting his head back, he exhaled slowly. Tension seemed to drain from his body along with the coils of fragrant, silvery smoke. It shimmered in the sunlight, dissipating into the breeze. A tendril of it reached my nostrils, filling them with the fragrance I'd long thought of as "Lero's scent."

Apparently, it wasn't just the cologne he used that made him smell so good, but also the cigarettes he smoked. What were they? I didn't smell a hint of tobacco in the smoke.

"I'm glad to see you've healed well," he said in a much smoother voice. His expression of detached politeness snapped back in place with another drag of his cigarette.

By the calming effect it had on Lero and by the desperation with which he smoked, I wondered if the cigarettes contained some kind of drug—a substance I'd certainly never smelled anywhere but on him.

"Shall we continue, Mademoiselle Alarie?" He offered me his hand to help me up the path to the manager's cottage.

I inhaled a cleansing breath and straightened my spine.

"Certainly, Monsieur Sauveterre." I matched his tone. Calm, detached, professional—it left no doubt what we were to each other, what we ever could be, an agent and a client.

⎯⎯⎯◉⎯⎯⎯

"THANK YOU, MADEMOISELLE Alarie. We'll be in touch." Lero shook my hand when we got back to the charter company's dock in Miami.

I kept my hand in his fingers longer than was necessary. Catching myself trying to memorize the sensation of his touch, I quickly let go. With a courteous nod, he headed off to the limo that had come to pick him up.

Would we really "be in touch?"

Even if Lero went ahead with the purchase, he'd deal with Javier directly from now on. I'd just filled in for today because of my boss's family emergency. Chances were, I would never see Lero again.

I watched him get into the vehicle and drive away, out of my life. As quickly as he'd appeared, he was gone.

What did I expect? A warm, friendly smile? A goodbye hug?

Would a smile or even a hug have made this odd feeling of abandonment easier to bear? Why did I feel so empty inside, watching him go? What was there for me to miss?

Lero had never really been a part of my life for me to miss him when he left.

All he'd ever given me was a few minutes of kindness when I was fourteen. Back then, I'd had an aunt who thrived on controlling me, a father who saw me as little more than the means to restoring his wealth, and a mother who had dedicated her life to her husband, caring little about me, her only child. I needed human kindness more than the air I breathed while growing up, yet I got nothing from the adults around me.

The neglect of my family might've amplified the effect Lero's one act of kindness had on me as a teenager, resulting in years of dreaming about him after.

Today hadn't been about kindness, though. His sudden reappearance in my life brought more harm than good, now that I was a grown woman. Seeing him again had added new, vibrant layers to the image of Lero I held in my mind. I worried it would now take even longer to wear off and fade away. How was I supposed to fight them now, when the memories of him were so new and fresh?

And so titillating?

"This time, you'd better make sure you're gone for good, Lero," I thought bitterly.

Chapter 3

STELLA

A month and two days later.

I didn't have an island, but I did own a piece of property—my very own condo the size of a studio apartment. It wasn't on an island either, not even on one of the Venetian Islands in Miami, but it was "in the epicenter of downtown," according to its real estate listing.

Returning to it after a long day of showings truly felt like coming home. There was always a sense of pride, too. I loved my place because I'd bought it entirely with the money I'd earned.

My dad used to think my rich aunt was strict with me because she cared about me. I always believed her behavior toward me simply stemmed from her inherent need for control.

Her death proved me right. Aunt Beatrice died childless, with no heirs but my father and me. She willed all her money to a few carefully selected charities, leaving nothing to either of us.

The only benefit for my future came in the job offer made by Javier Moreno, whom I met at my aunt's funeral. His real estate company had been tasked with selling some properties my aunt owned all over the world. Javier gave me my first office job and encouraged me to get my real estate license.

Javier had also been the one to sell me my condo, after giving me a substantial Christmas bonus that year. The property came from the listings of our agency. He'd negotiated a great price for me and helped me arrange for the mortgage with amazing terms.

Javier, a complete stranger, ended up giving me more support and showing more interest in my future than any of the people related to me by blood.

"If you work for me, we're family, Stella," he'd say every time I would attempt to put into words the deep gratitude I felt for everything he'd done for me.

In another, less law-abiding life, I believed Javier could've headed a cartel in Mexico or a *famiglia* on Corsica. He had that air of power and influence around him, rewarding those loyal to him, despising those who'd ever done him wrong.

The comparison of Javier to a mafia boss made me smile as I pulled into the underground garage of my condo building. My home might be the smallest unit in the building, but it came with the full use of all on-site amenities like the swimming pool, the exercise center, and the spa. I also got a great parking spot in the garage.

As it often happened, the last viewing had ended late. Most people went house hunting after their working hours. To accommodate them, I worked late into the night on most days.

It didn't bother me. I had no one waiting for me at home, not even a pet. For now, my job was my priority. Neither was I worried about walking alone late at night. My building was safe, even the underground garage. Spacious and brightly lit, I was never concerned about being in it on my own.

Tonight, however, the uneasy feeling of being watched nagged at me the moment I climbed out of my car. I locked the car and headed to the elevator, faster than usual.

The clipped staccato of my high heels hitting the concrete floor echoed through the deserted garage. But there was another sound—an indistinct shuffling of someone else's footsteps that seemed to come from the row of cars behind me.

I whipped around, scanning the vehicles and the surrounding space, but saw nothing out of ordinary.

Another sound, a low rumbling, rolling in from all sides made my insides freeze. Fear brushed against the skin of my arms, pricking it with goosebumps. I darted my gaze between the rows of parked vehicles and the concrete support columns.

No one was there.

Yet when I started walking again—keys clutched in my sweaty hand—the sound of someone following me came again. I slid the narrow blades of the keys between my trembling fingers, fully intending to fight back if attacked.

A distinct sound of breathing behind me spurred my fear into panic.

I ran.

There was no doubt left, someone was after me. And they were running, too. Their labored breathing came closer and closer. Instead of soles of shoes, their footfalls sounded softer, like paws, with the screeching of claws against the concrete floor.

Too terrified to glance back, I slammed into the closed elevator doors at full speed, frantically hitting its call button, again and again. The doors wouldn't open. The elevator was slowly crawling down from the upper floors somewhere. When it'd finally get here, it might be too late...

The hoarse breathing of my pursuer was now right behind me.

Cornered, I had no choice but to fight.

I swiveled on my heels, lashing out with my hand—the keys clutched in my sweaty fist, their sharp ends sticking out between my fingers.

My breath choked me, lodging in my throat, when I came face to face with my pursuer.

It was no human.

Whoever or whatever it was, the creature must've come straight from a nightmare.

It stood on all fours, its great paws spread wide. Lips drawn back, it bared its white teeth—narrow, long, and sharp like rows of slightly curved spikes or needles. Saliva dripped from its mouth. When it hit the floor, it sizzled, sending tendrils of steam up in the air.

The creature's large, red eyes glowed in the artificial light of the garage—wild and unhinged.

And... Oh, my God... Were those horns? Sprouting, straight and spikey, from the side of its head?

What was this monster?

Unable to tear my eyes away from the hellish creature, I kept hitting the elevator's call button mechanically, like a broken robot.

Would the elevator even help me if it came? Now that the beast was barely a leap away from me?

It jerked my way. I jumped, squeezing out a pitiful, choked sound.

Instead of leaping at me, the beast shoved away from the concrete with its front paws, then rose on its hind ones.

It appeared even bigger now, towering over me, seven or eight feet of flesh and thick black fur.

Frozen in terror, I couldn't scream. I could barely breathe. My knees shook, my legs growing too weak to support my weight. I leaned back against the elevator doors. Did I even want them to open now? Even if I made it inside, the doors would never close fast enough to lock the beast out. Then, I'd risk being trapped in the elevator with this murderous monster from hell...

Tipping sideways, I inched to the right, toward the corner of the wall that enclosed the elevator shaft.

The long things I'd mistaken for horns turned out to be the creature's ears. They twitched, then moved back as the monster flattened them against its skull. Tossing its great head back, it roared. So loud, the deafening sound pressed against my chest. The parked vehicles around us appeared to shake.

How did no one hear this? Why was nobody coming to my rescue?

I staggered one more step to the right. The wall behind me ended abruptly, and I tumbled backwards to the ground. My ass painfully hit the concrete floor around the corner of the enclosed elevator shaft.

The ding of the elevator finally announced its arrival, followed by the swishing sound of the doors opening. Scrambling to my hands and knees, I carefully poked my head around the corner.

Was there any chance at all for me to sneak into the elevator and get out of here? The stairs weren't an option—the monster stood right between me and them.

The creature remained on its hind paws. No longer roaring, it was sniffing the air in deep hurried breaths.

Could it smell me?

I ducked back, taking cover behind the wall instead of trying to get into the elevator in plain sight of the monster. Even if the beast couldn't smell me, my heart pounded so hard, I feared it would hear me.

"Get him! Now!" A male voice shouted out of nowhere.

I glanced out again to find a group of men surrounding the beast. Several of them held a black net stretched between them.

The animal must have escaped from the zoo or a circus. Thankfully, the people got here just in time to capture and return it where it belonged. That explained everything.

I slumped against the wall, relief draining the fear and tension out of my body.

The beast must be a bear, a panther, a large wolf or something just as ordinary. Fear had simply made it look "monstrous" to me.

I didn't know exactly what animals were housed in the Miami Zoo. Neither had I heard of any circus coming to town. But I worked a lot and didn't always keep up with the events in the city.

Sitting with my back to the wall, I remained out of sight, waiting for my breathing to return to normal. This had turned out to be quite a night.

The roar of the animal tore through the garage once again. Sharp and loud, it reverberated under the ceiling, bouncing off the surrounding concrete.

I looked out of my hiding place again, to see whether it was safe to come out.

The men threw the net over the animal, wrapping it around. Red sparks flashed along the net where it touched the fur of the animal. It roared again—the sound filled with agony.

The poor thing was clearly in pain.

I gripped the concrete corner with my fingers.

The net obviously hurt the animal that growled and fought desperately against it. The red streaks of light that flashed along the thin black rope of the net left smoldering scorch marks in his fur.

Whether the net had electric current running through it or had been soaked in some kind of harmful chemical, why did these people have to resort to such cruelty? Why not just use a tranquilizer to subdue the animal?

"Steady, *voukalak*," one of the men gritted through his teeth. "Do what you're told, and you and your sweetheart will live."

Sweetheart? What did he mean by that?

What kind of animal control people were these, anyway? I looked for any lettering or insignia on their black t-shirts and found none. They were incredibly similar in their appearance, I noticed. Tall and well-built, all of them were bald and had identical tattoos covering their necks and right arms. Their behavior was closer to that of a gang than to people who worked with animals.

Dread trickled cold down my back. Whatever these men really were, it no longer felt safe for me to come out at all. They didn't appear to have spotted me, and I decided to remain hidden, furtively watching them while being unseen.

One man came closer to their newly captured trophy, securing the net tighter around the tormented beast. The animal struggled against his bonds, then jerked his head, snapping his jaws at his captor. The red sparks appeared to jump off the net, running up the man's arm tattoo.

"Careful, Dez! Watch out for his teeth," another man warned.

Dez shoved the heel of his heavy boot into the animal's snout.

"His teeth will soon be added to Madame's jewelry collection if he doesn't smarten up," he scoffed.

The elevator doors closed at that moment. Someone from the upper floors must've called the elevator up. I jerked back and out of sight once again.

"The girl?" Dez yelled. "Where did she go?"

My heart sped up again. They knew about me. What on earth could they want with me?

The sound of the elevator going up filled the dead silence that followed Dez's questions.

"That must be her," another man suggested. "She escaped in the elevator."

"How much do you think she saw?" someone else asked.

"It doesn't matter." Dez's voice didn't sound too concerned. "Now that we've got him, we don't need her anymore." The sound of another shove of his boot came, followed by a groan of pain from the creature trapped in the net.

"We don't need her anymore."

Had they come for me, at first? Why? I didn't even know who these people were. What could they possibly want with me?

"What if she tells someone what she saw?" another man asked.

"Who would believe her?" Dez scoffed. "Come on. Take him to the truck before anyone else sees us. *Two* live witnesses would be a problem."

Afraid to move or even to breathe, I sat on the floor long after the sounds of their heavy footsteps quieted in the distance.

Only when someone else, a young couple, came to the elevator much later, did I venture out of my hiding place and into the elevator with them.

Back in the safety of my condo, I locked the door, turned off the lights, and climbed into bed. Then, I watched the reflection of the city lights on my ceiling until uneasy sleep finally claimed me.

Chapter 4

LERO

"So, where is he?" a female voice filtered through the thick fog of pain and rage.

It sounded familiar, but he couldn't place the voice, couldn't focus enough to even comprehend where he was. All-consuming anger dominated his mind. It burned through his brain with the same intensity as the pain that tormented his body.

"Aw, there you are," the woman cooed. "Lero, sweetie, we need to talk."

The familiar scent of *womora* hit him with a puff of air in his face. He drew it into his lungs with hungry, ragged breaths.

Awareness sharpened with each tendril of smoke filling his chest. The rage became manageable, but the pain got more acute. It concentrated around his ankles and wrists where cold metal cuffs held him in place.

His vision cleared as the smoke dissipated, bringing the woman's face in focus. Beautiful, youthful features, framed by vividly red waves of hair. Eyes black as night, with astute, ancient expression in their depths.

She stood in front of him, calm and free, while he was locked in restraints, chained to a concrete wall.

"Ghata..." he exhaled, his tongue and mouth finally able to form words instead of just growls and snarls.

Relief relaxed his muscles, aiding the effects of *womora*. Ghata couldn't be here to harm him. They had a long-standing agreement between them, born from necessity and strengthened by survival.

They both were criminals on the run.

Disgraced and pursued by her former followers, Ghata had helped him escape persecution for crimes he'd committed one grim night during a fit of Moon Madness. She'd shown him how to cross the River of Mists to come from Nerifir to this world.

"Not Ghata, sweetie. It's *Madame Tan*. For now, anyway." She took a long drag from the cigarette clasped in the holder on her finger then released another thick cloud of *womora* smoke in his face.

There were times when his kind had fervently worshipped Ghata. As the werewolves' goddess, she channeled the magic of the Moon. But she had abused her powers, corrupted the magic, and used it for her own gain. Eventually, she'd lost the faith of her followers and triggered their wrath instead.

"Remember how devastated I was, having to run away here?" A fragile note slipped into her voice—intentionally or not, he couldn't tell.

He'd seen Ghata at her most vulnerable when they'd first crossed into this world. Stripped of most of her powers, the little that remained depleted by the crossing, she'd appeared simply as a young woman to him, fragile and unwell.

He had taken care of her and Zeph, the orphaned siren boy who'd come with them from Nerifir. Besides learning how to navigate this new, often confusing world, he'd had two other lives depending on him.

Ghata leaned closer, sliding her finger along his jawline A layer of fur muffled the sensation of her touch. Despite the clearer mind and the ability to speak, he must still physically be a beast, partially at least.

"This world proved to be perfect for my re-birth after all, Lero," she murmured. "Big things are coming, my friend. When I use my old name again, it will be *Goddess* Ghata, as it was meant to be."

Even after Ghata had recovered physically, he had supported her financially. She'd spent their first few years in this world secluded in the small apartment he'd rented for her in Paris. He'd paid the living expenses for the three of them while she'd mourned the loss of her former splendor and the vast armies of followers.

In turn, she had promised him a life-time supply of *womora*. She was able to acquire it from Nerifir though her *bracks*, the werewolves who'd sworn their lives to her and become her slaves in exchange for immortality and the glory of being her priests.

Before the night of the full moon, he needed to smoke the leaves to retain control of his mind for as long as possible. Without *womora*, he wouldn't be able to lead the normal life he'd built for himself and Zeph, whom he'd raised as his own son.

Unlike the fae that Zeph and he were, *bracks* were capable of not only crossing to Nerifir and back, they always returned to the same *when* and *where* Ghata was. Their connection with her pulled them back to her across time and dimensions.

Bracks!

The memory of the black net burning his skin through his fur scorched his body with pain again. The *bracks* were the ones who'd caught him. Dez, Lero's own brother, had been the one leading the attack.

The net was gone. He was in a dimly lit room with no windows, his back pressed against the cold wall. The confinement of restraints on his arms and legs speared through him with panic and rage.

"Release me!" He strained his muscles against the hard metal. The restraints burned his wrists and ankles like acid. They must be made from iron brought from Nerifir.

"Hush, sweetie." Ghata puffed out another cloud of the calming smoke, enveloping them both. "You will be released. Soon. All I need is one small promise from you first."

With another deep breath of *womora*, understanding finally crushed him.

"You did this!"

"This, and so many other things." She laughed, a melodious sound like a trill of silver bells. Deceivingly innocent.

"Why?" he bellowed, indignant and enraged.

Ghata laughed again, not at all intimidated by his anger. She actually looked amused by it.

"Because I missed you." She pouted.

The mask of innocence slipped off her face then. A cold, calculating expression took its place.

"Lero." She leaned in so close the strands of her long red hair tickled his fur-covered chest. The hem of her scarlet silk kimono slicked against his knees. "This world is full of opportunities for creatures like us. Humans are weak and pathetic, but they're so easily influenced. They're starving for miracles and longing for a higher power. Born followers, they're eager to serve. And best of all, they're so easy to corrupt using their own greed and thirst for power. Humans are weak, but you're not human. You're fae. You have the strength and magic of your people. Join me, and we'll conquer this world together."

Dread chilled his spine.

"What are you talking about? What have you done?"

"It's not what I've done but what I'm still going to do that's important, my sweet Lero. Will you help me accomplish everything I've planned?"

As a fae, he could not break a promise given. He knew better than to commit to something as vague as "everything." What Ghata demanded sounded very much like slavery. Her plans, whatever they were, worried him.

"Remember why we came to this world, Ghata. Here, we got a chance to earn our redemption through a simple life of peace and restraint. The point was to blend in with humans, not to corrupt and conquer them."

She huffed a laugh, derisive and harsh this time.

"Blend in!" she scoffed, shoving away from him. "With *humans*? I was never meant to be one of them—the pathetic little creatures, with not a spark of magic in them. Their only strength is in their thoughts, their inner world. They don't even realize how much power there is in their beliefs. But they're lost. Can't you see, Lero? Their very nature is that of slaves, searching for a master. They were meant to be subservient. To me."

Ghata was a goddess. Disgraced and powerless at the moment, she would rise if people started believing her a deity again. Instead of learning humility, she'd used her time in this world to plan a return to what she'd been punished for in Nerifir. Except this time, her targets were the defenseless humans, void of any magic to protect themselves.

"You can't," he breathed out, stunned by her revelations.

"Oh yes, I can. And I will. The only question that remains..." She plucked the cigarette out of the holder, tossed it to the floor, and stepped on it, depriving him of the thought-clearing smoke. "Where do *you* want to be, my dear, when it all happens? By my side, as the master of these creatures, or as one of them, serving me?"

Without the *womora*, the power of the Moon began slowly sucking the calm out of his body and the awareness out of his mind.

He blinked, struggling to concentrate.

What did Ghata want from him?

"A promise, Lero," she reminded him, as if sensing his confusion. "I need you to make the *brack's* vow to me."

Her soft lips brushed his. The way his nose touched hers told him his face had its usual shape at the moment, not that of the beast. Or maybe it was something in between as the sensation of the fur on his back, shoulders and arms hadn't left. He was not a man anymore but not quite a beast either—a true monster, frozen mid-shift, his mind suspended between his two forms.

"Swear your life and your loyalty to me," Ghata whispered, her warm, fragrant breath fanning across the side of his face. Then her lips touched his cheek. The sensation of the caress tingled along his skin, spreading down his chest and belly and rushing blood to his groin. "Call me Madame until I am called Goddess Ghata again. Be one of the masters over the humans. Rule this world with me."

She slid her hand down his abs. His cock strained toward her touch, like a marionette puppet on a string. His mind homed in on the downward glide of her hand, his body shaking with anticipation.

"Fuck!" he growled, thrusting his hips forward.

"Yes, sweetie," she cooed ever so tenderly, tickling the tip of his throbbing cock with her fingers. The tease was torture, he needed so much more. "Give me your promise, and I'll let you fuck me. Only you. All night. No one else."

The decades-long practice of fighting his lust helped him wrestle it under control once again.

"Becoming a *brack* wouldn't make me a master, Ghata, but your slave." He attempted a laugh, but it turned into a groan of agony as she squeezed his erection, digging her long nails into his shaft.

"I can wait," she hissed, leaning in. "There is still plenty of time, which will fly fast for me. For you, however..." She dragged her sharp nails up his belly, leaving hot, swelling welts on his skin. "I'll make sure the time goes *torturously* slow. Dez!" she yelled over her shoulder.

Through the thickening fog of madness and pain, he saw a large dark figure step in from the door.

"Yes, Madame," his older brother replied.

"Oh, how often I've wished you were the eldest son in your family, Lero," Ghata lamented. "I would've loved to have you instead of your brother."

This was said intentionally loud for Dez to hear. And judging by the glare his brother hurled his way, he heard her loud and clear.

"You're in charge, Dez," she said. "Keep him in this location, for now. I don't want him at the menagerie just yet. It's best to keep my VIP acts separate, especially since this one can only really perform during the full moon. He can start working from here. I already have some clients who wish to watch him turn next month. That's what I do, *my dear*." She squeezed Lero's cheek painfully. "I make humans pay to see a 'miracle.' They're starving for the *extraordinary* in their mundane world and are willing to pay a lot of money to see someone as special as you or your little siren, who, by the way, turned out to be a gold mine."

Zeph!

The sudden realization slammed into him. No longer restrained by *womora*, rage filled him to the brim.

"What have you done to him?" he bellowed, yanking against the iron manacles. "Where is Zeph?"

"Shh." She patted the side of his face soothingly. He snapped his teeth at her hand. "Feisty, are we? Down, boy." She jammed her knee into his crotch.

Sharp pain made him double over as far as the chains would allow. With his arms spread and his wrists chained to the wall, his shoulders nearly dislocated from their sockets.

He howled in agony.

"That's better." Ghata's voice flowed, thick with satisfaction.

"You swore to me you didn't know where he was!" he growled, furious rage numbing the physical pain and making the agony of loss and fear for Zeph burn that much stronger. "You *promised* to search for him with me!"

"Oh, Lero." She shook her head, her tone mocking. "Unlike your kind, promises do not bind me. I give and break them as easily as humans do, which is the only thing I have in common with these wretched creatures."

"Unlike you, they have honor!"

She chuckled, retreating to the door.

"Thankfully, not all of them."

Her laugh, melodious and so misleadingly sweet, filled the grim space.

"You know it's all your fault, my sweet. You've been searching for the siren so well, I worried you'd find him soon. So, I had to get you, too. You've failed to protect everyone you've ever cared about, Lero. And now, there is no one to protect *you*."

Her laugh stopped abruptly.

"You and the siren are mine," she said firmly. "And I'm not stopping with just the two of you. Gorgonians, gargoyles, maybe even the sky fae themselves. Why not? I can have them all. Whether you want it or not, all of you will help me become what I was always meant to be. A Goddess."

Chapter 5

LERO

He had only a vague idea how much time had passed. As Ghata had promised, it crawled torturously slow, every moment filled with pain, rage, and lust in any combination of the three.

Sounds and images reached his mind at random, but he lacked the mental power to fully process them. He believed the constant fog hanging over his mind's vision had something to do with the things he ate, but he had no power to refuse food. It was scarce, and he was hungry. So ravenously hungry.

"I've got something for you, *voukalak*."

The voice brought some vivid images to his mind. A memory?

He knew this person. He had spoken to him before, in another world and in what felt like another lifetime.

A narrow, barely visible path in a forest. Crisp air. Tall pine trees, their needles glistening with early morning frost. The ground dusted with snow.

"Come on, Lero!" The older boy laughed. "If you don't improve your aim, the only meat you'll ever eat would be whatever prey you manage to catch in your beast form during the full moon."

The boy ran to the tree trunk, yanking Lero's arrow out of the bark. Lero had aimed for a spotted squirrel, but missed. Again.

"Here you go." Dez, his older brother, handed the arrow back to Lero, then patted his shoulder. "Maybe we'll get lucky and see another one soon. If it's a rabbit or a virleth pig, though, the shot is mine. No offence, but we're not wasting it on anything bigger than a squirrel just so you can practice. We need to eat, too."

Memories of emotions flooded in, along with the images.

The desperate desire to impress his brother. The disappointment that he'd missed. The warm gratitude for Dez's kindness and patience.

There was not a hint of kindness in Dez's voice now. Cold and hard, it felt the same as the circle of metal the *brack* put around his neck.

"Here you go. A necklace for you."

Sharp spikes inside the collar pierced Lero's skin, reaping a hiss of pain from his throat.

"You don't like it, do you?" Dez smirked. "Good. I dipped the spikes in *womora*. It'll keep you from shifting unless Madame allows it. After all, she is the goddess, higher than the Moon."

Fog might be clouding Lero's mind, but it was Dez who was delusional. No one was higher than the Moon. *Womora* only lessened the effects before or after the night of the full moon. Nothing ever stopped his transformation the night the full moon rose in the sky.

"Now, eat this, beast. It has some special seasoning, just for you."

Hunger tore at his insides, depriving him of any sense of caution. He swallowed the pieces of raw meat in seconds. Then, the bitter aftertaste in his mouth brought another series of images to mind.

A puffy yellow mushroom with bright orange dots on its squishy cup. It looked like a toy, fun and whimsical, half-hidden behind the trunk of a tall birch tree where the seven-year-old Lero found it. It felt soft, like a sponge in his hands. The smell of the mushroom reminded him of his mother's warm, freshly baked bread.

He licked the mushroom. Its flavor was pleasant, though a hint of bitterness coated his tongue a second later. He opened his mouth wider, ready to bite off a little.

"Don't!" Dez ran at him from behind, knocking the mushroom out of his hand. "Kibia mushrooms bring on Moon Madness without the full moon. If you eat them, you won't be able to speak, and your bones

will hurt as if you were shifting." He grimaced, watching the discarded mushroom roll into the grass like a squishy ball of rubber. "*It also tastes bitter.*"

Back then, Dez didn't want Lero to get hurt. Now, he was the one doing the hurting.

"The *kibia* mushrooms will urge you to turn, *voukalak*. The *womora* on the collar spikes will prevent you from turning. You'll get stuck mid-shift, no longer a man but not yet a beast. You know that torturous moment between the two forms? You're going to live that moment forever, for as long as I want. Madame makes money on you every full moon. The rest of the time you're mine to do with as I please. When she finishes with you, she's promised I will be the one to end you."

Dez's voice dripped with hatred, deep and unexplained. Nothing that Lero had done in the short years he and Dez knew each other as children could've caused his brother to hate him this much.

It was Ghata.

She'd changed the boys brought to her temple, making them her *bracks*. She'd altered their emotions and perception of things when she'd turned them into her slaves. The strong affection Dez used to have for his younger brother had been warped and corroded into a hatred even stronger.

Images of a gray winter's day entered Lero's mind. The day when Dez turned fourteen and left their family home for Ghata's temple. Lero cried, though their father told him it was a joyous day. The goddess had accepted his brother to serve her. In exchange, he would live forever.

Once a boy from their village entered her temple, he never returned. Though still young, Lero knew Dez would never come back, either. They'd never go hunting in the woods together again. For him, that day felt like the day he was losing his brother.

The next time he saw Dez, it was months later. Lero barely recognized him. His brother's raven-black hair was gone. An elaborate tat-

too covered his entire right arm and circled his neck like a collar of servitude. Dressed in the ceremonial clothing in Ghata's colors, red and black, Dez was taking part in a celebration at her temple, along with the other men she'd claimed as boys and turned into bracks over the centuries.

The villagers had been invited to the temple to participate in the festivities. Lero stood with his parents, holding his mother's hand. His gaze crossed with Dez's. His brother's eyes were no longer gray but dark brown, almost black. There was not a spark of recognition in them, no life, no kindness, just red streaks of cold fire.

"Why?" he croaked. His voice sounded more like an animal growl. The ability to speak the *womora* had just given him was already being taken by the *kibia* mushrooms. "Why are you doing this, Dez?"

His brother leaned closer, hissing in his face, "Because if you're not a *brack*, you're a werewolf—one of those who disgraced and banished us. You're an enemy. You deserve to suffer, and I'm here to make sure you do."

Lero closed his eyes, blocking the view of the man who once was his brother and was now his jailer and torturer.

"You've failed to protect everyone you've ever cared about."

The memory of Ghata's words brought a bigger agony than anything Dez could ever do to him.

As his voice broke and distorted into a roar and his bones twisted with pain, he thought of the people she'd spoken about. Those few whom he cared for and ruined.

He couldn't stop his father from giving Dez away to Ghata.

He'd failed to protect Amelie.

Now Zeph...

Ghata was right. He'd failed so many.

But he had managed to keep one name off that list—Stella.

He'd learned the *bracks* had spotted him with her the morning she was showing him the island he'd ended up buying. She was only a real estate agent, replacing the man he was supposed to meet that day. But the *bracks* had seen something else between them. The stupid goons imagined he had some special feelings for her. That put her on their radar.

He now knew that when he'd come too close to discovering Zeph's whereabouts, Ghata had ordered her slaves to take Lero. Unable to locate him at that point, the *bracks* had targeted Stella, hoping he would come for her. He took the bait. The moment he'd learned she was in danger, he'd rushed to protect her.

Stella wasn't *his* woman as the *bracks* believed she was, but he couldn't let them have her.

It'd happened right before the full moon. He'd been getting ready to go to the island that night, to prowl and rage in solitude until the sunrise. But he'd found out that *bracks* had come to Miami for Stella, so he had to get to her before they did.

The sun set when he was but a few blocks away from her building. He turned into the beast in a dark alley and ran to her place on all fours. In his effort to warn her, he scared her. Despite the lust that consumed him at the mere sight of her, he kept in control, getting ready to fight the *bracks* who were after her.

But then she ran. His control snapped. The predator in him leaped out to chase the prey...

At the end, he had protected her after all. When the *bracks* got him, they lost interest in Stella. She was out there somewhere, free and unaware of the horrible fate she'd so narrowly escaped.

That knowledge was the one ray of light in this mind, now. He'd gladly suffer if it meant no other life was ruined because of him.

The memories of Stella shone through the darkness of pain that racked his body. They kept him sane through the torment. If he were to die here, in this cold concrete room with no windows, he wished he could kiss her first.

He dreamed about that, delusional from pain. Would her kiss have the same flavor as her scent and the taste of her blood?

He knew, in reality, the kiss could never happen. Even if he ever made it out of this basement, the best thing he could do for Stella was to stay as far away from her as possible.

But for as long as he could before his mind blanked out from the agony his body was going through, he held on to the memory of her.

HE'D BEEN PUT INTO a cage. Bright light shone on him, hot and blinding. He couldn't see them, but he sensed other people in the room, outside the thick, rusty cage he was in.

Someone removed the collar with the in-turned spikes that kept the wounds on his neck permanently raw.

The energy of the Moon flooded him, unimpeded. Despite the torture it brought, he welcomed it—there was an end to the pain now.

The Moon magic coursed through his veins, twisting his bones and re-shaping his muscles. His voice grew stronger, not as a speech but a roar. Loud and liberating, it tore from his chest as he rose to his hind paws.

Every coherent thought moved to the background. The pain disappeared. Only rage and feral lust remained.

He'd *turned*.

For one night, he was fully a beast. Locked in the cage on display for others.

"AW, IT'S SO NICE TO see you again, Lero," Ghata purred. "I missed you. Now that you're finally here, in my menagerie, I can come see you whenever I want."

Is that where he was now? He'd fully become part of her freak-show.

Aside from being allowed to shift fully on the nights of the full moon, his body had been kept in the torturous state of mid-shift. It had been so many months, his mental state had suffered. He'd been hardly aware of his surroundings when they'd moved him. Only vague, fragmented memories remained of being loaded into a crate and then transported here.

Instead of the musty air of the concrete basement, the space around him smelled dusty. The sound of Ghata's voice didn't bounce off any hard walls here but was muffled either by rugs or fabric.

He'd learned during his search for Zeph that Ghata had a traveling show. Sometimes, she'd rent a more permanent place for a while. But more often, she operated from large tents set up at fairs and other public events.

Prying his swollen eyelids open, he saw the red-and-yellow canvas that formed the walls of the room where the metal frame stood with the restraints that held him upright.

"Are you ready to give me what I want, Lero?" Ghata's voice slithered like a serpent around him, dangerously seductive. "Just one word, and all of this will end. You'll eat as much meat as you want. No more *kibia* mushrooms, I promise. No cages or chains. You'll sleep in silks, with me." Her hand, warm and soft, slid down his belly. "You want me, don't you?"

He'd want *anyone*. The state of the perpetual arousal with no release had been a torture on its own. Not only had he no control left, but he was barely self-aware, driven to madness by hunger, pain, and lust. By now, he'd fuck anything that moved. The iron restraints were the only things that stopped him from lunging on her.

"Join me," she whispered, sliding her face against the side of his beast snout. "I want your life and your loyalty. Give me your promise, my sweet, and I'll give you the release you crave."

Her cool fingers wrapped around his hot, straining cock. Tenderly, almost lovingly, she slid her hand up and down along his length.

His knees trembling, his insides catching fire, he released a long, tortured groan, frantically pumping his hips into her hand.

"Is this what you want, beast?" she scoffed, flexing her fist around him. Tight. "One word, and you can have it all—"

The pressure spurred his arousal. It shot through him like a lightning, bringing on the long-denied orgasm instantaneously. Relief pumped from him in thick, creamy spurts.

"Ew!" Ghata jumped away from him, shaking her hand out. "Disgusting animal! You have no self-control whatsoever!"

"Madame?" Dez rushed to her from between the fabric partitions. "Did he hurt you?"

Dez slammed a heavy fist into Lero's face. His head rang with a bright flash of pain.

Ghata stopped the next blow with a gesture.

"Guh! I need to go wash my hands." She glared at Lero, her lips curved with disgust. "Apparently, he has even less self-restraint than any of you. Gross and pathetic!"

———————◆———————

"I'M LEAVING TONIGHT to get ready for the exhibition in London." Dez's voice reached him through the fog of the semi-consciousness he'd been suspended in for gods knew how long. By Dez's tone, dismissive but without the usual hatred, Lero assumed Dez wasn't talking to him. "You'll have to take care of this one for me while I'm gone."

A shove of Dez's boot against his shin rattled the chain of the manacle around his ankle.

"W-What is...this?" an unfamiliar female voice whispered shakily, so quietly he barely heard it. The woman sounded as if she hadn't used her voice often.

A female?

The blood in his veins heated anew. A ray of awareness made its way through the dark fog in his mind. His base instincts homed in on her.

With his face swollen from the most recent beating by Dez, he could barely open his eyes. When he managed to peer through the slits between his swollen eyelids, his vision proved too blurry to make out any details. All he could see were two indistinct shapes created by lights and shadows.

"This is one of Madame's VIP exhibits. He's been kept elsewhere. But now that the siren is gone, and the gorgonian is playing hard-to-get, Madame ordered this one to be brought here. Not that you need an explanation." Dez cut himself short. "Just do what I say until all of you have arrived in London, Amira. Then, I'll be taking over his care again. I love looking after him."

Another hard kick in his leg landed. The pain was easier to ignore this time as his awareness was entirely on the girl.

"Is it... Is it an animal?" she asked timidly. "He's standing upright, like a man..."

Apparently, that was all that remained of the man in him—his upright position in the frame, supported by cuffs and chains.

He drew some air through his nostrils, filtering her scent from the smell of metal, dust, and blood.

A human.

The female was without a doubt just a human. There was not a hint of magic in her scent. Filled with sweet femininity, it brought another woman to mind. The one whose blood he'd tasted—Stella.

That night in Paris, he had simply wanted to comfort a crying child. So, he'd licked her wound, reducing her pain.

A mating bond was not possible, even between different fae species, and he certainly didn't hope for a bond with a human. Yet meeting Stella as a grown woman proved unforgettable. Somewhere deep on a visceral level, he'd felt a pull toward her. A pull powerful enough to distract him from the scent of the female who was standing in front of him right now.

Instead, he tried to focus on her conversation with Dez.

"Feed him *only* the meat I showed you in the bucket in the kitchen trailer. Once a day, today and tomorrow. No food at all during the flight to London. His crate will be locked, anyway," Dez instructed. "Smear the spikes of his collar in the substance from this jar—thoroughly, you can't miss a single one. Very important. Got it? The full moon is tomorrow. We don't want him to cause any trouble for the rest of the guys who'll be finishing the packing. Do you understand?"

The woman didn't make a sound this time, but the shift of one of the blurry shapes in front of him might have meant she nodded.

"Here," Dez continued, "this is how to take his collar off. Put the noose around his snout first. Stay away from his teeth, they're dripping poison. If it gets on your skin, you'll die."

Dez's voice remained even and business-like as he coolly went over the steps of his cruel daily routine.

The woman's breathing sped up, however. She was frightened.

"Why me?" she whimpered, weakly. "Why don't you ask someone else to do it? Nerkan or Vuk?"

"Because if I ask a *brack* and he messes it up for any reason, Madame will order him whipped. If *you* mess up even a tiny little thing, she'd kill you. You know it as well as I do, Amira. She barely tolerates you lately, waiting for an excuse to end you. That gives you the best motivation to follow my instructions precisely."

Chapter 6

LERO

A thick leather noose wrapped around his face, but there was no brutal force with which Dez would normally yank at it. Instead, a much gentler touch moved his head aside with a soft tug. The scent of the human woman told him it was she who tended to him to-day—Amira.

She removed the metal collar from his neck. The spikes tugged painfully at his skin before letting go.

Next came the sound of water before she pressed a cool, wet cloth to his skin, cleaning the puncture wounds around his neck. That was not part of the routine. In Dez's "care," Lero got hosed down only on the nights Ghata put him on display. No one had ever bothered to tend to his wounds before, although quite a few of the *bracks*, not just Dez, had come by to inflict some of them.

With Dez gone, however, there hadn't been any beatings today, allowing for the swelling to come down. He could open his eyes completely.

The woman was young, with pale skin and dark hair. Her lanky body was drowning in an oversized black hoodie and a pair of sweatpants. A wide, black scarf wound around her neck, concealing her chin.

She stared at him with large, haunted eyes, while turning the rusty, iron collar in her hands. A bucket of water, pink from his blood, stood nearby, a piece of cloth floating in it.

The moment their gazes crossed, the woman dropped hers to the floor. Holding his collar in one hand, she produced a plastic-wrapped package of meat from the pocket of her hooded sweatshirt.

He roared through the noose around his snout, lunging for the meat with uncontrollable hunger. The restraints threw him back. Her eyes open wide in fear, the female jerked and dropped the meat into the bucket of water.

"Amira!" Ghata shouted from somewhere outside the canvas walls of the room.

At the sound of her voice, Amira shook so much, she dropped his collar. It followed the meat, splashing into the bucket.

He hadn't eaten since last night. His insides twisted with ravenous hunger. However, with no *kibia* mushrooms for the past twenty-four hours, his mind had started to clear.

"Where is that girl when I need her?" Ghata yelled again.

Amira bent over, snatching his collar from the water, then jerkily yanked a jar with *womora* from her pocket.

Ghata appeared between two partitions of the striped canvas wall.

"How long am I supposed to yell for you? He needs a bath." She thrust a small pink animal toward the startled Amira.

With the jar in one hand and the collar in the other, the poor girl had no way to accept the animal, which was a two-headed *virleth* pig, Lero realized. The creature usually had three heads. He'd hunted plenty of them back in Nerifir. Never did he expect to see one in this world, however.

"Don't just stand there." Ghata stomped her foot. "Take him!"

Amira dropped the collar to the floor and shoved the jar with *womora* back in her pocket.

The pig twisted in Ghata's arms. One of its heads nipped at her elbow, making her yelp in pain and drop the animal.

The pig landed on its side with a piercing squeal. Scrambling to its hooves, it dashed to Amira and hid behind her legs.

"Get him, you useless human!" Ghata screamed. Yanking the beaded leather belt off her waist, she lashed at Amira, who ducked to pick up the pig.

Ghata furiously whipped the girl across her shoulder blades.

Amira only winced with a muffled groan and bit her lip. She took the next hit of the belt just as stoically, not uttering a word of complaint. Holding the pig in her arms, she cowered behind her elbow, protecting the animal and her face from Ghata's belt. It whipped around her elbow, the studded end lashing across her chin. A deep cut bloomed red on her pale skin, the welt quickly filling with blood.

Amira's eyes brimmed with tears, yet she remained quiet, word-lessly taking the abuse.

A *brack* Lero hadn't seen before barged in.

"What's going on here?" he demanded, as if he had any right to demand an explanation from Ghata.

Bald like the rest of them, this *brack* looked slightly different. A full beard covered the bottom part of his face. To Lero's knowledge, *bracks* lost their hair after swearing their lives to Ghata, including all facial and body hair, except for eyelashes and brows. How did this one manage to keep his voluminous, dark-brown beard?

Ghata whipped around to face him. Raising her free hand, she slapped him across his cheek in the same movement.

"This stray runt you've found will not live long enough to die of old age!" she raged. Tossing her belt at Amira, she spun on her heel and stormed out of the room.

Amira crouched on the floor, her arms around the pig, head drawn between her shoulders, and her face hidden in the wide folds of her scarf.

"Amira," the *brack* kneeled at her side. The warm note of concern in his voice caught Lero's ear as extremely unusual to hear from a *brack*. "Let me see."

He gently lifted her face out of her scarf. Blood dripped from the split skin on her chin. Her eyes closed, she sobbed quietly as he leaned in and licked the blood off.

"It'll be okay."

"No..." She shook her head with determination Lero hadn't witnessed in her yet. She freed her face from the *brack's* hands. "It won't be okay, Radax... Not if I stay here."

He caught her by the shoulders. "Amira, what are you saying?"

She cupped his chin with her hands. Her slim fingers disappeared into his beard. The pig squeaked in her lap.

"Tell me how to get to Nerifir, Radax," she said in a soft but resolute voice.

"What?" He shrank back, staring at her—his dark eyes opened as wide as hers.

"How do I open the portal? Please, I need to do it, Radax." Letting go of his face, she wrapped her arms around the *virleth* pig again.

"Why? To save the pig?" he mumbled, looking flabbergasted.

She gently placed her hand on the red spot blooming on the side of Radax's face where Ghata had slapped him.

"To save *you*." She sighed. "And myself. You've been like a family to me, Radax. I love you like a brother. She knows it, and she can't stand it. Can't you see she doesn't miss any opportunity to hurt you for my mistakes. I try so hard to please her, but I just can't do anything right by her. She hates me, and she won't rest until she kills me. She's hurting you too... I need to get away."

Radax slowly moved his head from side to side. When he spoke again, his voice was lower, subdued.

"I can't go to Nerifir, Amira. Even if I could, she'd pull me right back to her. I'm a *brack*. I'm tied to her for eternity."

"I know, Radax." She sighed again, so deeply her breath came out with a soft, sorrowful moan. "I know you can't leave her, but I can." She cautiously glanced over her shoulder at the narrow gap between the partitions, then proceeded in a hushed half-whisper, "If I'm no longer here to mess things up for you, you'll be safer, too. You can finally stop risking your life to protect mine. She nearly choked you to death when the siren escaped because of me. You had to give up your position as leader of the *bracks* to Trez in exchange for Madame keeping me alive. Can't you see? She's been using us against each other, punishing you for my mistakes. She hates you being attached to anyone but her. Neither of us will ever be safe unless I leave."

Had Zeph escaped? Did Lero hear her right?

She'd been speaking so softly, that the acute hearing of the beast was the only reason he'd heard her at all. Now he remembered Dez mentioning that the siren was gone, too.

His heart hammered against his ribs with excitement. If Zeph was free and safely away, he could endure anything Ghata and Dez threw at him.

Radax sat on the packed-dirt floor, dropping his massive shoulders.

"I can't watch over you in Nerifir, Amira. I can't go back and forth like the rest of the *bracks*. And even if I could, the *bracks* land in different times and locations in Nerifir, too. If you leave, I'll never see you again."

He stared at her intensely.

"I love you, Amira, like the daughter I never had or the sister I've lost. You are my only family in this world or any other. Please, let me take care of this. Let me find a safer place for you here, in this world. At least then, I'll be able to check on you now and then and make sure you're safe."

She shifted closer to him. Holding the pig to her with one arm, she took his hand in hers.

"I can't stay in the same world as *her*, Radax. You know she'll search for me, if just out of spite. And eventually, she'll find me."

"I'll divert her efforts. I've been doing it for the siren, too."

"And when she finds out you're hiding me from her, she'll do something even worse than murder. You know what she's capable of. Radax, please. I need to leave this world."

The *brack* stubbornly shook his head, gripping Amira's hand, as if anchoring her to himself.

"You don't know life outside of these tents, girl. Nerifir can be a dangerous place. You won't be safe on your own."

She dropped her gaze to her lap, where the *virleth* pig snuggled peacefully.

"I won't be alone," she said, barely audible.

"What do you mean?" Radax frowned. "*Who* will be with you?"

"The gorgonian. His name is Kyllen. He promised to come with me."

"The gorgonian? Amira!" the *brack* exclaimed, and she hushed him by frantically waving her hands at him. "Have you been talking to him? You know it's strictly forbidden."

"He'll die here, Radax. Madame ordered us to deny him water. He can't survive without it. She is killing him, slowly."

"The gorgonian is a fae. He's much more resilient than you realize. Madame needs him, she won't kill him. Gorgonians are extremely deadly. You can't be around him. I don't trust him to protect your life."

"If I don't leave, there'll soon be no life to protect." Amira exhaled a shuddering breath. The fight appeared to leave her with it. She sat with her shoulders down, looking deflated.

His muscles cramping, Lero shifted involuntarily, rattling his chains. The sounds startled both the *brack* and the woman. They stared at him, both obviously having forgotten about his presence. Or maybe they hadn't paid him much attention because they didn't care about an animal hearing their conversation.

"Are you done with him for tonight?" Radax jerked his chin at Lero.

Amira glanced at the bucket with Lero's dinner on the bottom, concealed by the bloodied water.

"Almost." She pressed her hand against the pocket with the jar of *womora* but didn't take the jar out.

Instead, she grabbed the spiked metal circle off the floor, then approached Lero.

"Are you going to bite me?" she whispered softly, raising the collar to his neck. "Do you want me dead, too?"

The noose remained around his snout, but Amira didn't tighten it and didn't use it to turn his face away. If he wanted to, he could probably shake the leather belt off, free his jaws, and...

The violent beast rose inside him, drawn out by the Moon. This close to the full moon, he needed *womora* to tame the aggression rising to the surface. The beast longed to burst free, to escape the stifling fabric walls and tear to shreds any living creature in his path to freedom.

Whatever was left of the man in him didn't want to see the girl hurt.

He closed his eyes, forcing his rage deeper while her light fingers secured the collar around his neck. Only the threatening rumble of a growl in his chest betrayed the feral bloodthirst that seethed inside him.

"Come." Radax tugged Amira away by her arm. "I'll think of something, but we shouldn't discuss anything with *him* around."

A calculating expression flickered in her dark eyes.

"He is just an animal, isn't he?" she asked, slowly.

"Amira." Radax shook his head. "You of all people should know that in Madame's establishment nothing is what it seems."

Chapter 7

LERO

Something sharp poked him in the arm. He opened his eyes to find Amira standing in front of him again.

Hadn't she just left with that *brack*, Radax?

Or had it been hours ago? A day ago? The concept of time had been hard to grasp.

He tried to focus.

It must be the day after she'd had that conversation with Radax. The full moon would be tonight, he could feel it approach. Amira hadn't given him any *womora* last night. Without it, he felt the Moon magic in his bones acutely. It pumped through his veins, making his blood boil. His mind was about to catch the fever of madness.

Soon, he'd have but two urges—kill and fuck. Everything else would move into the background and stay there until the sunrise.

He sucked in the air, rich with feminine scent. Bloodthirst and lust shot through his system like an electric charge, swelling hot between his legs and pounding hard inside his skull.

Want.

Need.

Her flesh.

It had started already.

In addition to the Moon wreaking havoc in his mind, the lingering poison of the *kibia* mushrooms Dez had fed him for too long, weakened and hurt his body.

Oblivious to the storm raging inside him, the girl calmly lifted her hand, holding up a crown—a high diadem. The black and white spikes arranged in the intricate aged-gold setting of the crown must be what she'd poked him with.

"The black thorns in this crown are werewolves' claws," she said, her voice ringing in his ears, echoing inside his head like in a church bell. "The white ones are their teeth. Both are just like yours." She gave him a penetrating stare before leaning just a little closer and lowering her voice to almost a whisper. "You're a werewolf, aren't you? From Nerifir?"

Her image floated in a red haze that clouded his vision. His focus narrowed to the scarf around her neck. The neck he'd bite first...

Want!

The word vibrated up his throat and exploded into a roar. He yanked at the restraints lunging at her.

Startled, the woman cowered, jumping away from him.

No! Closer!

He roared again. The distance she'd put between them diluted her scent, reducing his madness.

"Can you speak?" she asked softly, desperation shining in the hopeless darkness of her eyes. "Here." She dropped the crown to the dirt floor and yanked two objects from her pockets. One he recognized as the jar of *womora*, the other, a large chunk of meat wrapped in a piece of foil.

"Dez said to give you both daily until we leave tomorrow. I've given you neither because I don't know what they'll do to you. Which one will help you speak, now?"

She held both objects up, one in each hand.

The wild hunger for the bloodied meat made him jerk that way.

"The meat?" She gave it a suspicious look and warned, "Dez laced it with something, a yellow powder. Are you sure that's what you want?"

Want!

The beast craved blood. Hunger ravaged his insides. He'd had no food last night. And even when he had been fed here at the freak-show, it had never been enough.

"Will it make you able to talk to me?" she demanded in a quiet but firm voice.

The *kibia* mushroom powder in the meat would deprive him of any coherent thought. Without the *womora* on the collar spikes, the mushrooms would aid the Moon in turning him into the beast faster and completely.

The girl wanted to communicate with him. Maybe she could tell him more about Zeph?

Zeph!

He needed to hear what she had to say.

Calling on whatever reason of a man he still possessed, he tore his gaze from the meat and directed it at the jar in her other hand.

"Will this help you speak?" She raised the jar slightly.

He released another roar, making an effort to soften it to a groan.

She nodded, quickly shoving the meat package back into her pocket. When she came closer with the open jar in her hand, his control cracked. The beast lashed out. He growled, snapping his teeth at her.

She jumped back again, clutching the jar in her trembling fingers.

"This needs to get into your bloodstream, under your skin," she muttered. "But I'm not coming anywhere near your teeth again." She slid her gaze down his body. "It should work here, too, right?"

She approached his left hand that was chained to the metal frame. The iron cuffs had rubbed through his skin when he'd thrashed against them during the fits of madness and the beatings by Dez. The Nerifir iron prevented the wounds from healing. The sores remained permanently open under the metal cuffs coated in rusty layers of blood.

Amira dipped a finger into the jar and spread the honey-like substance around his wrist under the iron cuff.

"Sorry if it hurts," she said softly.

The initial contact of the *womora* syrup burned. He jerked against his restraints with a deep snarl. A cooling sensation quickly replaced the burn. It spread from his mangled wrist, up his arm, calm settling in his chest.

He groaned, leaning his head back against the frame that held him prisoner.

"Better?" Amira whispered.

She carefully stepped around him to his right side and spread the *womora* substance in a thin layer around his right wrist, too. Dropping to her knees, she also applied the *womora* to his ankles under the manacles.

He breathed deeply, focusing on the cooling sensation that spread through his body and soothed the heat of Moon Madness.

Amira stepped back, watching him with wide-open eyes.

"You... You're changing," she breathed out in awe.

He must be, as *womora* combated the effects of *kibia* mushrooms. The spikes of his collar slipped out of his flesh as his neck shrank closer to the shape of a man's, losing the bulge of the furry scruff on the back.

"Thank you," he exhaled in a croak.

"You can speak!" Amira hurried closer. "And you look more like a person, now."

Sliding down his body, her gaze reached his crotch. She quickly diverted her eyes, a blush spreading up her pale cheeks. With the fur gone, his private area became exposed. At least he sensed his erection subsiding, now. Her scent no longer drove him crazy.

The generous amount of *womora* she'd spread on his arms and legs made him feel almost himself again. At least until sunset.

Something clanked deep in the tent somewhere, making Amira freeze, horror floating in her dark eyes.

"They're packing up to move," she whispered, her hot breath hitting his bare chest as she leaned closer to him in fear. "They'll be here soon to put you in the crate. We need to hurry. Quick, tell me how to open a portal to Nerifir."

He recalled her conversation with Radax. Despite the *brack's* pleas and assurances, the woman obviously hadn't changed her mind about leaving. After having witnessed the way she'd been treated here, he couldn't blame her.

"You don't *open* a portal," he rasped, clearing his throat. "You *find* one."

The River of Mists flowed between the worlds. Its stream brushed their borders, breaking into the realms and connecting them all.

An expression of deep satisfaction spread across her face.

"I knew you'd know. You weren't abducted straight from Nerifir, were you? How do I find a portal, then?" she demanded.

"The one I came through is near Paris, France. It's the only one I know."

There were more, he just wasn't aware of the exact locations of the others. Scattered throughout the worlds—the innocuous, misty patches of air—the portals tended to show up over a body of water late at night or early in the morning. There was nothing particular or spectacular about their appearance. If spotted, humans wouldn't think twice about them.

"Listen," he said. "I'll tell you everything I know about it, but you'll need to answer some of my questions, too. Deal?"

She chewed on her bottom lip, contemplating his words. Whether she knew anything about the perils of making deals with a fae or not, she proved smart enough to think it through carefully.

He had no plans to trap her, though. All he needed was information and a moment or two of clear mind to process it.

"I'll set you free if you take me to the portal," she counter-offered.

Free.

That was so much more than he'd hoped to get out of her tonight. Now that it was on the table, the anticipation of freedom tingled under his skin, lighting a flicker of hope in his chest.

"How would you free me?" He needed to know she could deliver on her promise before he let the hope grow.

"The key that opens your collar is the same that opens the locks on your restraints. I overheard Dez telling the others to shoot you in the head with a human-made gun before moving you into the crate. They worry you'll cause trouble when they try to shove you in. A bullet from this world won't kill you, but it'll make you pass out long enough for them to pack you in. And it'd hurt." She gazed at him, a flash of compassion in her eyes.

Dez had said something about moving. To London?

"Where is Gha...Madame going?"

"To Europe. She has shows booked there. England first, then France. If you say the portal is near Paris, I can pack you into the crate now, with your help of course, so they won't have to shoot you. Dez is in London already. He went ahead with some other *bracks* to get the new venue ready." She rubbed her cheek in thought. "He'll take the key away from me when we get there. I'll have to find a way to release you as soon as we land, while I still have the key."

"No." Now that freedom was so close, he couldn't spend another minute in the restraints—not to mention hours in a crate—and risk getting back into Dez's cruel hands. Besides, Stella was on *this* continent. If he escaped, Ghata would most certainly send the *bracks* after her again. He had to stay here to protect her. "Let me go now. I'll tell you exactly how to find the portal. I'll also tell you the rules of traveling through one."

"There are rules?" She shot him a concerned look.

He nodded.

"Rule number one," he started, impatient to nudge her into action of getting the cuffs off him. "Once you cross over, you will never be able to come back to this world again—not to this time or place, anyway. If you try to cross back to Earth, you may end up a month in the past or a thousand years into the future. There is no way to predict with any certainty."

She drew in a shaking breath. "That's what he said, too."

"Who? Radax?" he asked. "Or the gorgonian?"

He remembered Amira speaking of a captured gorgonian whom Madame tormented by denying him water. Gorgonians lived in the Lorsan Wetlands of Nerifir, far from the werewolves' Plains of Sarnala. Ghata had been expanding her reach, it seemed.

"Never mind *who* said it," Amira dismissed quickly.

"It does matter if you're planning to take him along to Nerifir," he insisted. "Your travel companion has everything to do with rule number two."

"What is rule number two?" She frowned.

"I need you to answer *my* questions first."

Faint sounds of shuffling and packing came through the canvas walls. The *bracks* were nearby. He needed to get more from her since they could be interrupted any minute.

"We don't have much time," he reminded her.

"Fine. What do you want to know?"

"You said something about a siren before?" he started carefully. "Zeph?"

"Was that his name?"

She shrugged. "That's what the girl who escaped with him called him."

"What girl?"

"She never told me her name. I never asked, either. Names mean friends. It's best not to make friends in Madame Tan's menagerie." She pressed her lips together.

The name didn't matter to him right now, anyway.

"How long was Zeph here?"

Amira cast a sideway glance at him, more curious than suspicious.

"For over a year, I believe. But he is no longer here. He escaped in November."

Escaped.

The confirmation flooded him with relief.

"What month is it now?"

"January. The twenty-second," she said, then added the year.

His heart nearly dropped into his stomach when he realized he'd spent sixteen months as Ghata's captive—almost exactly as long as Zeph had. Zeph had been taken about three months before him and escaped two months ago, just before he got this chance to do the same.

He barely remembered anything of the time he'd spent in captivity, and what memories he did have, he wished weren't there.

"Has Madame been searching for Zeph, do you know? Does she want to find him and bring him back?" he asked Amira.

"She tried, but he killed a whole bunch of her *bracks*. Radax is in charge of looking for him now."

"I'll divert her efforts. I've been doing it for the siren, too." Radax's words from earlier came to mind.

"And Radax is not that enthusiastic in his efforts, is he?" he guessed.

"No. He made a deal with the siren." Her eyes narrowed, and she brought a finger to his face in warning. "But you cannot say anything about that to the *bracks* or to Madame, do you understand?"

"I'm not exactly on speaking terms with either of them," he dead-panned.

"I mean it." She shook her finger menacingly. "Not a word."

"Promise," he vowed. "I won't say anything to either *bracks* or Madame about Radax's deal with Zeph."

The mere idea of a *brack* making any agreements on his own, be-hind Ghata's back and against her orders, felt absurd. Radax didn't appear to be an ordinary *brack*, though. Lero wanted to question Amira about that, but time was precious, and he had more pressing matters to resolve. *Womora* had provided only temporary relief. Be-tween the Moon and the leftover mushroom poison in his blood, racking his body with pain, he could barely think straight as it was.

"What other fae does she keep here? Other than the gorgonian?"

"Um... I don't think there are more," she replied uncertainly.

"They may be kept in different forms, but they would be male," he explained.

To his knowledge, there hadn't been any other fae in this world before. With the gorgonian being here now, Ghata must have started kidnapping fae directly from Nerifir. She wouldn't risk returning there herself, which meant she was using *bracks* to do it for her.

Bracks always returned to Ghata when crossing the River of Mists. The fae they acquired in Nerifir, however, risked ending up elsewhere unless Ghata used her power to pull them through the mists to her too, helping the *bracks* haul their victims to her. Her female energy would make it much easier to drag male captives through.

Though, that didn't mean that the *bracks* couldn't take human women from this world over to Nerifir. He wouldn't put it past Gha-ta to resort to trading women from this world for magical goods from Nerifir.

"What do you know about Madame's trade to supply her menagerie, Amira?"

She shook her head.

"Not much. She doesn't talk to me about her business."

He recalled Ghata had mentioned gargoyles and sky fae when he first got into her clutches. "Are there any winged creatures in this establishment?"

Amira nodded. "Many, from the bird-snakes to—"

"Bigger than a bird-snake. My size," he urged.

"Only if you count the statue. The dragon-man..." Her voice trailed off as understanding spread across her face. "He's not just a statue, is he?"

"Nothing is what it seems," he repeated Radax's words.

If Ghata held other fae prisoners, they would have to be released, too. He had to set them free—a rather ambitious idea, since he was still locked in restraints.

"Can you unlock my manacles now, please?" he asked her, keeping his voice low as the noise of the *bracks'* tearing down the tents and packing had moved closer. "I'll have to escape before they get here."

She produced the key from her pocket but held it tightly in her hand, not making a move to unlock anything. "You haven't told me how to get to the portal yet. What is rule number two?"

"Right." His bones ached harder. Sunset must be getting closer. "On your own, you can only cross back to the world where you came from. To travel to Nerifir, you'll need a fae or a *brack* to accompany you, someone native to that world."

She nodded in visible concentration. "I'll have Kyllen with me. I'm not leaving him here."

If Amira freed the gorgonian, it would make his task of liberating the rest that much easier. He'd only have to worry about the gargoyle. Once he was free himself, of course.

"Where does Madame keep the 'dragon-man?'" he asked as she removed his collar.

"He's already been shipped to London, along with other heavy objects. It's just the tents, some equipment, and the live animals here now."

A loud noise of something heavy being dropped startled them both into silence. The noise was followed by *bracks* yelling.

"Amira, please hurry," he pleaded, urgently rattling at his chains. "I'll talk as you unlock."

"Okay," she conceded, dropping to her knees to release his legs.

"Listen carefully," he started. "Once you make it to Paris, take the train to *Parc des Brouillards*, just outside of the city. It's private property, so be careful when getting in." He winced, recalling the guards chasing Ghata, Zeph, and him across the park's lawns when the three of them had first arrived. That had been their first introduction to this world. "The portal only opens for about twenty minutes at three o'clock each morning. It's a small cloud of mist over the water of the pond, at the back of the park."

"Is it there every day?" She unlocked his arms next.

He stumbled away from the frame, the poison of the mushrooms making him dizzy.

"The portal *should* be there every day." He staggered back, grabbing the side rail of the frame to steady himself. "The flow of the River of Mists changes, but very slowly. It's been over forty years since I was last in *Parc des Brouillards*, but it would take centuries if not millennia for the River of Mists to alter its course enough for a portal to disappear."

She paused for a moment, giving him a penetrating look.

"How do you know all of this?"

"Let's just say I spent some time with a goddess when she used to be a more benevolent creature, inclined to share things with me." He sighed in regret. There had been a time when he genuinely cared about Ghata and wished her well. Now, it felt like he'd lost an ally in her for good and gained a foe instead—a cruel and powerful one.

The Moon magic twisted painfully inside him, reminding him who was in charge tonight. He stifled a groan.

"Be careful when crossing to Nerifir, Amira," he warned. "There is danger and hostility in that world, too, maybe even more than in this one."

Her chest rose with a long sigh under the voluminous hoodie.

"I don't really have a choice. I can't stay here. Madame holds my life over Radax's head, forcing him to do things he doesn't always want to do."

It was a statement worth pondering. Amira obviously had no idea how incredible her connection with a *brack* was.

He had no time to linger much longer, but he had to know.

"Why is Radax not like the rest of them?"

She bit her lip, sliding her gaze aside.

"Madame blames me for that. Radax found me when I was little and saved my life. He says I remind him of his sister who died young. Madame says he is...damaged, and she doesn't let him go to Nerifir anymore." Tears glistened in her eyes, and she wiped at them with a sleeve of her hoodie. "Radax's life will be so much easier without me. He can't escape her, but he won't have to worry about me anymore."

His heart ached for this girl who'd been through so much yet still cared for a *brack*—the last person who needed her tears, in his opinion.

"Amira, I wish I could come with you to help you get to the portal, but I can't. The minute my escape is discovered, Madame will send *bracks* to hurt an innocent woman simply because they believe I care about her. I need to make sure she's safe."

He would do nothing more than that, he vowed to himself. Stella needed to get out of Ghata's reach for a few days after the goddess discovered his escape. Once it was safe for Stella to go back, he fully intended to let her be. He would cause no disruption to Stella's peaceful life. He merely wanted to ensure her safety.

"I see." She nodded in understanding, obviously familiar with Ghata's ways. "I'll have to manage on my own, then."

He stepped closer and placed his hands on her shoulders. She flinched but didn't move away.

"Stay with the menagerie until you get to Paris," he instructed, wishing to help this brave, timid woman with all his heart. "I've sold all of my properties there but one."

He gave her the address of the last townhouse he'd lived in before Zeph was taken. He couldn't part with that one. It was his last connection to the city where he'd seen Zeph last.

"In the main bedroom, under a loose floorboard under the bed, I have a safe box with some money. Remember the lock code." He slowly said the string of letters and numbers in the correct order to open the built-in safe, then made her repeat it. "Take as much as you think you'll need—all of it if you have to."

"You keep money under your bed?"

Seeing her innocent confusion made him smile for the first time since the night he was trapped and ended up at Dez's mercy.

"I keep money in a lot of places. In this world, money is more important than magic. But one can never know for sure when and where it may be needed."

"Thank you," she said with genuine gratitude. "You know, I can buy you some time to get to that woman."

"How?"

She ran to one of the canvas walls.

"Come here," she said, swinging a fabric partition aside to reveal a large wooden crate. "Help me load your metal frame in here."

"Why?" he asked, but did as she said.

His knees shook, and his fingers trembled when he lifted the massive frame. Normally, his inhuman strength would make the task easy, but the long captivity and the poison coursing through his body had weakened him. Thankfully, the approaching full moon gave him enough strength to drag the frame to the crate and shove it in.

"I'll throw some of these in here, too." Amira started grabbing the sandbags piled up behind the crate and dragging them into the crate. "To make up for your weight."

When the frame and a few bags were in, she lowered the crate's lid back into place, closing it.

"I'll hammer a few nails in it when you're gone," she explained. "And I'll tell them you've been loaded."

"Will they believe you managed it all on your own?"

If this was discovered, Amira would be punished severely. He hated to think what Ghata would do to her.

"Nerkan is with the group of *bracks* loading the animals in the truck outside of the main tent, and Vuk is with those who are breaking down the tents from the inside." She gestured toward the noise of shuffling feet, rustling of fabric, and clinking of support posts that had been steadily getting closer. "I'll tell Vuk that Nerkan helped me to load you. Then I'll tell Nerkan that Vuk did it. Both are too lazy to break into the crate to check. They'll just be happy to know that it's done, and they won't have to load you themselves."

She appeared to know well those she'd been living with side by side. Both the *bracks* and Madame definitely underestimated this pale, skinny woman.

"Thank you for thinking of that."

"It'll buy you some time." She shrugged awkwardly. "They aren't planning to feed you during the flight. With any luck, no one will know you're gone until the rest of us are in London."

"You'll get in trouble whenever it happens," he warned.

"Well." She heaved a breath. "I may just have to run away before the menagerie moves to Paris. Which wouldn't be that bad, trust me. The sooner I get out of this place, the better."

The sound of voices and feet shuffling appeared to be coming from right behind the next partition, now.

"Come," Amira whispered, creeping away from the noise along the canvas wall. "They'll be coming here next."

She slipped under a fabric flap, gesturing for him to follow. He snuck into the narrow, dusty place after her. The strings of lights high under the ceiling of the massive tent struggled to illuminate the space, separated by several rooms and walls from the center.

He concentrated on not losing sight of the small figure in the baggy sweatshirt as she led the way through the maze of fabric walls and narrow passages.

"Here." She yanked up one of the canvas walls. Fresh air rushed in, chilling his legs and cooling the wounds on his ankles. "There're no *bracks* or people on this side right now. The fair ended today. It wasn't that busy to begin with, I've heard. You'll need to climb over the chain-link fence to get out of the fairgrounds."

"Where are we right now?"

She told him the name of a small town he knew he'd forget soon enough. It didn't matter, anyway. What mattered was that it was only about a hundred miles north of Miami and Stella. In the beast form he was about to take, he'd be able to cover that distance in a single night. Which meant he had just enough time to get to Stella before the crate arrived in London and his escape was discovered.

"Well, goodbye, Amira." He gently touched the hand holding up the canvas for him. "Thank you for everything. Good luck and may you find your happiness in Nerifir."

"Good luck to you too." She hesitated for a fraction of a moment before asking, "What's your name?"

Names meant friends, as she'd said earlier.

"Lero." He smiled.

"Be careful out there, Lero," she said softly.

He crouched by the opening that led outside.

"Um... Do you need any clothes?" she asked tentatively, and he could almost feel her gaze on his bare ass.

"No." He chuckled, slipping under the canvas. "I'll have lots of fur to keep me warm, soon."

The fresh air of freedom licked his skin when he crawled out of the stuffy tent that had been his jail.

It was almost dark already. The muddy yellow of the streetlights along the chain-link fence aided the deep red of the dying sunset. The power of the rising Moon flooded his veins, filling his body with the strength he needed.

He scaled the fence and ran across a dirt road to a field beyond it. The night was fresh. The ground under his feet cool. Coarse dry grass cut his feet as he ran across the field, but he hardly noticed.

As every trace of daylight vanished, moonlight illuminated his way. He felt it in his bloodstream, coursing through his veins and pumping his muscles with strength and speed. His bones screamed in pain, twisting out of shape.

He surrendered to the power of the Moon, letting his body take the form it longed to be in.

Rage, lust, bloodthirst, and pain filled him. He used all of them to run faster, heading south. To her.

Chapter 8

STELLA

I shut the door of my car but lingered near it. The key fob clutched in my hand, I wasn't pressing the button to lock the doors yet. Sweeping my gaze over the vast space of the underground garage, I didn't know exactly what I searched for when I strained my eyes. A flash of black fur? A red spark of the net? A glimpse of a bald head or a muscled, tattooed arm?

It'd been well over a year since I'd witnessed the wild animal being captured here—sixteen months, to be exact. Nothing scary or unexplained had happened since. Yet every time I parked, the eerie feeling of unease filled me. My skin would prickle with warning, and my breathing would speed up.

A man in a business suit parked in a row ahead of me. I locked my car and hurried to join him on his way to the elevator. He smiled, hitting the button, and I nodded in greeting when getting in the elevator with him, glad not to be alone.

During the months since that night, I'd tried to get an explanation for what had happened. I'd even filed a police report, hoping to get some information that way.

The men who'd captured the beast hadn't wanted to be seen—probably because what they did wasn't legal. If they ran an illegal rare animal trade, they needed to be stopped. The cruel way they'd treated the beast brought tears to my eyes and filled my heart with anger every time I thought about it.

As Dez had predicted, however, no one had believed me. The police officer I'd spoken to had listened with interest at first. When I'd come to the description of the fantastic beast, his expression had grown skeptical. He'd quickly ushered me out of his office and hadn't provided me with any updates since, no matter how many times I'd called.

There was no evidence to back my words. For some unexplained reason, the security cameras in my building had no footage of the incident.

With time, I started believing the whole thing might be a figment of my imagination. The one lasting effect of that night was an uncontrollable fear whenever I was in the garage on my own.

Safely back in my condo, I ate a dinner of cereal and avocado toast, then went to bed. Lying on my back, I watched the lights and shadows dance on the ceiling as the curtains on the open door of my tiny balcony moved in the night breeze.

Over the past year, the memories of the incident in the garage had faded. The nightmares rarely came, now. Instead of worrying about the beast while falling asleep, I thought about Lero once again.

The memories of him were always there—sometimes more vivid, other times just a faint echo of themselves. Nothing could get him out of my head for good, though.

I knew he had closed the deal on Blue Cay within days after the viewing. My agency couldn't provide me any updates on him after that, of course. We didn't stalk our clients, no matter how much some of us—me—might wish to do so. Unless Lero decided to buy or sell another property, I wouldn't hear anything about him ever again.

Instead of allowing me to move on, the idea of never seeing Lero again troubled me.

I tossed and turned as the pale disk of the moon gazed at me through the balcony doors, the cool, blue moonlight drowned out by the warm yellow of the streetlights.

After the stress of a busy day, if I allowed myself to revel in the memories of Lero at night, it relaxed me. He'd been my safe place for so long. I loved to recall his image during those few moments of semi-consciousness just before drifting asleep. After our last meeting, I'd had some fresh memories to relive.

Closing my eyes, I remembered the sensation of his strong hands on my waist when he helped me off the plane; the image of his face, breathtakingly handsome but always with a frown; his intense gray eyes offering but a glimpse into his stormy mind.

Thinking about him, I fell asleep smiling.

I wasn't sure if I ended up dreaming about him that night. A loud thud on the balcony snapped me out of sleep just before sunrise.

The sky had brightened along the horizon, with just a sliver of the sun peeking out. It was way too early to get up.

My unit was located on the third floor, high enough from the ground for me to feel safe, even while sleeping with the balcony doors cracked open to let in some fresh air. The sound, however, appeared to have been made by something large enough to be scary.

Sleep flew away.

I grabbed the first thing I could find that would serve as a weapon—a shoe. The convenience of living in a tiny condo unit meant that everything was just a step away, including my closet. The shoe had a stiletto heel—hard and sharp.

Stealing along the wall toward the balcony door, I also grabbed my cell phone off the shelf that served as my night table.

The shoe in my right hand, my left thumb hovering over the emergency call button of the phone, I tiptoed closer to the door.

Something large crouched on the balcony's floor. It growled and grunted as I came closer. Dropping the shoe, I leaped to the door to close it. I'd worry about figuring out what the hell that thing was once I was safely behind the locked door.

"Stella..." came from the balcony in a low, strangled voice.

It knew my name? How did this thing...

A person!

It wasn't a thing, but a man.

He rose to his feet, unsteadily holding on to the door frame. The pale light of the rising sun washed over him in waves of blush and gold. His face came into view, framed by a long, shaggy mane and a full beard. Despite the unkempt appearance, I recognized his silver-gray eyes right away. I could never mistake them for anyone else's.

"Lero?" I exhaled his name, pressing my hands to my chest to calm my thundering heart.

The man of my dreams had literally just dropped onto my balcony. Or was I still dreaming?

"I didn't mean to scare you," he croaked. Swaying in the doorway, he gripped the frame with both hands.

The details of his condition finally registered with me.

Lero was naked. Completely. Not a thread of clothing on his body. His hair was much longer than I'd ever seen on him. Tangled and matted, it fell past his shoulders. He sported a full beard, also wild and unkempt. I'd only ever seen him elegantly dressed and impeccably well-groomed before. It was a miracle I'd recognized him at all.

Deep circular wounds marred his ankles and wrists. Dirt and scratches covered his legs and arms. And... were those half-healed puncture wounds at the base of his neck?

He stumbled on his feet, with a groan and a full-body shudder.

It snapped me out of my shocked stupor.

"God... Lero, are you okay?" I rushed to him and grabbed his arm in an attempt to steady him. "What happened to you?"

I glanced over the railing of the balcony, searching for anything out-of-the-ordinary. All seemed normal for this early in the morning—the courtyard of my building was still deserted.

With another soft groan, Lero let go of the doorframe and dragged a hand over his face, leaning heavily on me.

"You... You can't stay here," he muttered.

"Right. Let's get inside." I led him into my unit.

My bed was directly in front of the balcony entrance. My place wasn't big enough to space the furniture out much.

Lero tripped over his feet, and I let him sink onto my bed. I gave him a long once-over, noting all the wounds and scratches, as well as his pale skin, chapped lips, and the deep shadows under his eyes. My heart ached at the sight of him. Whatever had brought him to this state couldn't have been good.

"You're hurt. I'll call an ambulance." I lifted the phone in my hand.

"No," he rasped, heaving himself up on an elbow. "No ambulance."

He reached for my phone. The wound around his wrist was raw in the middle, its edges ragged and in various stages of healing. An identical wound on his other wrist made me believe he'd had his hands tied long enough to create the wounds and keep them from healing.

"Who did this to you?" I whispered in horror.

"My brother." He winced.

Lero had a brother? What kind of a man was he to treat a person—his own family—like that?

"We need to call the police, not just an ambulance." My voice came out hollow and sharp.

"No phone calls, please." He shook his head resolutely.

"Why not?"

What was he afraid of?

Unless he was a criminal, too. What did I really know about this man? Other than he licked little girls' legs and bought multi-million-dollar islands in the Bahamas? Both of which fell well in line with criminal behavior.

I clutched my phone tighter in my hand, unable to tear my gaze away from the man who was clearly suffering right now. Maybe he was a criminal, but if I had a choice between the police and an ambulance, I'd still go with the ambulance first.

"Lero—" I sat gingerly on the edge of the bed next to him.

"Stella, please listen to me," he rushed out, interrupting me. "It's very important. Someone will be coming for you shortly."

"What?" I either didn't hear him right or he was in so much pain, he was getting delusional.

Why would anyone want anything to do with *me*? However, his solemn expression and the serious voice triggered an alarm in me, raising the fine hairs on my arms.

"Who?" I shot a cautious glance toward the balcony.

"It doesn't matter *who* right now." He swallowed with an effort then licked his dry lips. "What's important is—"

"Is it the same people who did this to you?" I gestured at his wrist. "Your brother?"

Fear vibrated through me, now. Though, I still had no idea why anyone would be after me.

He let his head drop back on my pillow.

"Yes."

I leaned over him, crawling closer. "Why? How do they know about me?"

His chest rose with a sigh. "They've seen you with me. When we went to the island."

"Oh... Lero. That was a long time ago."

He stared at the ceiling. "Time doesn't matter to them."

I ran a hand over my face. Where would I go? What could I do? This couldn't be real.

"What do they want with me?" I asked through the hand over my mouth.

"To get to me," he said, trying to rise on his elbows again to look at me. "They've already come for you once and got me, instead. They'll do it again."

What was he saying? That I'd been hunted, and I didn't even know it?

"Why?"

"Because they think I care about you. That if they take you, I'll come for you."

They think.

Didn't mean it was true. Or was it? Did Lero care about me? Well, he did care enough to come here to warn me about the danger, at least. The danger that threatened me because of him. What had I gotten myself into without even realizing it?

And why would they hunt him to begin with?

I rubbed my forehead. All of it was extremely overwhelming.

"I have so many questions," I muttered.

"But there's no time for answers. You need to get to Blue Cay, right now." He closed his eyes tight, frowning in concentration. "In the main house, in the master's closet, there is a security system panel. You'll have to engage it when you get in. Make sure to arm both the house and the island."

"You want me to go to your island? Alone? What about you?"

"I—" He tried to sit up. His arms shook with strain, and he dropped back to the pillow. "I don't think I can manage it right now. The sun is up, and I'm exhausted." He closed his eyes. "Go. I'll be there as soon as I can."

A grimace of pain distorted his handsome features. I couldn't stand watching him suffer. Rushing to the kitchenette, I filled a glass with water.

"Here. Drink this, Lero." I held up his head, helping him drink. "We'll go to the island together. Okay? Once you've rested and recovered. Then, you'll tell me everything that's going on."

"No. You need to go, now." He fell back on the mattress and mumbled, "They're flying to London this morning. By evening, they'll know I'm gone, if they don't know already. There's no time..."

With a long, pained groan, he rolled to his side, clutching his middle with both arms and drawing his legs up to his belly.

"Lero? Please... You're hurting." I grabbed his shoulder. All my questions and doubts moved to the background. Right now, I just wished to ease his suffering in any way he would let me.

"The *kibia* mushrooms..." he gritted through his clenched teeth. "He fed them to me for too long. It'll take a while to wear off..."

What on earth was he talking about?

"I can't leave you here like this."

"Go..." he ordered, not moving.

"Lero," I pleaded, but he no longer responded at all. I shook his shoulder, then shook it again, harder. He remained motionless.

Whatever had been done to him, most certainly had been done over a course of time. The man lying on my bed right now looked nothing like the Lero I knew before. He looked like he'd been kept in a cage for months. Dread chilled my spine at the thought—maybe he had.

If I left him and ran, he'd be completely alone—weak and defenseless in his current state. The cruel people he was talking about would easily get him again.

"I'm not leaving you," I said with determination.

However, I respected his wish not to call the police, not until I learned more about his reasons of avoiding going to the authorities in the first place.

Picking up the phone, I dialed the number of the building's lobby, instead.

"Hello."

Hope filled my heart when I heard the voice of the doorman on shift. Chris and I were on good terms.

"Morning, Chris. It's Stella. Listen, I need a small favor. My, um...cousin had a bit too much to drink last night. If he doesn't make it home right away, his wife will totally kill us both. I'll drive him home, but he is, kind of, a bit...well, passed out." I winced, cursing my inability to come up with a better story on such a short notice. "Would you mind bringing one of the wheelchairs you guys keep on hand for accessibility?"

The building management's memo clearly stated the wheelchairs were provided upon request to assist elderly people and those with health concerns and mobility issues. They were definitely not there to transport passed-out drunk cousins, but Chris was a nice, understanding guy. He and I often chatted outside while he was on a smoke break, and I waited for a friend or a client to take to a viewing.

I released a breath in relief when he cheerfully replied, "Sure. Just give me a minute."

A minute suddenly seemed way too short as I dashed around my place, trying to pack. How long was I leaving for? When would I come back, if ever? I was supposed to be at work in a few hours. Should I call Javier? What would I even tell him?

Instead of Javier, I dialed the phone number of the charter company. The mention of Javier's name helped me arrange the flight to Blue Cay on hardly any notice at all.

Lero remained in bed, motionless and uncommunicative. I checked his pulse and breathing to make sure he was still alive. His heart beat wildly, but he didn't speak. He wouldn't even open his eyes anymore.

Yanking off the oversized t-shirt I'd been wearing to bed, I slid it on him. This was probably the only piece of my clothing that'd fit him. Well, maybe also my bathrobe.

I got into a pair of jeans and a long-sleeved shirt. The early-morning weather was chilly this time of year, even for someone like me who was born and raised in New York. Then, I grabbed my white bathrobe from the bathroom.

The doorbell rang as soon as I'd gotten the bathrobe on Lero's uncooperative, limp body.

Chris stood in the doorway when I opened it—a wheelchair in front of him and a bright smile on his well-tanned face.

"Oh, thank you so much!" I gushed, forcing a smile in reply.

"Do you need any help with this?" He gestured at the wheelchair.

My instinct was to decline and send Chris away before he spotted the abused, half-naked man on my bed. Logic told me, however, there was no way I'd be able to lift Lero's tall, muscular body on my own.

"Oh, that would be fantastic, if you don't mind." I opened the door wider, allowing Chris to roll the wheelchair in.

"He's right here," I said cheerfully, trying to act like my biggest worry in the world was getting my drunk cousin home to his wife, not being pursued by someone who were into imprisoning and torturing people.

I quickly threw a sheet over Lero, in addition to the clothes I'd managed to put on him, then drew the hood of the robe over his sunken face smeared with dirt and dried blood.

"Is he okay?" Chris maneuvered the wheelchair to the bed.

"Oh, he's fine!" I waved my hand, with a nervous giggle. "He just can't hold his liquor. He was at some crazy costume party last night." I desperately hoped that would explain Lero's current outfit of a t-shirt, a bathrobe, and a bed sheet. "He stopped by my place for just one more drink this morning. Not that he needed any more, obviously."

Chris looked doubtful, and my heart sank in fear that he might demand further explanation or make me call the police after all.

"I've already called his wife," I added, hurriedly. "She's furious. Poor guy is going to have a hell of a hangover. But first, I need to get him home ASAP. Otherwise, I'm afraid she'll divorce his ass."

I kept blabbering nonsense, hoping that my chattering would distract Chris from any logical thoughts he might be having right now.

"Shall we move him, then?" I grabbed hold of Lero's legs wrapped in the bed sheet.

"Right..." Hooking his hands under Lero's arms, Chris tentatively lifted his torso off the bed.

Lero groaned, rolling his head to his shoulder, the bathrobe hood and his beard thankfully concealing most of his face. The groan was a sign of life. It proved to Chris I wasn't trying to get rid of a dead body, at least. I tried to calm my nerves.

"Dude, are you okay?" Chris asked Lero after we'd placed him in the wheelchair the best we could.

I grabbed the duffel bag with my things.

Lero groaned again.

"Fucking *kibia* mushrooms..." came from under his hood.

"Mushrooms?" Chris gave me a knowing grin. "It's not just the alcohol problem, then?"

"Yeah, well..." I quickly tucked the sheet around Lero's feet, then yanked it up his lap too, to better hide the wounds around his ankles and wrists. "I'll let his wife deal with him."

"Are you okay to drive?" Chris asked when we'd made it down to the garage and approached my car.

"Sure. I didn't drink or, you know, do *mushrooms*." We loaded Lero into the back seat, and I arranged the sheet over his lap. "Just in case he throws up in the car," I explained to Chris.

"Well," he said, eyeing the duffel bag I had slung over my shoulder. "Call me if you need anything."

"Thank you. I'll be good now." I threw the bag in the passenger's seat, relieved he didn't ask why I was bringing an overnight bag while supposedly driving my cousin home. I'd lied more than enough for one day already, and the day had just begun. "Thank you so much, Chris. Can't wait to dump his drunk ass into his wife's lap already."

Thankfully, the plane was ready when I got to the dock of the charter company. Jose, the pilot, helped me load my "rich, drunk client" into the plane with only a few questions. He'd seen me with Lero on the day of the viewing, and he was obviously aware that Lero was the new owner of Blue Cay.

"You know how it is?" I swept the loose strands of hair from my sweaty forehead after buckling Lero into his seat. Loading and unloading a limp body had proven to be quite a workout. I panted, nearly out of breath. "Once you have enough money, you can buy whatever reputation you want. Then if you let loose and go wild one night, you can hide on your private island until you sober up and are ready to face the world again."

"Right." Jose gave me a disapproving look, as if he suspected that I was one of the "rich client's" vices as well.

I had no energy and no imagination left to defend my reputation. If he thought I fornicated with clients then cleaned up their messes for publicity purposes, then so be it.

The sun was high in the sky when we approached Blue Cay. Lero had barely moved during the flight. Keeping an eye on him, I couldn't stop myself from comparing this trip to the last one I'd made to this island. My travel companion was the same, however, his state and our circumstances were much different now.

"There's no dock," Jose informed me as we got ready to land. "I'll have to land on the water then beach the plane."

Lero hadn't waited long to go ahead with the changes. The docks indeed were gone. Strings of faint blue lights encircled the perimeter of the island.

"What are those?" Jose asked me, descending to the small bay surrounded by the white-sand beach, the closest one to the main house.

"I'm not sure." I really had no idea.

"Is it even safe to land here, now?" he sounded doubtful.

I remembered Lero's instructions to "arm the island." Could the lights be a part of his security system? If so, I hoped it wasn't armed right now, because the last thing I needed today would be an alarm blaring or something worse.

On the other hand, Lero hadn't mentioned I'd face any problems getting into the house.

"It's fine," I said, injecting more confidence into my voice than I felt. "Go ahead. Land. These are just, um...solar-powered lawn lights."

After landing on the water, the pilot masterfully backed the plane right onto the beach then tied it to a nearby tree.

Together we dragged Lero—semi-conscious and largely uncooperative—to the house and dropped him on the bed in the main bedroom. I scraped together whatever cash I had left in my wallet after the generous tip I'd given to Chris and handed it all to the pilot.

"Thank you so much, Jose," I said, feeling incredibly grateful for this part to be finally over.

"No problem." He tipped his chin at Lero. "That's going to be a bitch of a hangover later."

"Yeah... He definitely overdid it this time." I rubbed my forehead, thinking about everything else I still had to do.

After Jose left, I walked through the house, making sure all doors were locked. There were so many of them. In addition to the main entrance and several sets of glass double doors in the dining and living areas, each of the six bedrooms had a walkout to a patio with a path to one of the beaches.

Once that was done, I went to the master bedroom closet in search of the security system Lero had talked about.

I opened the closet and stepped back, stunned. Instead of a code panel or a small screen, the entire wall of the spacious room had been converted into a surveillance center.

Flat screens lined the wall. A long panel with hundreds of keys and buttons stretched in front of them. The dresser that'd stood in the middle had been replaced with a computerized workstation.

The lights in the closet lit up the moment I'd opened the doors. That seemed to bring to life the rest of the equipment, too. The screens glowed pale-blue, and some of the buttons on the panel lit up with a rainbow of colors.

I came closer, inspecting the setup that appeared to have come straight from a spy movie or spaceship.

From what I could understand, the entire perimeter of both islands was under surveillance. Judging by some of the labels on the keys and the commands glowing on the screens, I doubted the system would simply blare an alarm when triggered. I wondered if by arming it I'd somehow be loading an actual weapon.

To arm, the system demanded a fingerprint for identification.

Through the open closet doors, I glanced back at Lero on the bed. His arms spread wide, my sheet still swaddling his legs, he seemed to be asleep. His chest rose and fell evenly. His body must've finally conquered the pain enough to allow him some rest. I'd hate to disturb him again to drag him to the closet to obtain the stupid fingerprint.

Then I remembered that he'd wanted me to come to the island on my own. Neither he nor his finger were supposed to be here at all.

How did he mean for me to activate this thing, then?

Tentatively, I pressed my own palm to the screen. Shockingly, it turned green, accepting it.

When did Lero have the time to set this up? How did he know I'd be here? Did he plan it all along? And if so, what had I allowed him to drag me into?

None of these questions could be answered yet. I'd have to wait until he was well, awake, and ready to talk.

Having armed the system, I felt relatively safe, for now anyway. The physical and emotional stress of the past couple of hours had worn me out.

Making it back into the bedroom on shaking legs, I collapsed on the bed next to Lero.

Chapter 9

The ache in my shoulders woke me up when I turned in bed. I winced, stretching my arms. My muscles throbbed as if I'd been digging in a garden or doing pull-ups.

...or dragging a tall, well-built man to and from planes and automobiles.

I quickly opened my eyes as the memories of that morning rushed in.

Lero lay next to me on his side, his arm thrown over my waist as if in an embrace. His eyes were closed, and his expression was so peaceful.

With the afternoon sun already tipping toward the horizon, I must have slept for hours. The sea, visible through the glass door to the patio, was calm, the sky blue. It wouldn't be much of a stretch of the imagination to believe I really was here on vacation with a man I'd had a crush on since my early teens.

Lero looked much better than he had this morning. Some smudges of dirt remained on his face, but the shadows under his eyes had lightened. His skin tone had improved. And his lips no longer appeared dry or chapped. The beard suited him, as did the longer hair. I doubted anything could ever mar this handsome face.

Unthinking, I reached out and moved a long, wavy strand of hair that had fallen over his forehead.

His thick, black eyelashes fluttered in the warm sunlight that flooded the bedroom. He opened his eyes, meeting mine.

"Stella?" he murmured, his voice soft and dreamy. "This is the most beautiful dream yet..."

He gave me a smile, the first I'd ever seen from him. It was gentle and undisturbed by reality.

"Hi, Lero."

I had so many questions to ask him. All of them could wait a few more moments, though. Lying in bed with Lero like this, side by side, smiling at each other, felt surreal and so peaceful. I wished to enjoy it for a little bit longer.

Lifting his hand, he gently slid his knuckles along my jawline.

"Kiss me," he demanded, suddenly. "There's no harm in kissing in a dream, is there?"

It certainly felt like a dream. After all, I'd spent so much more time with him in dreams than in reality.

Lost in the silver-gray of his eyes, I hardly realized I'd been leaning closer to him. My lips hovered a hairbreadth from his. He rose on an elbow, closing the distance.

His mouth captured mine in a kiss that was so much better than any dream could ever be. Air rushed out of me in a moan, and he swallowed it, sliding his lips along mine.

My heart pounded in my chest, the swishing of blood echoed in my ears, making me blind and deaf to the world around us. There was nothing else but Lero's mouth on mine, his hand in my hair, and his body so close to mine.

I didn't want this to end, pulling away just a little to catch my next breath between his kisses.

"Gods, this is heaven," he exhaled, pressing his forehead to mine. "I don't want to wake up."

Wake up?

He still sounded somewhat delusional. Clearly, the effects of what had been done to him hadn't worn off yet.

The realization was as sobering as a bucket of cold water dumped over my head. I'd just kissed a man who hadn't come out of a delirium. He wasn't fully himself yet, couldn't be. I couldn't blame it on anyone or anything but myself. Unlike Lero, I had been awake and fully conscious, taking advantage of him.

"Sorry," I mumbled, awkwardly backing off the bed. "I'll get you some water. You must be thirsty."

I hurried out of the bedroom, found two glasses in a kitchen cabinet, and filled them with water. I emptied one myself, drinking in huge, thirsty gulps. I desperately wished the cool water could drown my mortification and erase the memories of Lero's lips on mine.

After that, I stood over the sink for as long as it took for my heart to calm down and my blood to cool off.

The sensation of his kiss still tingled on my lips, however, buzzing through my body with a thrill I'd never known before. The effect this man had on me was stronger than anyone I'd ever been with. And that was just a kiss, he hadn't even touched me anywhere else...

I closed my eyes for just a moment, breathing in deeply. Then picked up his glass, willing my hand not to shake, and headed back to the bedroom.

"Water," I announced in an upbeat voice, walking through the door.

Lero was sitting in bed, looking rather confused. "What happened?"

He'd gotten out of my bathrobe and was now wearing only my long t-shirt with *I "heart" coffee* written on it in pink and brown letters. It looked so out of place on him, I smiled despite everything.

"What *do* you remember?" I asked.

He winced, spearing his fingers through the tangled mane of his wavy hair.

"I have some memories. But I'm not sure which are real, and which are just echoes of illusions..."

I sat on the bed, handing him the glass. His fingers brushed mine, sending sparks up my arm straight to my heart. He obviously felt nothing like that, calmly taking a drink.

"Okay, so." I swallowed, clasping my hands in my lap and making sure no part of my body touched his. "You showed up on my balcony early this morning, not looking very good. You said your brother did something to you... How are you feeling?"

He put the glass on the nightstand by the bed.

"Good." He rubbed his wrist.

His wounds had healed incredibly well over the last few hours. The scars were still there, but they seemed old, as if at least a week or two had passed between this morning and now—no more fresh blood or open sores.

"You look... better." I frowned, confused while visually assessing his injuries.

I'd had no time to treat his wounds that morning. However, they appeared to not need any treatment at all. The small round scars I'd seen on the side of his neck between his hair and his beard were barely there now. Just this morning, they were clearly visible, even in the muted light of the new sunrise. The scratches that had thickly covered his arms and legs a few hours ago were all but gone now, blending in with his skin.

"Nerifir iron prevents wounds from healing," he murmured distractedly, inspecting his wrists.

I had no idea what he was talking about. I understood most of the words he'd said, but together they made little sense.

"Lero," I said slowly. "We need to talk."

We did. But where would I even start?

"How did I get here?" he asked, glancing around the room.

Physically he had obviously been improving, but his mental processing had not quite caught up yet.

I sighed, thinking back to our physically and emotionally exhausting journey to the island.

"With a lot of muscle power and the kindness of strangers."

"Did you put yourself in danger for me?" he asked sternly.

"Hardly." I shrugged. There was no point going into the details of schlepping his barely conscious self all the way from Miami. "We're both here safe and sound, aren't we? That's what matters."

He stopped his gaze on me, as if really seeing me just now.

"Thank you, Stella."

God, I loved hearing my name from his lips. And now I was thinking about his lips and what he'd just done with them. Would our kiss remain a dream for him forever?

I cleared my throat, forcing my thoughts in another direction.

"How did you heal so fast?" I pointed at his wrist. "I mean, I'm happy you're feeling better, but I don't understand..."

He inspected his hand again, as if seeing it for the first time. With his skin healed, the dirt stood out more prominently. Sliding his other hand along his jawline, he winced.

"I need a shower and a shave," he said as if he hadn't even heard my question.

"You want to shave it off?" I felt a slight pinch of regret. Lero's disheveled appearance made him a little more approachable in my eyes. Besides, the beard and longer hair suited him.

He scratched his chin, his lips curved with distaste. "It feels too much like fur..."

Tossing the sheet aside, he paused, staring at my t-shirt with the picture of the pink heart and brown letters stretched over his broad chest. The shirt almost reached my knees when I wore it. On him, it barely covered his private area.

I cleared my throat, once again.

"That's my shirt. You, um... You weren't wearing any clothes when you came over this morning."

He arched an eyebrow in a slightly amused expression. "I see. Well, thank you. I'm sorry about showing up naked."

Holding on to the bed post, he heaved himself out of bed. The metal frame groaned as he leaned heavily against it.

"That's okay." I stepped closer, just in case he needed my help. "You were barely conscious. Lero..." I took a long breath. "Those who did that to you need to be held accountable. I haven't called the police yet, but I think—"

"No police." He shook his head with the same resolution as before.

"Can you explain why? Please?"

He blinked, jerking his gaze aside. "I need to think... I..." He looked straight at me, as if having made a decision. "You must be hungry. I certainly am. There must be some food in the pantry. Help yourself to anything you like, just check the expiration date first. I'll have a shower, then we'll talk."

I nodded reluctantly.

He let go of the post, taking a shaky step toward the bathroom.

I rushed to his side, grabbing his elbow. "Are you sure you can manage? Do you need help?"

"In the shower?"

"Well, um... If-if necessary." I stumbled through my words, feeling my face heat up with a blush. The thought of washing Lero in the shower... Well, it deprived me of any other thoughts.

His smile was a shade too wistful to be considered flirty. "Thanks. I'll be fine."

Taking a deep breath, he carefully moved around the bed on his way to the bathroom. His movements were a little slow but got steadier with each step.

I watched the door close behind him, then listened for any sound of distress or a call for help. When I was satisfied he was indeed fine in there on his own, I took his glass and went back to the kitchen.

Hunger rumbled in my stomach. I hadn't eaten anything since yesterday. The huge double-door fridge in the kitchen was sparkling clean and completely empty. The spacious pantry, however, was fully stocked with non-perishables.

A variety of grains and pasta were displayed in clear, air-tight containers. Rows of canned fruit, meat, and vegetables neatly lined the white shelves. There were also boxes of crackers, spice cookies, and cereal.

I regarded the bounty for a few minutes, then grabbed two cans of chili, a pack of crackers, a can of fruit salad, some cookies, and a box of tea.

After hauling my loot into the kitchen, I found a can opener in a drawer and an electric tea kettle on the counter in the small room behind the kitchen. I vaguely remembered the sales brochure calling that room "the butler's pantry." Small appliances were lined up on the counter there, including a fancy coffee machine I was not even going to attempt to figure out how to use.

So far, the food in the pantry, the state-of-the-art small kitchen appliances, and the security system seemed to be the only things that Lero had added since taking the possession of the island. Otherwise, the house looked very much the same as it had during the viewing.

I wondered what that meant about Lero and his priorities. The more time I spent with him, the less I knew him. Right now, he was an even bigger enigma than that night in Paris, now more than fifteen years ago.

I divided the chili from one of the cans into two bowls then warmed them up in the microwave. While waiting for the water to boil for tea, I arranged the crackers on a plate and put fruit salad into two dessert dishes.

It wasn't the greatest dinner, but I worked with what I had. It still turned out better than some of the frozen meals I'd had in my lifetime of living alone and working late.

The tea smelled amazing and tasted delicious. The packaging looked expensive, too. Lero obviously loved living in style.

I took the dishes to the round breakfast table in the casual dining area off the kitchen.

The sound of the bedroom doors opening came soon after I'd set the utensils next to the bowls of chili. Lero walked in, freshly showered and fully dressed. Now, he looked much closer to the elegant man I'd sold this island to over a year ago than the exhausted, delirious person I'd found on my balcony this morning.

Dressed in a white shirt and light-brown pants, his beard completely gone, and his long, damp hair slicked back, he appeared well-rested and refreshed. The last several hours almost felt like nothing more than a nightmare, chased away by the bright afternoon sun. And our kiss seemed even more like just a dream.

"Dinner?" I made an inviting gesture toward the table before taking a seat.

Lero's nostrils flared as he sighted the food. His movements stilted, as if he were forcing himself to hold back, he sat at the table across from me and lifted his spoon.

"It's not fine dining," I said, apologetically.

I'd done my best with the dinner, considering the circumstances. Though, I wouldn't have done much better if I'd had an entire farmer's market of fresh food available. Cooking wasn't exactly my forte. Back in Miami, I didn't eat much better than this—canned foods, cereal, and frozen meals. Fast and easy.

Lero didn't seem to mind the lack of class or flavor in our meal. I'd only taken a few spoonfuls of chili by the time he'd completely emptied his bowl and polished off more than half of the crackers.

"You weren't kidding when you said you were hungry." I took a sip of my tea to hide my astonishment at the speed at which he ate.

"You have no idea," he growled, practically inhaling his fruit salad.

I wondered how long it had been since he'd eaten last. The thought that he might've been starved twisted my insides, driving away my appetite.

Moving aside the empty bowl, Lero regarded it for a moment, looking almost surprised with himself for finishing it. His gaze fell on the second can of chili on the counter over my shoulder. He got out of his chair, heading that way.

"Canned stuff is disgusting." He made a face while eating the cold chili with a spoon straight out of the can. "I'm going to order proper food for us tonight."

Disgusting or not, he ate the entire can of chili before returning to the table to finish the remaining crackers.

With a deep breath, he leaned back in his chair. Taking a small bite of the spice cookie I'd put on the table, he sipped his tea in a slow, dignified manner.

"How long has it been since your last meal?" I asked softly, dreading to hear his answer.

He put down his cup, not meeting my eyes. "Stella—"

"How long have you been gone?" My voice rose, along with my hurt and indignation for him. "How long did they have you, Lero?"

He cleared his throat.

"It doesn't matter."

"It doesn't? How can it possibly not?" I leaned over the table, my heart speeding up as my anger heated. "You said some people—your brother—took you. I can only assume, against your will. They kept you in deplorable conditions, judging by your state this morning. You have wounds, for goodness sake. Did they restrain you? Torture you? And you're going to let them get away with all of that? Why?"

"Because right now, making them pay is not my priority." He leaned in, too, though his voice and expression remained calm.

"What is?"

"Keeping you safe."

"Me?" I stared at him in confusion. "*I'm* the priority? Why?"

"Human lives are short and fragile. I can't concern myself with vengeance or retribution until you're safely back home with no further danger to your life or freedom."

I loved the idea of nothing threatening my life or freedom, of course. But all of it sounded rather vague.

"But, you—"

"I'd like to go down to the beach," he said suddenly, pushing his chair back.

"Wait." I reached over the table for him. "I need you to answer some questions first."

He rubbed the back of his neck uneasily. "Questions are a tricky thing."

"Not if you have honest answers."

He raised an eyebrow, avoiding my eyes. "You see, Stella, I may not have answers, not the ones I can share anyway. And I really don't want to lie to you."

That didn't sound promising.

"Well, tell me what you can at least. Why don't you want to call the police?"

He made a face, shaking his head. "It'd be useless. Human police wouldn't be able to do much, anyway."

"*Human?*"

"*The police,*" he corrected himself quickly. "The police won't help here. It'd be a waste of time, in the best-case scenario."

I opened my mouth to argue, then closed it, thinking about my last visit to the police to report the parking garage incident. The visit and the report had been a waste of time. It wasn't the same as what had happened to him, of course, but I understood his mistrust to some degree.

"Just tell me one thing, please," I said. "Do you have something to hide from the police yourself? Have you done anything illegal, Lero?"

He stared straight ahead, not answering. The pause was less than a second, but it proved long enough to scare me.

My mouth felt suddenly dry like sandpaper. I swallowed heard. "Did you... Lero, what have you done?"

His expression remained somber, but he finally moved his gaze to mine. "Ever since I came to this world, Stella, I've been trying to keep those around me safe while leading a peaceful, productive life and obeying all laws of society."

"Trying?" I clarified. "Have you succeeded in living a peaceful, law-abiding life, Lero?"

His chest rose with a sigh as he heaved himself up to his feet. "Keeping others safe is where I've failed."

I got up, too. "What do you mean? Who are the others?"

He held on to the back of his chair, though his stance was much more confident now that he'd eaten.

"*You* are, for one," he said. "I bitterly regret disrupting your life, Stella."

"Well, from what you've told me, it wasn't your fault, right?"

He shook his head, muttering, "I wish Javier had done the showing that morning."

"Would you rather Javier be their target, instead of me?"

The steel-gray of his eyes softened with a barely-there smile.

"The reason you've been targeted is their belief I have a romantic interest in you, Stella. In this case, Javier would've been safe," he added confidently.

"*Do* you have a romantic interest in me?" I blurted out, immediately feeling mortified. Out of everything he'd said, did my mind need to zoom in on *that*?

He let his gaze linger on my face for another moment. My skin warmed up under it like under a ray of sun.

"My priority right now, Stella, is to make sure you can go home as soon as possible. Then, I hope for your sake, our paths never cross again."

———————— ◉ ————————

ROLLING HIS PANT LEGS up to his knees, Lero waded into the sea while I remained on the sand. I'd come with him after our canned chili dinner, worried he might trip and fall on the path, though he was recovering incredibly quickly. In fact, he had even ended up supporting *me* on some steeper parts of the path.

My head was still reeling from the last words he'd said back at the house.

"I hope our paths never cross again."

Hearing it from him had been brutal. Though, I realized he'd never promised me anything. Nothing Lero had ever said could be considered "leading me on." My attraction to him had always been one-sided, and I had no one to blame but myself for letting it grow.

The disappointment and rising anger I felt now were directed at myself.

Maybe it was good for me to hear it directly from him like that. That should help me get my head on straight, too. My daydreaming about Lero was not unlike a celebrity crush—I'd never known him as a person. I still didn't know him at all. The reasons I'd found myself on the island with him were shady at best. And so far, he'd refused to clarify anything.

Lero stood ankle-deep in the water, small waves rolling softly around his legs and onto the beach.

"How long do you want me to stay here?" I asked.

He stared out to the horizon.

"I'm not sure yet."

"I'll have to call Javier," I said. "Taking vacation days won't be a problem, but I'll need to give him some kind of an explanation for my absence."

Technically, as a real estate agent I was self-employed with the flexibility to take a vacation whenever I wanted. In reality, I rarely took any at all. I had ongoing listings and viewings scheduled year-around, which would now need to be taken care of by someone else while I was gone. Also, since I worked from Javier's office, I had to account to him for my whereabouts. I couldn't drop out of sight with no explanation.

Lero folded his arms across his chest. With the long sleeves of his shirt rolled up, the wound around one of his wrists came into my view. Clean of dirt and blood, it was but a bangle of pale scar, now. I obviously had been mistaken that morning when I'd thought it raw and fresh. It simply couldn't have healed *that* fast.

"Tell Javier you'll be away for a week, maybe two," he finally said. "I'll call him myself if it takes longer than that. I don't want you to have any problems over it."

"How much longer might it be?" I asked.

"I really can't tell yet." He shook his head. "But I will let you know as soon as I figure out more. Did you bring your cellphone?"

"Yes. But it's off." I'd turned it off back in my car, afraid someone might trace where we were going.

"Good." He nodded approvingly. "You can use the phone I have in the surveillance room to call your work and your family. Tell them you're taking a trip. I don't want them to start worrying or report you missing."

"There is no one to worry about me outside of work." That was true. My job had become my entire life, slowly taking over whatever personal life I used to have. I'd let it, because there hadn't been that much personal life to begin with, and I found my advancement at work satisfying enough for now.

"How about your family? Your parents?" Lero asked, regarding me with interest.

I blinked under his stare and glanced down to where the waves churned around his ankles. They rolled back then rushed in again, rising up to his knees and spraying his pants with foam and mist.

"I don't keep in touch with my parents," I said. "Other than a call once a year, at Christmas." Those were very brief strained conversations, too.

Since the death of Aunt Beatrice and the "inheritance disaster," as my father called her omitting us from her will, my parents and I had hardly spoken at all. Mom had finally succeeded in convincing my father to sell their apartment in Manhattan with just enough equity left for them to buy a modest bungalow upstate. They'd been living there ever since. Mom spent most of her time at a quilting club at their church, and Dad sitting in a rocking chair on the porch blaming his sister, me, and everything else under the stars but himself, for depriving him of the money and status he was "meant to have by birthright."

"We've never been close," I replied, sensing Lero's questioning stare. "My father openly disliked me for as long as I can remember. And Mom... Well, she told me that she saw herself as a wife first, not a mother. She never planned to have children. I was an accident..."

She'd said it more than once, enough times for me to believe her words weren't something one would say in the moment of anger while dealing with a moody teenager. Enough times for her confession to lose the sharp quality of a knife stabbing through my heart when I heard it. Enough for me to believe her and accept her words as the truth. Enough time had passed for me to deal with it and move on, becoming my own person, even if she wasn't thrilled to have me as her daughter. Yet saying it out loud, especially to Lero, practically a stranger, felt raw again. As a kid, I'd blamed myself for being unwanted even by my own mother, thinking something must be horribly wrong with me.

Afraid to see his face, lest I find judgement—or even worse, pity—there, I kept staring out to sea.

"Do you have any close friends?" he asked after a little while.

"At work." I nodded, with more enthusiasm.

The lack of a family connection in my life had been easier to deal with thanks to the family-like atmosphere at work. There were plenty of people about my age at the office. We had parties, went out for drinks, gathered in each other's houses. I did have friends, they just also happened to be my colleagues.

"I'll call them to let them know I'll be away for a while."

"How about—" He stopped in the middle of the next question, and I stared at him expectantly.

His mouth pressed into a firm line. It appeared he didn't want to continue with what he was about to ask.

"Do you have anyone...closer than a friend, Stella?" he said finally. "A man?"

"You mean a boyfriend?"

Over the years, I'd had a number of casual dates. All of them remained just that—casual. Now, I wondered if that was because both my mind and my heart had been occupied by Lero all my adult life. My bed remained the only place free for another man. Maybe that was why none of my relationships had ever moved past the bed...

"No, no one in particular," I said softly.

His chest rose with a long breath, but he said nothing more.

I watched the waves stroking the shore for a few seconds.

"What's going to happen now, Lero?"

He cast a long look out, toward the horizon, as if searching for something out there.

"You'll stay here, safe. You can go swimming any time, just stay close to shore and away from the reef. I may have to leave at some point."

"Leave? Where're you going?"

"Europe. Not yet, though. First, I want to make sure it's safe for me to leave you here by yourself. Then I'll ask you to remain in the house, with the security engaged."

His words spurred another question that had been lodged in my brain since that morning.

"How come my palm print is in your alarm system?" I asked, narrowing my eyes at him.

"Fingerprints," he corrected. "Not the entire palm. Individual fingerprints are easier to obtain. Which we should replace with the full hand scan—now that you're here."

"You've obtained my fingerprints? How?"

He had the decency to look somewhat ashamed. "I got them shortly after the viewing. You touched things around the house."

I glared at him. "Have you planned this? Me being here?"

He winced, rubbing his forehead.

"Not *planned* but got *ready* for it. The system can accept handprints of more than a dozen individuals. I used as many as I could think of—anyone I had around me at the time."

"Anyone? Your friends maybe..." It made no sense to me. I was no one to Lero, a real estate agent who'd showed him a property once. When giving access to a security system, people normally chose close family members or trusted friends.

"I have few friends, Stella. Their palm prints are logged, but so are those of several of my former employees, the hotel manager where I stayed in Miami, Javier's—"

"Javier's? But why? The more people who have access to your security system, the less secure it becomes. Even I know that, and I don't even have one."

"I didn't install it to keep *everyone* off the island, Stella. I just wanted to prevent certain individuals from coming here to harm those I needed to protect. From the very beginning, Blue Cay was supposed to be a safe place for me and whomever I'd bring here. In my case, the more people who had access to the system, the better. Because I couldn't predict with certainty whom I might have to send here."

I needed time to wrap my mind around all of this.

Lero appeared to care about me—about my safety and wellbeing, at least. I believed I could trust him on those accounts, even if I didn't understand his actions and motivations.

The sun crept toward the horizon.

"Shall we go back in the house?" I asked.

"Soon." He nodded, not moving out of the water. "Just another moment."

At our viewing, I'd gotten the impression he didn't like the ocean that much. Yet he'd insisted on wading in the water then, too.

"You said you didn't like swimming."

"Swimming?" He made a face, as if the very notion was absurd. "No. Other than the shower, I detest getting wet."

"You just like getting your feet wet, then?" I glanced down where the receding wave churned the sand around his toes.

"Not really." He followed my gaze. "Baths are especially unsettling," he muttered under his breath, staring at his feet. "I really don't understand humans' desire to submerge themselves in water any chance they get when they can't even breathe in it."

I snorted a laugh. "You sound like an alien from another planet. Like you aren't one of us 'humans' yourself."

He blinked, moving his gaze to my face.

"Do *you* like swimming, Stella?"

"Sure. When the weather is nice, why not? I love going to the beach. Snorkeling should be really fun around here."

"Zeph would be great to snorkel with," he said, glancing out to sea, the same wistful expression I'd seen before crossed his features.

"Who is Zeph?"

He ran his hand over his overgrown hair.

"A friend of mine. A very close friend. Water is his life."

This was the first time Lero had spoken of someone close to him.

"Will he come visit you here some time?"

"Maybe. I hope very much he will."

Chapter 10

LERO

It'd been two days since the last full moon. He still had weeks before the next one. But sleep had been escaping him already, leaving him tossing and turning in bed. Without *womora*, calm was a thing of the past, a distant dream. Blood churned in his veins like sea water, rising and ebbing with the call of the Moon. The sensation was gentle for now, like the soothing caress of waves on the beach protected by the reef. In a couple of weeks, however, he knew it would grow into a true tempest.

Hopefully, it would be safe for Stella to return home by then.

Reports from the people he'd hired to keep an eye on Ghata revealed she was too preoccupied with her European tour, and possibly something else, to send anyone to hunt for him. He worried about her true plans, which so far, he'd been unable to decipher.

Giving up on sleep, he climbed out of bed and walked out onto the patio. The large swimming pool had stood empty ever since he'd ordered it drained and the gap into his bathroom boarded up. He had no use for a pool and didn't care to maintain it.

Zeph would've loved having a house with a swimming pool that extended into his bathroom. Lero had bought the place with that at the back of his mind. But Zeph wasn't here, and there hadn't been any news about his whereabouts from the extensive network of humans that Lero had employed to search for him. The more time passed without word about Zeph, the more worry racked him.

Dressed only in the light pair of white lounge pants he wore to bed, he walked down the patio steps then climbed down the slight incline to the beach.

Wading through the water had become his obsession as he anxiously awaited news from Zeph. He had no way of knowing where the siren was, but he knew that as long as he remained in the ocean, Zeph had a way to find him. As a water fae, Zeph could sense people's emotions through the ocean, no matter the distance.

Lero walked to the small beach behind the house then followed the receding wave. The water ebbed then rushed in again, rising to his knees. He forced himself to remain in place, fighting the urge to get out and shake every drop of moisture off his body. The swelling of the waves unsettled him.

Breathing in the fresh night air, he turned his face up to the sky. It was overcast, the moonlight but a puff of silver behind the thick shroud of clouds. He would've found the Moon even if it was completely obscured, though. The awareness of it never left him even on the darkest of nights or the brightest of days.

He had more than three weeks before the effects of the approaching full moon would become unbearable. Without *womora*, they would be much more difficult to resist before the Moon turned him completely. A shudder ran through his body. There were a few brief moments of utter exhilaration right after a shift, then the wild nature of the beast took over, depriving him of control.

Until that night came, however, he had a few important things to do and verify.

He had no way of knowing if Amira had made it to Nerifir, but he'd heard she and the gorgonian had fled Ghata's show shortly after landing at Heathrow in London.

Ghata had fewer and fewer fae to exploit. According to Amira, she still had a gargoyle in her possession. In Nerifir, gargoyles took human form during the day. Here, it appeared she was somehow keeping him in his stone form around the clock. Lero had been working on a plan to free the gargoyle. If it worked, it would leave Ghata with no high-earning exhibits at all.

Logically, it made sense for her to focus on recapturing him and Zeph, as well as on sending her *bracks* to Nerifir in search for more. According to his sources, however, Ghata no longer seemed interested in restocking her menagerie with sentient fae. It should make him happy that he no longer needed to worry about *bracks* coming for him or hunting Zeph. But it worried him instead. Ghata wasn't retiring. She had most likely moved on to the next stage of her plan, and he needed to find out what exactly that was.

Whatever came, having a secure place was more important than ever.

He'd had the idea of a private island for years. He knew Zeph's powers over water would be best utilized here. The two of them would also attract much less attention here compared to densely populated places like Paris. The only reason he'd waited for so long was his desire to raise Zeph as a normal human boy. Lero wanted to give him a real chance at becoming a part of this world. Maybe then the young siren wouldn't feel like an outsider, the way Lero always did.

That decision had backfired, as Zeph ended up wanting everything humans had, including human connections and relationships. Lero desperately wished for Zeph to avoid making the mistakes Lero had made, though he wasn't sure *how* best to stop that.

The cloud cover had thinned, letting moonlight shine through stronger. It reached down to the water, rippling with silver streaks through it, in a magical, shimmering path that stretched from the horizon toward him.

The ripples glowed brighter, no longer fueled by the Moon but by something moving through the water to him. His heart leaped with anticipation even as in his mind, he was still afraid to believe.

The glow brightened and grew, approaching. Impatient, he waded deeper into the water. When it reached his hips, the turquoise glow surrounded him, and the head of the man he'd raised as his son and loved as his only family popped out of the water.

"Zeph!"

The siren grinned at him, blinking droplets of sea water off his long, dark eyelashes. "Found you!"

Not waiting for Zeph to fully emerge from the waves, Lero grabbed him in a big hug, splashing and splattering in the surf.

"I've searched everywhere for you." He squeezed hard, so hard a human would have been screaming for mercy, but Zeph just laughed, hugging him back.

"I've been blending in, Lero, just like you've taught me."

He had taught Zeph many things but assimilating into the human society had always been one of the most important lessons. Humans generally didn't respond well to anyone different than themselves. If discovered, Zeph and Lero could have been detained, locked in a lab somewhere, or simply killed.

"I've searched for you, too." Zeph leaned back from the hug but kept holding on to Lero's shoulders. "I went to Paris and got your note from the cabaret. *'You'll know how to find me when the time comes.'* That didn't tell me much."

Lero had kept the message he'd left for Zeph brief and vague for a reason. He didn't want Zeph to stick his head out in search for him and risk putting himself in danger. There had also been the risk of the note landing into the wrong hands.

"I also wrote *'stay near the water.'*"

"Right. That's what I've been doing, swimming every chance I got, scanning the ocean for you. I know you don't like water much, but is it the first time in months that you got your feet wet?"

"I've practically lived in the ocean for the past two days!" He laughed. Happiness spread thick and warm through his chest at finally seeing Zeph, safe and sound. His limbs grew light with relief.

"Well, I work on land—"

"Where? You don't have to work anymore. You know we have enough money to last both of us until the end of our days."

Zeph inhaled deeply. "A job helps us blend in, remember? One needs to have it, like humans do. I sing. It's the most natural thing for me to do. People pay me for it."

As a siren, Zeph's need to sing was more than simply for recreation. Music was in his blood. He needed to sing as much as he needed to breathe.

"We can find you something in the Bahamas if you want." There were bars and clubs on the islands nearby where Zeph could continue singing for an audience.

Zeph glanced along the beach then up at the house over Lero's shoulder.

"What is this place? Why are you here?"

Lero turned to look at the house, too. From here, it appeared even bigger than from the front—walls of glass and light-gray stucco, with stone on the bottom. The light in Stella's room was off. She must be sleeping. Maybe he'd dream about her tonight. Those always were the best dreams if she was there.

"This is a safe place," he said to Zeph. "I've been trying to make it as safe as possible. Ghata—"

Zeph groaned, his long eyebrows knitting into a grimace of distaste.

"She held you captive," Lero stated.

"You know?" Zeph cut him a glance.

He rubbed the back of his neck, the phantom pain from the collar spikes making him wince. "She got me too."

"When?" Zeph staggered back as if punched in the chest.

"I escaped three days ago."

"Fuuuuck!" Zeph speared his fingers through his white-blond hair, aimlessly wading through the water. "I had no idea you were there! I should've looked for you before taking off myself."

"I wasn't there. Not at the same location as you, anyway." Lero followed him, concerned by his distress. "She kept us separated. I was brought into the menagerie tents only after you'd escaped."

"It wasn't the tents. She was running her show from a building in Niagara Falls, in Canada, when I escaped."

"She went back on the road sometime after that, then." He placed a hand on Zeph's shoulder and squeezed it tightly. "There was nothing you could've done to free me. Getting out of there as quickly as possible was the best thing to do, trust me."

Zeph heaved a sigh.

"Did she exhibit you, too?"

Lero nodded, chasing away the muddy memories of shifting inside a rusty cage.

"With her exhibits escaping, Ghata doesn't have many left," Lero said. "She may still decide to recapture us. We need to be vigilant and prepared. Zeph, I want you here, safe with me."

"I can take care of my own safety, Lero. I'm no longer a kid, you know." The siren pressed his mouth into a hard, stubborn line.

"Together we're stronger, Zeph." He paused, wondering if he should say anything about his fears, as vague as they were. Zeph needed to know, though. He had to warn him. "I'm afraid Ghata is planning something much bigger than anything she's done so far. She was talking about taking over the world."

Zeph lifted an eyebrow, with a hint of amusement—he obviously didn't believe Lero. "And how is she planning to do that? By stealing the moon or firing a giant laser from outer space?"

Lero gave him a look that hopefully conveyed exactly how unimpressed he felt at Zeph's making light of what could be a serious issue soon.

"Through corruption of faith," he said. "Ghata is a disgraced goddess, remember? She longs for power. The power of a deity lies in the faith and number of her followers. She must be secretly recruiting new believers. The more she gets, the more powerful she becomes."

If Ghata succeeded at regaining her former strength, the Earth would suffer the fate of Sarnala, the land of his people.

Zeph was too young to remember Nerifir, but Lero had heard from the elders about how the power of the Moon changed under Ghata. The magical bond that connected his people warped. Instead of freedom and love, the werewolves craved more violence. Aggression had gradually taken over their beasts. Instead of celebrating the full moon by making love and hunting together, they roamed the Plains of Sarnala, craving murder and blood.

Nothing good would come to humans under Ghata's reign, either.

"Whatever comes, we need to stay together."

Zeph studied him closely from under his brow.

"I'm not alone, Lero," he warned.

"What do you mean?" He frowned in confusion, then it dawned on him. "Ah... The girl." Amira had mentioned that the "siren man" had escaped Ghata's menagerie with a girl.

"Her name is Ivy." Zeph's tone hardened.

That sounded familiar.

"Is she the one from Paris?" The vague memory of a shy young woman gasping for air in the back court of the cabaret he used to own came to mind. It was the one and only time Lero had met her. She'd just seen Zeph perform. The experience had proven too intense for her, and she'd come out to the courtyard to get some fresh air, catching Lero smoking *womora* there.

"Yes. We met in Paris first. Later, she saw me at Ghata's."

"How?"

"Coincidence." Zeph shrugged.

"Are you sure?" After Ghata's betrayal, it proved hard to trust anyone.

"Listen..." Zeph sank his fingers into his hair again. Shorn short on the sides, the longer tresses on top draped over his forehead reaching his nose. "Ivy is my everything. I trust her implicitly. If you don't believe me—"

"She is a human, Zeph." He hated to break the boy's bubble but chasing happiness with a human had a price Lero never wanted his friend to pay.

"She is mine." Zeph glared at him, with a hard, silver glimmer in his sea-blue eyes.

Lero heaved a long breath, calling on his patience. The stubbornness of the younger man had caused him a lot of frustration in the past.

"We've talked about this, Zeph. Humans are much weaker than us. They're not fae, we can't bond with them. If you try, you'll end up damaging them. Irreparably so."

The memory of a life he'd ruined painfully clawed at his heart with guilt that never left.

"I don't care about the fae bond." Zeph shook his head, sending a spray of droplets from his hair out in a semi-circle. "I've never had it or even witnessed it in others. The bond is nothing but an abstract concept to me. Don't you understand? Ivy is real. I love her. The connection between us is unbreakable. I'm not leaving her."

Lero dug his heels into the soft sand under the water. Both of them had moved a little closer to the shore while talking. The water now barely reached their knees.

"She is just another liability," he said. "In times like these—"

"What are you talking about?" Zeph laughed. "Ivy isn't a liability. She is my strength. My reason to live. My *everything*."

"If you really love her, the honest thing to do would be to let her live her life in peace. She'd be better off without you. Think about it, without a bond, she'll age and die way before you do."

"But I will be with her until the day she dies," Zeph argued, passionately. "No one—fae or human—can offer her more than that."

"Being with fae is dangerous for humans. You can kill her just by hugging her. What if she pricks her skin on one of your spikes and dies? Zeph, it's not just selfish and irresponsible on your part. Keeping her around is criminal."

The poison in Zeph's fins was just as potent as that in Lero's teeth. Unlike his long fangs that he only acquired during the full moon, however, Zeph had the ability to open the fins on his back, arms, and legs any time. Sometimes, they'd open spontaneously on their own.

When Zeph was little, he'd come to Lero's bed at night after having a bad dream. After waiting for him to fall asleep again, Lero would quietly go to the boy's bedroom to change the shredded, poison-soaked blankets Zeph had ruined during the nightmare. The fins used to open while he dreamed, spewing the deadly poison. Lero would then move to sleep in the living room for the rest of the night.

"I have much better control now," Zeph replied.

"Are you a hundred percent sure an accident will never happen? Remember Ivy only has one life."

Zeph spun away from him, without a reply. A swirl of water, fanning out around his legs wider than it naturally would, betrayed his agitation. It sprayed high enough to reach the siren's swim shorts.

"Could you live the rest of your life knowing you've killed the one you loved and were meant to protect." Lero couldn't give up now. "Think what you're dragging her into. We don't know exactly what Ghata is up to. There may be a war coming—"

Zeph whipped around to face him again.

"Then we'll fight it together, Ivy and I," he said firmly. "There is no separating us anymore, Lero. She is a part of me. And she is not as fragile as you think. Just because humans aren't as physically strong as us doesn't mean they don't possess a strength in spirit. You said it yourself, Ghata is planning to use their faith to become a true goddess once again. Human spirit is strong enough to create and topple gods."

"Humans are easily mistaken and easy to mislead." He shook his head.

"So are fae, aren't they? If what you've told me about Nerifir and Sarnala is true, then your people were misled by Ghata, too. They're no different than humans. What exactly are your people anyway, Lero? What *are* you? You've been hiding so well, even I don't know who you truly are. Have you been *blending in* so perfectly that you've completely forgotten your true nature?"

Lero's patience worn thin, his temper snapped. His voice thundered over the water, "That's enough, Zeph!"

He'd hidden his beast from everyone, even from those closest to him. Zeph had never seen him on the full moon night, he'd made sure of that. The one time someone had seen his true self, it destroyed them. Poor Amelie and her fragile mind.

"It's better that way," he said, running his hands through his uncomfortably long hair. "My true self is a hideous sight, Zeph. More than that. It's destructive and dangerous."

"Mistrusting," Zeph snapped, his expression grim. "Those who love you would accept you, no matter how hideous you think you look."

Spoken with the true naivety of youth. He sighed.

"Zeph. I want you to stay here. Now."

The younger man crossed his arms over his chest, taking a wide stance.

"Ivy is waiting for me." He backed out into the open sea.

"Zeph!" Lero shouted in desperation, knowing he had no chance of catching the siren in open water once Zeph dove in. "It's not safe out there on your own."

"I'm no longer on my own, Lero. And I'm capable of protecting those I love. I love Ivy, and she loves me. We live together and will fight together if needed. I won't let anyone stand between us, Lero. Not even you."

Chapter 11

STELLA

The sun was already over the horizon when I climbed out of bed. It'd been four days since Lero and I first got to the island. All this time, he'd been distant, as if lost in thought. He would probably say the same about me, as I tried to stay out of his way as much as possible. Lero's gorgeous house didn't exactly feel like a prison, but I certainly wasn't a guest here, either. I harbored no illusions, this wasn't a holiday.

I'd made phone calls and sorted out things in the real world. Javier had no problem with me taking some vacation time. We'd arranged for another agent to take over my viewings in the meanwhile. So, I could relax a little about my job, at least.

Wandering around the island on my own got old fairly quickly. After a day of doing nothing, I ended up working remotely, using one of Lero's computers. The other agent did the viewings, but I did everything else, from updating listings to answering emails. It had kept me busy for a few hours a day since.

This morning, the sun shone bright, and the day promised to be warm. I took off the t-shirt I slept in and shuffled into the bathroom.

After that first day when I had passed out in Lero's bed, I'd moved into a bedroom of my own. There were five rooms to choose from, and I went with the one closest to Lero's. Listening to him move about behind the wall felt comforting while I was falling asleep at night.

Not a sound was coming from his room this morning. He must be up and out of his bedroom already.

I had a shower then put on a pair of denim shorts and a blue flower print blouse. Having brushed my damp hair, I twisted it into a bun.

If I let it loose to dry in the humid ocean air, my hair would spring up and stick out like a wild mane. While living in New York or Paris, I'd occasionally managed to tame it by slicking it down into civilized auburn waves cascading over my shoulders. After moving south, however, fighting the frizz proved to be a losing battle. Eventually, I'd given up and resorted mostly to buns and occasional braids.

"Morning," Lero greeted me in the open-concept breakfast room separated from the kitchen only by the counter.

The back doors were open, the sheer curtains slowly moving in the breeze. The sunlight washed the room in a golden glow. Amazing smells wafted through the air.

"Breakfast?" Lero rose from his chair at the table. Shoving aside his laptop, he moved toward the counter.

Dressed in a white button-down shirt and beige pants—the outfit he seemed to prefer while being on the island—he'd left his dark wavy hair unbound. It lay on his shoulders in thick black locks, with the sun bringing out the streaks of copper highlights.

Smiling, I walked around the table, past the laptop he'd left open. Its screen was still on, and I couldn't help a glance at it.

A message in French lit the screen, next to the picture of a gorgeous flower arrangement in white and purple.

"Joyeux anniversaire, ma très chère Amélie"

Which meant *"Happy Birthday, my dearest Amelie."*

The words struck me like an electric shock, rooting me in place. This was a confirmation of a flower delivery. Lero had sent a bouquet to a woman, Amelie, for her birthday.

He'd never said anything about having a woman in his life. But I'd never asked him directly, either.

"My dearest Amelie..."

Could it be a sister? An aunt? People sent flowers to relatives all the time.

The problem was the word "my." When it came from Lero, it sounded especially intimate.

Not that it meant anything, of course. It wasn't *supposed* to mean anything. I was leaving here eventually, never to see Lero again. He was perfectly within his right to send women flowers and call them "my." None of it was my business.

Yet I just stood there, frozen in place like having been struck by lightning.

"Would you like some breakfast, now?" Lero's voice sounded right above my ear.

His hand came into view, closing the laptop.

I felt like I'd been caught snooping. It wasn't my fault he'd left it open for me to see, but I knew he hadn't done it on purpose. The way his eyes flicked away from mine and his brows furrowed told me Lero would've preferred to keep the existence of Amelie a secret from me.

I fidgeted with the edge of my blouse.

"Oh. I'll just get some cereal," I mumbled, gesturing at the door to the pantry.

Since our arrival to the island, we'd had groceries delivered by a charter plane. Milk had arrived as well.

"Cereal?" Lero made a face. "That's just for emergencies. I finally got some real food. We now have a good selection of cheeses and fresh cream, too. It's about time we had a decent breakfast."

Personally, I found Lero's obsession with fancy food endearing. Though, I didn't entirely understand it. It was like he created his own problems by stressing out about having an adequate wine selection in the cellar or a certain type of cheese in his fridge.

"Coffee?" he asked, making a move toward the butler's pantry with all the small appliances.

"Yes, please, but... I can get it myself."

It'd taken me a while but with Lero's help, I'd finally figured out how to operate the complex piece of equipment that he called a "coffee machine." Though, it still looked more like a spaceship to me.

"I'll get it." He placed a hand on my shoulder, pressing down gently for me to take my seat on one of the bar stools at the counter.

His frown had smoothed out, which put me more at ease too.

"Here you go." Lero returned to the kitchen a minute later and placed a warm cup of coffee topped with milky foam in front of me. "Just the way you like it."

He'd never asked me how I liked my coffee. It seemed he'd paid attention all along though, for it was exactly how a perfect cup of coffee should be, in my opinion—no sugar and lots of warm milk.

"Thank you." I took a sip. Closing my eyes in pleasure, I savored the rich creamy taste.

Lero's "emergency" supplies tended to be of a highest quality possible. He really knew his stuff when it came to tea, or coffee, or food.

I might have moaned a little, for when I opened my eyes, Lero was staring at me. The gentle half-smile curving his lips reminded me of the one and only time we'd ever woken up in the same bed, just before he'd dreamily asked me to kiss him and I'd so eagerly obliged.

He'd made his intentions clear since then. His goal was to get me off this island as soon as it was safe, and to never see me again. No more kissing. No more daydreaming about it, either. I was at his place out of necessity, not because he enjoyed my company.

"Something smells amazing," I said, dropping my gaze to the coffee cup in my hands. "Like baking?"

"Croissants," he announced, grabbing an oven mitt.

Opening one of the two ovens in the kitchen, he produced a tray full of golden, puffy crescents.

"You baked them?" I gaped at the tray as he set it on the counter.

Even without tasting one, I could tell that these did not come from a pack of frozen dough, either. The mouth-watering smell made my stomach rumble. I reached to grab one of the pastries.

"Too hot." Lero shifted the tray out of my reach. "Let them cool off a little while I make the eggs."

"Eggs?" A tray of freshly-baked croissants was a fine breakfast already, in my opinion.

"Do you like Eggs Benedict?" he asked. "It won't take me long."

Lero obviously wasn't a stranger in the kitchen. His movements were measured, practiced, and confident.

To me, whipping up a Hollandaise sauce from scratch required a level of skill I'd never even dreamed of achieving. But Lero made it look easy as he stirred the egg yolks, butter, and spices in the small pot on the stove.

Watching him, I now understood why he craved the luxuries of life. He'd been starved and tortured. There still was the threat of him being recaptured. Instead of freaking out or crying in the corner like some would in his place, Lero was baking croissants and ordering fine cheeses.

Maybe this was a part of how he was dealing with what had happened to him? By bringing the familiar routine back into his life. By ensuring he had the things he wanted and loved in his life again.

If so, who was I to judge him? Whatever his "normal" was, I wished he would get it back soon. I wished it would comfort him and help him recover from the nightmare he'd been through and from the horrors he wouldn't talk to me about.

"Do you always cook your own food?" I asked softly.

"I try to, yes. I prefer to eat what I make myself or the food prepared in one of my establishments."

"You own a restaurant?" That made a perfect sense. "Because if you don't, you totally should."

He tucked a strand of his hair behind his ear.

"I've had restaurants before. But my latest establishment was a cabaret."

"You mean like a *real* cabaret?" I gaped at him.

He glanced my way, a teasing spark lighting his eyes. "Are there any *fake* ones?"

I smiled, too, happy to see him more relaxed this morning.

"I've never been to a cabaret," I said. "Only saw one in a movie. It sounds exciting."

"A cabaret is only as good as its performers. A lot of talented people worked for me. Some were truly magical." His brow twitched with a slight shadow moving over his expression.

"What happened to your place? Where are the performers, now?"

"I sold the business, but most of the people who worked for me are still working there now. That was the condition of the sale—the people would keep their jobs," he said, poaching the eggs.

"Why did you sell?"

He glanced aside. "It was time. I'd had it for too long."

"Many people keep their businesses all their lives. There's no time limit on how long you can have it, is there?"

"In my case, there is." He placed a croissant on each of the two plates on the counter between us.

I watched him plate the rest of the food next. "Who taught you how to cook? Your mom?"

He shook his head.

"No, I learned from TV shows and cookbooks. By the time I started really appreciating the benefits of home cooking, my mother was no longer around to teach me."

"I'm sorry." I looked up, finding his eyes with mine. "How did she pass?"

"It's been a long time," he said calmly, not answering my question.

"How about your dad?" I ventured carefully.

He took the cutlery out of the drawer.

"He's passed away, too."

"Is it just you and you brother, then?"

"Yes."

I didn't exactly win a lottery with my own family, but Lero's murderous sibling was truly despicable.

"What happened between you and your brother, Lero?" I blurted out. "Why is he so...brutal to you?"

He stared past me, through the open doors and out to the horizon beyond.

"My brother..." he started slowly. "Dez isn't really himself, not how he used to be. I don't even know how much I can blame him for his actions, which doesn't make them any better of course."

"What happened that made him so?"

"He has been heavily influenced by someone, from a very young age." Lero appeared to be choosing his words carefully. "To the point that his actions or judgements can hardly be considered his own, now."

"Sounds like he's been brainwashed?" I studied his face. There was concern in his expression, even pain, but not as acute as a new hurt would be. Whatever was happening with Lero's brother must've been happening for a while now. "Did he join a gang? Or a cult?"

"Something like that." Lero nodded, heaving a deep breath. A long strand of hair slid down and over his face again. He released a frustrated groan, twisting his hair back.

"Here." I produced a spare hair elastic from the pocket of my shorts. "I have thick hair, too. It can be a real pain."

He glanced at the elastic in my hand. "What exactly do I do with this?"

"A bun. Or a ponytail," I suggested, getting up. "Is this the first time you've ever had long hair?"

"Since I was much younger, yes."

"May I?" I walked behind him and gathered the silky, fragrant mass of his mane in my hands.

He had to bend his knees a little and tilt his head back for me to do it properly. Then I quickly twisted his hair into a fairly neat knot on the back of his head.

"Better?" I stepped back, admiring my handiwork. "It'll be cooler too, now. Long hair can feel like a fur coat on your shoulders in hot weather."

"Fur... Exactly." He gave me a grateful smile over his shoulder. "Thank you. I wish I could order a haircut delivered."

"Well, you could always have a barber shipped over," I quipped. "Or, I could cut your hair, if you absolutely want to chop it off. Though, long hair looks good on you, I have to say."

The long tresses added a romantic, bohemian flair to his appearance, softening the sharp angles of his handsome face.

"You can cut hair?" he asked with a glint of curiosity in his eyes.

"I took a course during Christmas vacation one year," I mumbled, realizing how stupid my offer had been. He'd probably gotten his haircuts from some famous stylist in Paris.

Backing away, I stumbled over to my seat again, clutching my hands into fists to get rid of the lingering sensation of his silky strands sliding between my fingers.

"I'll keep it in mind." He moved back to plating our breakfast but kept looking at me every now and again. My heart skipped a beat every time our gazes crossed, and I wasn't sure whether it was the morning sun heating up the house or...something else.

"Do you like to cook, Stella?" he asked.

"Me? Oh, um... I don't cook much. I live alone, work late... I mostly stick with quick and easy."

Lero topped the eggs with the Hollandaise. That stubborn strand had made its way out of the knot I'd made, dropping over his forehead once again. His gray eyes glistened from under it.

"There're few pleasures in life, Stella."

He licked the sauce spoon, sliding his gaze down my body. If I didn't know better, I'd think he might be wondering what it would feel like to lick me, too. The idea of his tongue on my skin made my body feel both uncomfortably hot and pleasantly tingly.

"Why deny yourself the joy of good food?" He cut off a small piece of his creation, speared it on a fork, then offered it to me, not releasing the fork from his fingers. "Try this, but don't just *eat* it. Think about all the flavors, textures, and emotions that fill your senses and your heart while the food is in your mouth."

His voice turned softer and deeper as he spoke, tempting and full of promise.

"He is just talking about the food, Stella." I had to remind myself mentally before leaning toward him.

His attention was fully on me as I wrapped my lips around the fork, taking his offering in my mouth. The rich flavors of the sauce hit my senses, with the warm, flaky pastry practically melting on my tongue.

He leaned over the counter, watching me.

"More?" he said softly when I'd swallowed.

"Yes. Please." I licked my lips.

He didn't move, staring at me, his eyes lingering on my mouth.

My heart pounded so hard, I could hear the echo of his words from our first day here *"Kiss me"* in the thundering sound.

"Lero..." I had no idea what to say, but I needed a confirmation from him that this almost-palpable tension of attraction that crackled in the air between us right now was not just my imagination. Every nerve in my body stood on end, charging me with energy I thought would rip me apart, unless I... unless *he* did something about it.

He frowned and closed his eyes, leaning back with a long sigh, and my heart dropped into a pit of bitter disappointment.

"Of course you can have more, Stella," he exhaled, sliding the whole plate my way. "I made it all for you."

Chapter 12

"Is this the way you usually take?" Lero asked, as we strolled along the path toward the bridge connecting the two halves of Blue Cay.

"Yes. Unless I just go for a walk on a beach."

We'd started our second week on the island. Lero insisted it was safer for me to remain here for now. I hadn't argued too much against staying on the beautiful island instead of returning to the hustle of the city, even though he still hadn't answered many of my questions. Today, he had offered to accompany me on one of my "treasure hunting" outings.

"The tide is low right now." I gestured at the strait under the bridge. "I like coming here to see what the water leaves behind."

"Have you found anything interesting, so far?" he asked.

I nodded.

"A few neat pieces of coral. Oh, and a round piece of glass. The surf has polished it into an almost perfect oval."

Lero spent his mornings either in the closet room or in the spacious office in the front of the house. When I caught glimpses of him in there, he'd be on his laptop or on the phone.

I worked the first half of the day, too. The afternoons, we often spent together. Since he took on all the cooking, I did our laundry and vacuumed. Lero would get busy in the kitchen while I read a book on the tablet he'd ordered for me.

It was easy to forget about any danger that might still be out there. I didn't mind staying in this cozy little bubble of the island life we'd created.

"Careful." Lero grabbed my hand, helping me down the slope.

I accepted his help but let go of his hand the moment we reached the wet sand under the bridge. As much as I loved holding hands with Lero, it felt too intimate. He'd voiced his expectations—we were to part for good eventually. Not allowing myself to forget that, I carefully maintained the distance he'd established.

We waded in the ankle-deep water on the very bottom of the straight.

"Look!" I crouched to dig out a dark round object half-covered by the sand.

"What is it?"

"I believe it's a rock." I twisted the flat disk between my fingers. "But it's been polished flat and round, see?"

"Beautiful." He laughed. "Looks like a true treasure."

I tucked the flat rock into the back pocket of my jeans, intending to add it to the collection I'd started to assemble on a shelf in my bathroom.

We approached the south end of the strait. On the right, the beach ended in a rocky cliff that went on, all the way around the western shore of the Blue Cay and behind the manager's cottage.

"You know what a true treasure would be?" I said to Lero as we came closer to the rocky end with surf foaming around it.

He glanced at me. "Tell me."

"I saw a huge shell down there when I went swimming the other day." I gestured at the water beyond the surf. "It must be the queen conch. I don't think it has a mollusk inside. It's enormous, and it appears to be stuck in the rocks. Too deep for me to get it."

"Where exactly was it?" Lero waded into the water closer to me.

"Right there, just about twenty feet from here or so." I gestured with my hand. "Not far from the shore, but there is a drop off. It's deep—"

I turned to face him, only to find him ripping his shirt off over his head.

"Lero? No," I protested, guessing his intentions. "It's really deep there."

But he'd already taken his pants off and tossed them onto the sand, heading into the sea with nothing but a pair of black briefs on.

"Lero!" I hurried through the waves after him, more than a little concerned. "It's too deep."

"I'll be right back." He casually waved me off before diving in.

"But how well can you swim?" I yelled after him, as he disappeared from sight.

He'd said he *could* swim, but he'd also said he disliked water, especially being submerged in it. Which wouldn't be something a good swimmer would say, would it?

I couldn't believe it. Lero wouldn't even take baths or swim in a pool. Now, he dove headfirst into the ocean. Just because I said I wanted a shell from the bottom.

Unlike the northern beaches, the waves on the southern shore of the island were much stronger, unbroken by the reef barrier. They swayed me on my feet, reaching up to my chest, as I peered into the water, anxiously searching for any sign of Lero.

I hadn't thought about starting to count seconds the moment he went in. Now, it felt like an eternity had passed. He'd been down there for ages. Much longer than was humanly possible.

Panic rose in my throat with each passing moment. I wasn't a strong swimmer myself, but dammit I couldn't let him drown.

Taking a step into the waves, I was about to dive in after him when his dark head broke through the water.

"Lero..." I exhaled, pressing my hands to my chest to still my racing heart.

Sea water sluicing down his face, his black hair plastered to his cheeks and forehead, he smiled, holding up the freaking conch shell in his hands.

"Is this the one?" He beamed, coming closer.

Relief made me weak in my knees, the waves nearly knocking me off my feet as he walked me out of the water.

"Don't you ever scare me like that." Placing my hands on the shell, I pressed my forehead to his chest, saying a small prayer in my mind for getting him back alive, safe, and sound.

He let me hold the shell, moving his hands to my waist.

"You were right." His voice sounded soft and low. "*This* is a real treasure."

My heart all but skidded to a stop, then took off in a gallop at his touch. The warmth of his large hands seeped through the wet material of my blouse.

Suddenly, his body stiffened. Like a shield lowered over his features, replacing the warm expression with a deep frown of concern.

"A boat," he said, staring over my shoulder.

The sound of a motor reached me over the noise of the surf. Lero promptly crouched behind a shrub at the edge of the beach, taking me with him.

I peeked through the branches of the shrub. A small, white motorboat was slowly moving parallel with the shore. It kept at a safe distance, however.

"I don't think they're coming this way," I whispered, as if the people on the boat could hear me. Lero's concern had filtered to me, but I tried to calm him. "It's not unusual for watercraft to pass by."

"Have you seen boats pass by before?" he asked.

The location of Blue Cay kept it fairly isolated from the most populated islands and away from the traffic between them.

"No. Not yet, but—"

"I shouldn't have stayed here," he said firmly.

The boat kept gliding past Blue Cay, but I had a feeling it wasn't just this particular watercraft that Lero worried about.

"You said this was a safe place," I reminded him.

"It is, but my being here makes it no longer safe for you. If they come here searching for me..." A shudder rolled across his wide shoulders. "I need to leave."

"Leave me here alone?" I exclaimed. "How would that be safer?"

I didn't share Lero's fears, not to the same degree, anyway. He'd refused to give me any details about the threat. Whatever he was worried about remained very much an abstract concept to me. The idea of him leaving, however, had immediately cast a gloom over the sunny day.

"No one knows Blue Cay is mine, Stella. At least none of the people I don't want to know, and I need to keep it this way. Me being here may compromise that. In my mind, I always knew that. In my heart, however..."

He paused, keeping his eyes on mine. With me crouching sideways in front of him, my knees ended up propped against his naked thigh. His arms remained around me, his large body crowding me. This close to him was both the only place I wanted to be right now, and the one I knew I had to leave as soon as possible.

He cleared his throat, getting up.

"Your clothes are wet. You'll get cold," he said, helping me up, too. "We should go back to the house."

"Where will you go when you leave?" I asked, not worrying about my clothes at all.

"To Europe, as I've planned to do all along. It was selfish and foolish of me to stay here as long as I did." He took a long look out to sea, scanning the horizon, then picked up his clothes from the sand. "I'll go back to Paris, make sure I'm seen in Europe. If they want to hunt me, they can do it there, not here."

"You'll use yourself as a bait?"

He shook his head, a corner of his mouth twitching up in a smile. "Not bait, a lure. The last time they saw me, it was in North America. I'll have to make sure they know I'm no longer even in the same hemisphere. So they'll have no reason to search for me here."

"What if they catch you again?"

"They won't get me that easily this time. I'm much better prepared and far less trusting."

Despite his assurances, the restless worry gnawed at me from inside.

"What do they want from you, Lero?"

My heart squeezed painfully when I thought back to how I'd found him on my balcony—weak and broken. It must've taken hellish torture to break a strong man like Lero.

"Stella," he said as we headed up the path back to the house. "Please, trust me on this. It's best if you don't know any details. None at all."

His plan was to let me go back to my old life after all of this was over. In that he was right, I didn't need to know any of this to live the way I used to before. But could I really go back to the way it was after spending all this time here with him? After having learned even as little as I had?

"Lero, can I come with you?" I hurried up the path next to him.

"No," he said resolutely. "I'll worry less, knowing you're safe and protected here."

"But how would I know if something happened to you? What if I could help you? Maybe we could figure out how to stop your brother for good? Together?"

"Absolutely no—"

"Can you at least tell me who exactly these people are? The name of their gang or their...organization? How would I find you if they take you again?"

He stopped abruptly. Facing me, he took hold of my upper arms.

"Whatever happens, Stella, do not go looking for me. Do you hear me?"

I met his eyes straight on.

"What if you need help breaking free?"

He stroked the bare skin of my arms with his thumbs.

"I won't let them take me. Not again."

"Promise?" I demanded.

His gaze flickered away from mine. For someone who'd made me promise many things to him by now, he wouldn't make promises that easily himself.

<hr/>

THE NEXT DAY, LERO was gone. He calmly shook my hand before climbing into the sea plane cabin, as if I were just his real estate agent, nothing more. As if we hadn't spent nearly two weeks living under the same roof, sharing meals, walks, and conversations. My insides tightened with worry for him the moment he set his foot into the plane to fly away from me.

While he was gone, I did as he'd instructed. I kept the island security system on at all times. In the evening, I locked up the house and armed its system, too. In the morning, I thoroughly checked the feed from all the cameras before disarming the house security to go outside.

Once every few days, a sea plane delivered groceries and other supplies. But Lero had told me to stay in the house while the pilot beached the plane, unloaded the crates, and carried them to the front porch. I was not to talk to or be seen by anyone.

I worked for a few hours every day. In the afternoon, I read to get my mind off things or explored Blue Cay, making sure to stay out of sight of any passing traffic, either in the air or on water. Not that there were many of either.

By now, I'd learned every nook and cranny of the small double-island. Sometimes, I went swimming in the warm lagoon protected by the reef. Lero had sternly instructed me not to swim past the reef, and I wasn't a strong enough swimmer to venture that far, anyway. During low tides, I often went to the bridge, digging pretty shells, intricate pieces of coral, and sometimes polished colored glass out of the wet sand.

A week had passed. And another one was almost through. I hoped things would get better soon, safe enough for Lero to return to me. Though it would also mean that I'd have to leave him then.

At least, he called me almost daily. His calls were brief, and his words few, but I loved hearing his voice. It told me he was safe and free. Talking to him also made me feel connected with the rest of the world. Being all alone here, on the entire island, often felt like being set adrift.

I knew I shouldn't be thinking about him much. I had to use the time away from him to "cleanse" my system from everything Lero. If I had to leave here at some point, I needed to train myself to be without him. But it wasn't easy. The thoughts of him had long been a part of me.

To access the system controls in the closet, I had no choice but to go into his room daily, though I made sure not to linger. He hadn't been smoking lately—at least not in my presence—but the unique fragrance of his cigarettes still clung to his skin when he'd left. It lingered in his room, too, making me feel like he was close.

One morning, he called me while I was in the closet, watching the footage recorded by the cameras overnight. It was the most boring part of my routine—staring at the videos of waves, birds, and tall grass swaying in the breeze. Lero insisted I review them regularly, even if I didn't know exactly what I was looking for other than "anything suspicious."

"How was your night?" he asked, polite but distant.

I released a breath, glad to hear his voice again.

"Quiet."

"Quiet is good. You're not too bored?"

I wasn't bored as much as I was lonely, at times.

"Not really. I have some work to do every day. And I read."

"What are you reading?" He seemed to be in a more talkative mood today.

"A book. It's called *Rein*, by Bex McLynn. It's about wolf shifters."

"Who?" Unexpected interest rang in his voice.

"Wolf shifters. You know, people who sometimes turn into wolves? Kind of like werewolves. It's fiction, of course."

"Oh... And, how do you like the book?" his voice sounded guarded, now.

"I love it. It's..."

The love story was magical, the hero dreamy. And sex... Well, I wasn't going to discuss the amazing sex that took place in *Rein* with Lero.

"It's a very well-done story. It has everything—magic, suspense, mystery... Romance, too."

"Romance? With a werewolf?" A bitter note slipped into his voice. "Well, now I know it's fiction."

"Love knows no boundaries," I said, risking sounding like a hopeless romantic.

But wasn't it true? All of us were a combination of good and bad, weird and normal. The trick was to find a person who'd love the good in us enough to accept the bad, and who would be willing to take our weird as normal. At least I firmly believed so.

"And how are you?" I asked since he remained quiet.

"Good. Thank you. Could you please disarm the security at three thirty this afternoon?" he said. "I'm coming back."

My heart had no business jumping as high as it did then racing like crazy at his words.

"You're coming back?" I asked, afraid to believe. "Is everything...well then?"

"Yes. I'll be there in a few hours." Did I hear a smile in his voice, too? "Anything you'd like me to bring for you?"

Just you.

My chest swelled with longing. I hadn't even realized how much I wanted to see Lero again. So much for trying to "cleanse my system" of him, I sighed.

"No. Thank you. I have everything I need," I replied, willing my heart to slow down.

As soon as I finished working that afternoon, I hurried to the beach. I stared at the sky for so long, searching for the shape of a plane, that my eyes started to hurt.

When the sound of the plane engine finally reached my ear, I almost jumped up with excitement. Holding my breath, I watched the tiny form of the floatplane grow in the sky as it approached.

The pilot backed it onto the beach as he always did. As soon as he tied the rope to a nearby tree, the passenger's door opened and Lero jumped onto the float and from there to the beach.

Dressed in a light gray-blue suit, a tie, and leather shoes, he was bringing the air of the outside world with him. Somewhere out there, people wore business clothes, had meetings, and traveled, as opposed to wearing flip-flops, shorts, and wading along the same beaches over and over again.

He spotted me, lifted his hand in greeting, and smiled—a wide, happy grin of his I'd never seen before and now didn't want to live without.

Kicking off my flip-flops, I ran to him. The smile lingered on his lips, shining through his eyes. Warm and inviting, it drew me closer. When only a few feet remained between us, I stopped. I'd give anything to feel his arms around me. Despite his smile, however, the usual aura of polite distance hung around him, making even a friendly hug impossible.

"Hi." I peered at him from under a few strands of hair that had made their way out of my bun. My lips spread wide in a smile that couldn't be helped. "Welcome back."

The sea breeze played with his long hair, which gave him an especially romantic flair, as if he'd come from a fantasy world.

"Hi, Stella. It's very good to see you again." He lifted his hand to my face, caught one of the fly-away strands of my hair between his fingers, then gently placed it behind my ear. "I can never tell what color your eyes are," he said unexpectedly. "There is green, and brown, and gray. But right now, they're almost blue."

"Hazel." My face heated under his attention. The warmth of his gaze was spreading to my heart, erupting into a kaleidoscope of butterflies in my stomach. "My aunt used to say hazel is what you call the eyes like mine that have no particular color."

"Or have all colors at once." He let his hand linger just under my ear, the tips of his fingers nearly touching the side of my neck.

The breeze brought a faint whiff of *Lero's scent* my way, and I drew in a long breath, filling my lungs with it. God, how I'd missed him. The day had brightened somehow now that he was here.

If it was wrong for me to want him then why did it feel so right to have him here, with me again?

"Was it a good trip?" I asked, trying hard not to jump into his arms and make a fool out of myself.

"Overall, yes." His grin grew wider. Smiling made him even more handsome if it was at all possible. I loved seeing him happy so much, it could prove addictive.

"How about your brother?" I asked cautiously. "Where is he now?"

He glanced over his shoulder at the pilot who started unloading bags and boxes off the plane.

"All of them are moving East next, farther away from here, which I was glad to learn." He raked a hand through his hair. "I'll have to leave again in four days, Stella. But it'll just be a short, overnight trip."

In four days, I'd probably be leaving myself now that things were starting to look better. I didn't feel like bringing that up right now, though.

Lero turned back to grab one of the boxes.

"I got something for dinner tonight. Do you like lobster?" He lifted the box with a picture of two red lobsters on it.

"Who doesn't?" I smiled.

The breeze blew his hair over his face. My hand jerked to brush it away for him, but he beat me to it, shoving his hair back again.

All this time he'd been away, he never got the haircut he'd so badly wished for before.

"You left your hair long," I said.

He cleared his throat.

"I've decided to take you up on your offer to cut it for me."

"Well, if you trust me—"

"I do."

Chapter 13

STELLA

"I'm ready whenever you are." Lero placed a pair of barber scissors and a gray box with a picture of hair clippers on it on the table.

It was the day after our lobster dinner, another warm and sunny afternoon. I'd finished work a couple of hours ago, and Lero already had a casserole ready to go in the oven for dinner.

I set aside the tablet with the book I was reading.

"Are you absolutely positive you want to cut off your long hair?"

"It really bothers me." He yanked the hair elastic out of his thick, wavy locks.

Dark as night, they spread over his wide shoulders, sunrays streaking them with burgundy red. It'd be a crime to chop off this beauty. Though, knowing how he got the long hair in the first place, I understood the reasons why he wanted to get rid of it. It was a reminder of his time in captivity.

"And you're sure you want *me* to do it?" I verified.

He could've gotten a haircut during his trip since he'd found the time to get the scissors and the clippers. Instead, he'd been dealing with the long hair he despised, waiting to get home, for me to cut it.

"You offered." He tilted his head, holding my gaze.

"Fine." I smiled, getting up from the couch. "But I need to warn you, the result may not be what you're used to."

He speared his fingers through his mane, shaking it out.

"Will it be shorter?"

"*That* I guarantee!" I laughed.

"Then, I'm all yours."

I wish.

I blinked, ducking my head down to hide the sudden blush that warmed my cheeks at that thought.

"Where do you want me?" he asked.

"W-What?"

"Here?" He made a sweeping gesture around the sitting room. "In the bathroom? Or would it be better if we went outside?"

"Oh, outside would be best for cutting hair." Of course, that was what he was talking about—cutting hair. "We can go out on the patio?"

With a nod, he grabbed a chair from the table then walked out through the back doors.

Swiping the scissors and the hair clippers off the table, I ran to my room to grab a comb, then followed Lero to the patio with the drained swimming pool.

Apparently, Lero disliked swimming so much, he didn't even want to bother with the pool maintenance. He hadn't gone down to the beach lately, either. His obsessive wading in the water had stopped abruptly. The last time I saw him in the water was when he dove to get the conch shell for me. I still had it on my shelf with all the ocean treasures I'd collected.

"Here is good?" he asked, gesturing at the chair he'd placed to the right of the empty pool.

"Sure. But we need a towel or a sheet." I took a critical look at his crisp, white shirt. "You'll get covered in hair as I cut."

"Or..." He deftly unbuttoned his shirt then shrugged it off. "Would this work?" He glanced at me innocently, tossing the shirt aside. "I'll just take a shower after."

Cutting his hair while being presented with an unobstructed view of his tanned, muscular torso? He was obviously a brave man, unafraid of losing an ear to my scissors.

"Well..." I swallowed hard. "I need some water, you know...to wet down your hair?"

I ran back to the kitchen, filled a glass with water, and drank half of it. Taking a few deep breaths, I waited until some of my composure returned before going out again.

Lero took a seat in the chair, and I approached him from behind. It felt safer to stay here, out of his sight for now.

"Let's do this." I splashed some water on my hands then ran them through his hair. Silky and soft, with a slight wave, it reached below his shoulders.

"You have beautiful hair," I blurted, enjoying the sensation of it under my fingers. "It's almost a shame to cut it."

"Cut it," he said firmly. "Please. I hate how it feels against my neck." A shudder ran across his shoulders.

"Okay." I snipped a strand off. It fluttered down to the stones of the patio.

Lero remained quiet as I worked. I tried to replicate the stylish haircut he'd had the last time I'd seen him with short hair.

"I'm doing my best, but it won't be perfect." I felt the need to warn him again as I kept snipping at his hair.

"It doesn't need to be perfect," he reassured me.

While working, I tried hard not to pay attention to how smoothly his tanned skin stretched over the dips and valleys of his muscular arms and shoulders or how amazing he smelled this close. Keeping my focus proved incredibly difficult.

Once done, I used the hair clippers to clean up the shape on his nape and temples, then stepped in front of him to assess my handiwork.

Styling his now short hair with my fingers, I made sure I got the shape right. It wasn't just a trim, his hair had been too overgrown for me to follow the previous pattern. Surprisingly, it looked pretty good, better than I thought I could do. But then again, everything looked good on Lero.

I glanced down, and his gaze trapped mine. Gray like a rainy sky, his eyes focused on my face. I froze, staring into them, my fingers tangled in his hair.

My knees buckled, bumping into his. Deep inside, I knew I had to move away from him, but I forgot all the reasons why. More than anything in the world, I just wanted to keep touching him right now.

Instead of taking my hands off him, I flattened them, cupping his face.

Heat flashed in his eyes, reflecting red. His jaw muscles flexed, and his top lip lifted, displaying the tips of his canines. Grabbing me around my waist suddenly, he yanked me into his lap.

Air rushed out of me with a gasp. My hands dropped to his shoulders. The sensation of his bare skin under my palms spread through my body like honey, thick and sweet. Shockingly, the wild expression in his eyes thrilled me instead of terrified.

Silently, he slid his hands under my t-shirt and up my sides, bringing me closer. So close, I felt him grow hard against me through the material of his pants.

"Kiss me." His words rushed through my brain, once again.

Had I said it out loud right now, I had no doubt he would kiss me. He'd do more to me than kissing, I sensed. Tingling licks of heat ran up my inner thighs, pooling hot in my lower belly. I longed for his kiss and whatever else he wished to do to me.

His fingers digging into my sides, his body shaking with strain, he did nothing more but hold me.

Something was holding him back.

Amelie...

The name rose in my mind unbidden.

Lero had never been the man I wished to have for sex only. For years, I'd held a place reserved for him in my heart. I wanted him to come and claim it, or I didn't want him at all. With Lero, I couldn't do it half-way. It had to be all or nothing.

If there already was another woman, however... None of this would be what I wished to have with him.

"Lero. Who is Amelie?" I asked softly.

My heart sunk, as I watched the desire dim in his eyes at the sound of her name. He kept holding me tightly, but his entire body went rigid, as if every muscle in it flexed to the limit.

His eyes were no longer a serene gray. Rings of fire appeared to dance around his pupils. They throbbed and grew, flooding his irises with red.

"Your eyes..." I whispered, unsure about what I was seeing. Did my own eyes deceive me? Was the setting sun playing tricks on me? It looked surreal. Unnatural.

He shut them.

"Get off my lap, Stella," he growled low.

His voice sounded unfamiliar, foreign, and terrifying. But it was his words that hurt me the most.

I realized that was all he'd ever done. He'd lure me in with his kindness, then hold me at arm's length. He'd enthrall me with a smile, then build a wall between us. He'd let me glimpse the genuine attraction I longed for only to slam the door to his soul shut against me.

And like a starving woman, I'd been following the crumbs, unable to stop dreaming of the feast I'd imagine could be there one day.

I took my trembling hands off him.

"You can't do this," I said bitterly. "You can't pull me in, then push me away the very next moment."

Tears burned my eyes, from hurt as much as from the rising anger.

"Talk to me. Lero, I need you to explain—"

"Go! Now!" he roared, lurching up.

Alarm spiked through me at his outburst.

Lifting me by my waist, he deposited me in the chair he'd been sitting in. Without sparing me a glance, he jogged down the stairs to the beach.

Stunned and hurt, I watched as he made his way along the golden sand to the end of the beach then disappeared behind the trees to the right.

How could he make me feel alive with a smile then kill me with one word? Hot, bitter tears rushed out of my eyes. What had I done, for him to treat me that way, to literally toss me aside and run away from me as if I were...a disease?

Pain squeezed my chest like a steel band, making it hard to breathe.

Spinning on my heel, I rushed through the house and out of the front door.

Not willing to cross paths with Lero as he'd made it clear he wished to avoid me, I kept to the opposite side of the island.

I wanted to run without stopping, far away from here. But how far could I run on an island?

Soon, I made it to the bridge. Instead of using it, however, I crossed under it, wading barefoot through the water slowly rising with the evening tide. Climbing up a dirt path, I made my way to the second building on Blue Cay, the manager's cottage.

I hadn't been here since the viewing well over a year ago. Lero seemed to have done even fewer updates in here. The place looked very much the same as I'd seen it last.

Despite being called "the cottage," it was a full-size house, with four bedrooms and several spacious common areas. It had the same lavish finishes as the main house, too. Marble, expensive wood, and stylish furniture made it just a smaller version of the place where Lero and I stayed.

Well, I couldn't go back to Lero's house, now. Not tonight. I just didn't have it in me to face his usual cool composure when everything inside me bubbled and burned.

Instead, I locked the front door then went to the kitchen to pour myself a glass of water. Like in the main house, the cabinets here were filled with dishes. A number of small appliances graced the granite countertops. The pantry held a selection of non-perishables here, too. Lero obviously had accounted for the possibility of someone staying here. Except that I wasn't hungry at all.

The anger had simmered down somewhat, but the unsettled feeling still weighed heavily on my chest.

Mostly out of habit, I did a full walk-around, just like I'd done every night while at the main house, locking all doors and checking every window.

The backyard here faced west, the shore ended not in a beach but in a drop-off. White-crested waves rolled over it. The rhythmic sound of the surf reached me even with the windows closed, soothing my nerves.

With the glass of water in my hand, I sat on the couch, without turning on the lights, and watched the sky grow darker as the sun sat deeper behind the horizon and my thoughts kept circling around Lero.

Even after all this time, he had largely remained a mystery to me—a man made entirely of questions. The only question I no longer had was "What if?"

For fourteen years, I asked myself, "What if I met him as a grown woman?"

Then, after the viewing of this island, I'd asked, "What if we weren't a client and an agent?"

Now, there were no more "what ifs." I'd met him as a grown woman, I was no longer his agent, and I got my answer.

Nothing.

Absolutely nothing would ever be between us. Lero would never allow for anything at all.

Chapter 14

STELLA

I fell asleep on the couch. When I woke, the sun was up already. I didn't remember getting up in the night, but a cozy cotton blanket I'd never seen before covered me to my shoulders.

Someone had been here.

The thought jolted me awake. I bolted upright, looking around. "Who's here?"

All was quiet, the glass back doors closed, windows shut.

My gaze fell on the breakfast tray on the side table next to the couch. The dishes were covered with metal domes. An insulated cup was filled with coffee. I took a sip, it was just the way I liked it.

Lero...

I plopped back on the couch, hugging the mug with both hands and staring at the silver domes arranged on the tray. Among them stood a small, frosted glass vase with a bouquet of local tall grass and flowers.

As the property owner, Lero would obviously have a key to the cottage. He'd come earlier this morning to cover me with the blanket and deliver breakfast. He'd found the time to gather a bouquet for me on the way, it appeared.

I lifted one of the domes, finding a scone with cream and jam under it. When I broke the scone in half, it was still warm in the middle. He'd baked them fresh this morning...

I dropped the pastry back on the plate and buried my face in my hands.

Why would he do this? Why couldn't he just make it easier for me to grow cold with time, instead of warming my heart with any kind of attention.

Why did he need to continue taking care of me if he didn't *care*?

I lifted the other dome, searching the tray for a note, a card, a message, anything. Just a peach yogurt and a bowl of fresh fruit stood there. Not a word written anywhere. What was I supposed to make of this breakfast? And the flowers?

Was it a gesture to apologize? What kind of an apology, though? *"Sorry, I hope you had a nice stay on Blue Cay. Have a good life."* Or *"Sorry, let's talk. You mean something to me."*

I couldn't assume anything, definitely couldn't allow myself to read too much into his kind gestures anymore. Lero had always been polite and attentive. It didn't have to mean anything more than that. I was his house guest, and he was a classy host. Nothing more.

He'd told me—straight and clear—he never wanted to have our paths cross again in the future. I'd spent almost four weeks on this island now, and never once had he said anything about having a relationship with me other than that of my protector until it was safe enough for him to take me back home.

I might be angry, and my heart ached as if torn in two, but Lero had never made any romantic promises to me, so I couldn't blame him for breaking any of them.

Sipping the warm, fragrant coffee, I tried to distance myself from longing and heartache and think rationally.

Lero had been taking care of me ever since I got here. He'd cooked for me and made sure I was safe. He'd had fresh groceries delivered for me even while he was away. He dove into the ocean for me, despite his severe dislike of water.

But had he always been just a gracious host? Was I really nothing but a house guest to him? Had I let my imagination run wild, making more of his smiles than they really meant?

Was I the only one to blame?

I recalled the fire in his eyes. It'd been intense, undiluted desire—for me. I'd never seen such a feral need before, so I couldn't have imagined it to that extend. It had surprised me and excited me, too.

Lero wanted me, without a doubt. I'd felt the physical evidence of that, pressed hard against my core.

But he'd been fighting it. And that was the most important part. He didn't *want* to want me. He'd shoved me away because he *couldn't* want me.

He didn't care to explain his reasons, but I sensed they had everything to do with the woman named Amelie. Hearing her name had acted like the crack of a whip, snapping him out of his desire quicker than a cold shower.

Though, I didn't believe Amelie was the woman he loved. He couldn't love her. For if he truly did, why was he spending any time here with me?

One way or another, however, Lero was obviously unavailable. Which meant I had to get off this island as soon as possible. After yesterday, I no longer trusted him completely. I trusted myself even less around him.

Without even noticing, I finished the scone and yogurt, then started on the fruit, now thinking about the best way to leave.

Lero hadn't told me much about his captors, but after his last trip, I understood the situation must be improving.

He hadn't said anything about me going home, but I hadn't brought it up myself, either. Other than feeling lonely when Lero was gone, I'd been rather comfortable on Blue Cay. He'd made sure of it, by catering to my every wish and more.

A frank conversation on the subject of my departure was long overdue. Maybe I could catch a ride with the next airplane that delivered groceries?

I finished my coffee, gathered the empty dishes, and with a bracing breath, headed back to the main house.

The front door was unlocked when I got there, but I knocked before entering. This was the first time I'd ever knocked when entering Lero's house. This morning was different. I didn't feel I belonged here anymore.

"Lero?" I called, stopping in the hallway.

No one replied to me. I heard not a sound.

"Thank you for the breakfast," I said in a polite, neutral tone.

Again, no reply.

Maybe he went for a walk?

I made it to the kitchen, put the dishes into the dishwasher, rinsed and dried the serving tray to put it away. Then, I noticed the piece of paper on the kitchen table. The paper was weighted down by the conch shell he'd gotten for me from the ocean. It was a piece of stationery of *Monsieur L. Sauveterre*. On it, in wide, confident cursive stated,

"Stella, I have to leave earlier than planned. I will be back in three days. Unfortunately, I won't be able to call this time. Please stay safe. Lero.

P.S. There's food in the fridge and a bottle of wine."

I held the paper in my fingers long after I'd finished reading.

He was gone.

My heart pinched painfully, and I let it ache. It was time for my heart to learn how to go on without Lero.

The note was brief and to the point, with no excessive emotions or a hint of sentiment.

I sighed.

This was good. It was how it should be. He set the tone that would make it easier for me to leave him.

Ideally, I would've loved to leave right away. Except that it wasn't that easy to leave an island. I couldn't call the charter company to arrange for a flight using the agency's name again, not without having a very good reason and a detailed explanation for Javier.

Last time I'd done it, almost four weeks ago, it'd been an emergency situation. I *had* to get Lero and myself to Blue Cay. And even then, I'd only avoided having to explain anything to Javier because Lero had called my boss the very next day and settled the matter personally.

Since we'd just received a plane full of supplies yesterday, another grocery delivery probably wouldn't happen in the three days that Lero was gone. Which meant I wouldn't get the ride back to Miami with the pilot either. I was stranded here until Lero came back.

He wasn't even planning to call me this time, which was for the best. Since he wasn't here, I wouldn't have to face him or pretend anything. All I had to do was stay here for three days on my own, I'd been alone for longer than that before. It wasn't a big deal.

Once Lero returned, I would catch the same plane to go back home.

It was time.

———◦———

THE NEXT TWO DAYS WENT by, filled with my usual routine. I locked up the house at night, worked from morning until early afternoon, and ate the eggplant casserole Lero had made for dinner the night I'd spent at the cottage.

As he'd informed me in his note, he didn't call me this trip. Not once. And I couldn't help the worry for him.

I told myself Lero was a grown man who knew what he was doing. He didn't need or want my caring about him. But not knowing how he was doing while away scraped inside me with worry I sensed would never really leave me, no matter how far away I'd be from him in the future or how much time would pass.

To distract myself from thinking about him and fretting over whether he was well and safe out there, I focused on doing things I wouldn't be able to do as easily when I was back in Miami. These were my last days on Blue Cay, after all.

I sunbathed on the patio—naked because who was there to demand I cover up? I took naps, because why not? I went swimming, also naked, because it felt more comfortable without the strings of my bikini digging into my neck and hips. I read to my heart content.

On my last day alone, I made myself some spaghetti with the pasta sauce from a jar since Lero wasn't here to insist on making one from scratch.

If all went as planned, this would be my last dinner on Blue Cay. I might as well make a celebration out of it, I decided—my way to say goodbye to the island I'd grown quite attached to.

I set the massive dining table in the formal part of the house with a linen placemat and a matching napkin, put my spaghetti on a pretty plate, and even located a chunk of parmesan cheese in the fridge.

Before taking my seat in the chair with a high carved back at the head of the table, I remembered the bottle of wine that Lero had mentioned in his note.

It was white wine, I realized when I got the bottle out of the fridge. Obviously, Lero wouldn't leave a bottle of red in a fridge. According to him, red wine was supposed to remain in the "temperature-controlled environment" of the basement right up until its consumption.

Mostly, I drank white wine while on Blue Cay. I preferred its crisp, cool taste in the heat of the Bahamas. Tonight, however, my spaghetti dinner called to be paired with a glass of red. Spaghetti wasn't a seafood. It might only be the pre-made sauce from a jar, but it was supposed to be my celebration dinner, dammit. I needed a proper wine pairing to go with it.

Maybe I'd have something nice for dessert, too. I'd seen a box of chocolate-dipped macarons in the pantry. Then, I'd take a nice, long walk on the beach to say goodbye to this place.

The perfectly round moon shone bright like a streetlight through the large windows of the house. It illuminated every grain of sand on the beach. I wouldn't even need to bring a flashlight with me.

Leaving the bottle of white wine in the fridge, I headed down to the basement for some red instead.

The massive oak door to the cellar creaked when I shoved it open. Cool air enveloped me, refreshing after the lingering heat upstairs.

I rubbed the goosebumps out of my upper arms while walking along the floor-to-ceiling mahogany shelves that lined the walls of the room. Lero had done a good job stocking on wine. There was still plenty of free space, but dark bottles sealed with red, gold, or black wax glistened on many shelves. Knowing his tastes, some of the wine bottles here might cost as much as my car payment or more.

I grabbed one with a pretty gold label. The writing on it wasn't in a language I could read. Italian, maybe? Spanish? Or Portuguese? I didn't care where the wine came from. The important part was that it looked red, even in the reduced light in the cellar.

Holding the bottle, I turned to leave when a low, rumbling noise reached me. Muffled by the walls, it appeared to be coming from inside the house somewhere.

Dread chilled my chest. The sound reminded me of a growling of a large dog—deep, rolling, threatening sound.

How did an animal get in here?

Where would a dog come from on this island? The biggest creatures I'd seen here that didn't live in the water were birds.

Unless the dog came with someone, on a boat or a plane?

I kept the island security system armed at all times. The house alarm, though, was not set yet because I'd planned to go for a walk later. If some uninvited visitors had made it to the island somehow, bypassing Lero's defense system, they'd have no trouble getting in the house.

My heart beat faster. Pressing the wine bottle to my chest, I stopped to listen for any sounds of footfalls or of moving upstairs. If there indeed were intruders in the house, did they come here for me? And if so, would they think to search the basement?

Staying still as a statue, afraid to move, I heard another long rumble, much clearer this time. It didn't seem to be coming from upstairs but from right here, near me, just behind one of the walls.

Jumping away from the shelves, I spun around, taking in the place. Now, that I thought about it, the cellar looked smaller than I remembered from viewing it with Lero. I didn't recall the exact dimensions from the sales brochure, but it seemed shorter.

Carefully, I crept closer to the wall opposite to the entrance. Had it been here before? Or had it been farther back?

Upon closer inspection, one section of the wall shelving appeared to be set inside a frame that was big enough to be a door. Did Lero have a secret room in his cellar?

He always brought up the wine on the few occasions we'd had some with dinner instead of letting me get it. I'd never questioned it. It was in line with his overall chivalry. Now, I wondered if he'd had a reason to keep me out of the cellar.

I pushed on the shelves, trying to slide the section in, but it wouldn't budge. Setting the bottle down on the floor, I ran my hands along the frame, searching for a lever, a button, or whatever else people usually had to touch to open secret passages in the haunted castles in movies.

I found nothing. If Lero indeed was hiding something here, he'd been smart enough to make it hard to find.

Suddenly, another rumble broke through the dead silence of the basement. It appeared to be coming right from behind the wall with the door frame. I immediately changed my mind about trying to open it. Instead, I bent to pick up my bottle of wine, ready to bolt.

The growl grew louder, turning to a roar.

A crushing noise thundered through the cellar. Bottles crashed to the floor, breaking and spilling the precious wine all over the place.

I jumped back from the wall, tripped on the rug soaked with spilled wine, and fell down on my butt.

The framed section of the shelving was destroyed. Broken boards dangled on nails and brackets, pieces of the wall littering the floor.

Another roar thundered—loud and clear—the sound was no longer obstructed by anything.

Then, I saw *what* had destroyed the shelving.

Two giant hands—or paws? Covered in thick, black-as-night fur, tipped with sharp, curved claws. They tore through the remnants of the wall, ripping the dangling pieces of shelving and wall off and tossing them into the cellar.

I trembled with shock.

"God help me," I whimpered, crab-walking away from the nightmarish thing that was about to tear through the wall separating us.

What on earth could it be?

The creature's face came into view. And suddenly I knew *what* it was.

I'd seen this animal before, almost a year and a half ago, in the underground parking garage of my condo building.

The beast smashed out the remaining pieces of the wall and shelving, but I realized it couldn't make it into the cellar to me. The opening in the wall was barred with thick metal rods, keeping the creature safely away from me.

I drew in a shaky breath. My arms and legs trembled from fear, but I felt a bit safer with the bars between me and the monster. They appeared much stronger than the wall. The beast grabbed on to them, trying to shake or break them, but to no avail.

Its pure rage, however, proved intimidating enough for me to remain on the floor. Deafening roars reverberated through the cellar as the animal thrashed against the metal bars of the cage that enclosed it.

Cinder block walls were visible behind the hulking figure of the beast. Shredded rags littered the floor on his side. I was right, the cellar had been made smaller. A section of it had been barred and walled off to create a holding cell for the animal.

But why? How long had it been there?

There was no stench of filth or excrement coming from the cell. Who fed him and cleaned after him? How did he get here?

The last time I saw the beast, he'd been captured by a group of intimidating bald men.

Was Lero one of them? Did they work for him? Was that where his money came from, the illegal animal trade? The idea made me sick to my stomach.

I'd been on this island for nearly a month now. I'd never seen any cages or crates delivered here. Was this the only animal he kept here?

A feeling of disappointment and betrayal settled heavily in my chest. I trusted Lero with my life. I felt safe coming here with him. I accepted his right to secrecy. And he'd made me believe he led a law-abiding life.

Recognizing the beast as a victim not a monster helped ease my fear. Avoiding any sudden movements, I slowly rose to my feet.

"Why are you here?" I asked softly. I wasn't expecting the animal to answer, of course. I simply tried to calm the creature by using a soothing voice.

The beast must've heard me despite the racket he was creating by roaring and shaking his cage. At the sound of my voice, he quieted, his bright red eyes following my every move.

Slowly, I took a step forward, fascinated by the creature. Separated by the bars, I gave in to my curiosity and inspected it a little closer.

"*What* are you?" I took another step in the direction of the cage.

In the dim lighting of the cellar, the beast's fur appeared black, absolutely void of any color. The flaming red of his eyes stood out on his face like two burning fires in the night. Sharp needle-like teeth filled his mouth. Long, spiky ears rose on each side of his head with a wolf-like snout.

The clawed "paws" he had wrapped around the bars were monstrous, but they had opposable thumbs and looked very much like hands.

"You're like no animal I've ever seen," I said, watching him closely as he stared back at me.

He stood upright, and his hind legs ended in paws, not feet. A long, bushy tail lashed around his legs, menacingly slow. His tense posture made him look ready to pounce. I could only hope the bars would hold if he did.

I came as close as I dared, making sure to stay well out of the reach of his great paws, even if the beast stuck them out between the bars.

Thick fur covered his chest that seemed too wide for a quadrupedal creature. At the same time, it didn't appear like standing upright was entirely natural for the creature. He hunched, towering at least a foot or two over my height. He would be even taller if he fully straightened out, which I didn't believe he could.

"Where on earth did you come from?" I whispered in awe, tilting my head back to take him all in.

The thick bars were positioned too close to each other for him to get his entire arm through, I realized. So I moved just a little closer.

At this distance, a wisp of the familiar scent reached me. Faint and subtle, its impact was like a punch in my stomach.

It was Lero's scent! I could never mistake it for anything else.

"What's going on?" I mumbled, utterly confused.

Why did the beast smell like Lero?

He'd told me there were questions he wasn't able to answer. But the sheer amount of all the unanswered questions I had were now crushing me.

"Why is he holding you here? Why do you smell like him? Why..."

The blazing red in the beast's eyes wavered, drawing back like a curtain of smoke and fire to reveal the serene gray behind it.

"Oh my God..." I clutched my neck with both hands as it suddenly hurt to breathe. "Lero... It can't be."

He closed his eyes, wincing. Despite the fur, the snout, and the grotesque beastly shape of his face, it was *his* expression. I recognized it without a doubt. I'd seen it enough times on his human face.

It was impossible. It simply couldn't be real.

And maybe it wasn't? Maybe all of this was some kind of a delusion, after all? Who on this island would tell me what was real and what wasn't? There was no one here, other than this beast of a man and me.

Forgetting all about keeping a safe distance, I came closer, searching the face of the monster for traces of the familiar features. Now, that I knew what I was looking for, there were so many—the way he narrowed his eyes under my scrutiny, the way his lips curved in the corners, the way he jerked his head to toss back a thick clump of fur that hung over his forehead.

"Unbelievable," I breathed out. "Lero? Who did this to you?"

Bits and pieces of information I'd collected like crumbs along the way started to merge into a bigger picture.

Lero had been held captive, with obvious signs of sickness after he'd escaped. He'd been in pain. The glowing red in his irises that I'd spotted after cutting his hair had been the last and most unexplained symptom. Something had been done to him that had eventually transformed him into a beast.

The creature I'd witnessed getting captured in the garage wasn't an animal, either.

Dez.

It was the name of one of the men who'd captured the beast in the garage nearly a year and a half ago. Now, I remembered Lero had called his brother Dez, too, when he'd spoken about him earlier. Could it be the same person? It must be.

Lero couldn't be the same animal, of course, since he'd just transformed recently. There must be more like him.

Something evil had been done to Lero. I could only hope there was a cure.

"I'll need to find out who did this to you."

Dez, was the only name I had. It wasn't much.

Throwing his head back, the beast released a loud groan, then struck his hand out between the bars and grabbed my upper arm.

"No!" I jerked back.

Lero would never hurt me, not physically anyway. But how much of Lero was left in the beast? Trepidation vibrated through me.

His fingers dug in deeper, holding me in place. With one yank, he brought me closer. Pressed against the bars, I grabbed on to one, straining to push away.

His face hovered next to mine, so close, his breath was moving the hair above my ear.

"Watch out for his teeth." The warning of one of Dez's men from long ago rang through my mind.

Those terrifying teeth were less than an inch away from my skin, now.

"Please don't hurt me," I whimpered.

I used to trust Lero, but I'd just learned I knew absolutely nothing about this man. The beast could end me quickly and in many ways.

I heard him breathe in. His lethal teeth snapped next to my neck, making me jump. Fear made me tremble uncontrollably.

"Please..." I struggled against his hold on my arm.

Instead of a bite I felt a gentle touch to my neck—the cool press of his nose, accompanied by the soft tickle of his fur. The hard metal bars between us didn't allow him a real hug, but I believed that was what he was trying to do—not to hurt me but embrace me.

"Lero?"

Whatever had happened to him, I sensed he was suffering in this form. His reaching out for me suddenly felt like a plea for help. Compassion crushed my heart.

Instead of struggling to get away, I tentatively slid my hand between the bars and touched his arm. My fingers sunk into his fur—long, soft, and luxurious. I couldn't resist stroking up to his shoulder to feel the silky glide of his fur between my fingers.

"What can I do?" I half-whispered, overtaken by concern for him and at the same time, mesmerized by the wonder of this entire experience.

This close, his familiar scent enveloped me, the heat of our bodies warming the metal of the bars trapped between us.

He threaded his other arm through the cage—it fit only up to the elbow between the bars—and grabbed on to my waist. His sharp claws pierced through my shirt and dug into my skin without breaking it.

The surreal sensation of being held by him—half-man, half-beast—made me dizzy. Fog clouded my mind, mixing with his scent. His soft fur brushed against my skin. I was no longer sure whether it was a man or a beast holding me. Somehow it no longer mattered.

Either way, it was Lero.

"Who locked you here? How do I get you out?"

There was no predicting for sure what Lero would do if set free. I had no idea what to expect from him in this form. He clearly couldn't communicate with words. However, I couldn't possibly leave him in the cage now that I'd found him.

Searching around the bars, I noticed they were covered in blood where his hands had just gripped them. Alarm shot through me, my concern rising higher.

"Are you hurt?" I twisted to see the hand gripping my arm.

Smears of blood marred my skin where he held me. The white fabric of my shirt was also stained red by his hand at my waist.

He was bleeding.

I slid my hands up his arms to his shoulders then to his neck, gently feeling for injuries. My arms being thinner than his, I was able to fit them between the bars all the way up to my shoulders.

The hard cords of muscles flexed and bulged under his thick, soft fur. Despite being completely still, he was far from relaxed. A shudder ran through his body. His hands flexed tighter on me. He released a groan filled with pain.

"What is it, Lero? Where are you hurt?"

He pressed harder against the bars, holding on to me like to a life raft. With a sudden loud roar, he thrust his hips against the cage separating us. A hard length—not metal, but just as solid—poked me in my belly.

"Oh God..." I shrank back, with a shocked realization of what it was—his erection.

He yanked me against him with a long growl.

"No!" I fisted my hands in his fur.

He threw his head back, releasing a deafening roar that ended in a bloodcurdling howl.

Fear chilled my chest. Clamped in his grip, I could barely move. The more I struggled, the firmer he held, his claws scraping against my skin as his hands flexed.

Reaching down, I found his hard-on and squeezed it hard in return.

"Let me go," I threatened in a hiss.

Instead of fighting me, he thrust his hips into my grip with a deep, satisfied rumble.

I leaned back as far as his hold would allow. "Is that what you want?" I relaxed my grip but didn't let go, his shaft hot and pulsing in my hand. It also felt slippery.

Glancing down, I saw where Lero's injuries were. Deep scratches marred the velvety soft skin of his hard length, blood seeping from them and slicking it red.

He'd tried to touch himself, it dawned on me. With those sharp claws on his fingers, he'd only ended up hurting himself.

"What have you done?" I whispered around the hard lump forming in my throat. I relaxed my hand, releasing him.

Letting go of my waist, he quickly grabbed my hand, wrapping my fingers around his erection once again.

The terrifying red glow in his eyes ebbed with the tide of cooling gray again. It appeared like Lero was looking at me from behind the scary face of the beast.

"Lero... Honey, it'll hurt," I whispered, attempting to remove my hand.

With a soft rumble, he pressed my hand in place. Gripping my waist again, he thrust into my hand. Apparently, the pain from his injuries was less than the agony of arousal he was going through.

Tears swelled behind my eyelids. I stopped fighting him. Sliding my free arm between the bars, I snaked it around his neck, keeping my other hand gently wrapped around his straining length.

Resting his nose on my shoulder, he kept pumping his hips with fervent desperation. Holding him to me, I let it happen.

For years, I'd been craving intimacy with this man. Never in my darkest nightmares had I envisioned it would happen this way. The pain in his groans made it feel almost like an act of mercy. My tears dripped, sliding down the metal bars to be soaked up by his fur.

At the same time, there was something thrilling and fulfilling in it, too, despite the sadness. For those few moments, there was no beast, just a man who desperately needed me, and I reveled in being close to him. Right now, the bars between us seemed so much less of a barrier than the distance Lero had maintained before.

Stripped of his human appearance, he seemed to have lost his reasons to keep away from me, and I cherished it for what it was.

His growls grew deeper, stronger. He jerked violently against the bars, then the hot spurts of his release shot to the floor between us. The cage shook. His teeth snapped at my ear again, and he yanked his head back, keeping his mouth away from me.

Something grew beneath my fingers. Glancing down, I saw a thick bulbous swelling form at the base of his shaft.

"What's that?" I jerked my hand away, afraid I'd hurt him.

Lero no longer seemed to be hurting, however. His growls softened to a satisfied purr that vibrated through his chest.

Relieved, I rested my forehead against the cool metal of the cage, a little overwhelmed by it all. The tension and anxiety that had gripped my heart and weighed down my shoulders had drained, leaving just numbness behind.

With a soft snort, Lero fitted his nose between the bars and placed it on my shoulder again. I touched the side of his face, and he snuggled closer—so different from his previous behavior with me, back when he looked like a man and acted like a stranger no matter how much time we'd spend together.

"I need to get you out of here," I said softly. "Then, I'll have to figure out who did this to you and what to do next." I heaved a long, heavy sigh. "I wish you would've told me everything. Back when you still could talk..."

He relaxed his fingers, sliding his hands up and down my sides as far as the bars would let him.

"Is there anything on your computer system about this, Lero?"

The desktop in the closet room was connected to the island security system. Other than the request for a palm print, I hadn't encountered any other password prompts or restrictions. I hadn't snooped, but the current situation might warrant it.

The moment I made a move to leave, however, he wrapped his fingers around my arm again, keeping me in place.

"You want me to stay? But how will I help you from here? I need to go upstairs to search the system."

He stared at me with those clear gray eyes, one of the parts of the old Lero I recognized in the beast. His grip on me remained firm, as if my presence was the only help he needed.

It felt wrong to leave him here alone.

"Show me how to get you out of here." I inspected the metal box fitted between the bars on one side. Flat and solid, it appeared to have an opening on the other side. I couldn't see it, but I felt it with my fingers. If it was indeed a lock, the keyhole was on Lero's side.

"Do you know where the key is?" I asked.

Searching around the remnants of the broken shelves, I tried to locate anything that could hold a key—a box, a hook, anything—and found nothing. Logic told me that since the keyhole was on Lero's side of the bars then the key should be there, too. Though, it made no sense to keep the key in the prisoner's cell.

He didn't appear to be concerned about my efforts to free him. In fact, he seemed tired. His eyelids heavy, he looked like he would crash to the floor, exhausted, had he not held on so tightly to me.

"You look sleepy," I said.

With a long, rumbling exhale, he dropped to his knees, taking me down with him. I grabbed on to the bars, to keep my balance, though he probably wouldn't have let me fall anyway, his grip on my arm and waist as firm as ever.

There was nothing but torn rugs on his side of the bars, with spilled wine, broken glass, and pieces of wood on my side.

"I'll stay," I promised, placing my hand on his at my waist. "Just let me get some blankets and pillows first."

His eyelids flew open. He seemed fully awake once again, giving me a penetrating look as if searching for truth to my promise deep inside my eyes. Finally, he released me, slowly sliding his hands down my sides before letting them drop from me completely.

Carefully stepping over the broken wine bottles on the floor, I made it to the cellar exit.

From there, I glanced back. Standing on his knees, his massive, fur-covered hands gripping the bars of his prison, Lero's intense gaze followed me. There was so much longing in his eyes, my heart squeezed in sorrow for him.

"I'll be back in a minute," I promised, choked with compassion and struggling to hold back a new wave of tears.

I ran up the stairs to the main floor.

There, I grabbed a couple of cushions off the lounge chairs on the patio, then collected some pillows and blankets from my room. Piling it all up on top of the stairs, I rushed to Lero's closet.

No matter how crazy the night had turned out to be, he'd drilled into my head that safety was important. I quickly armed the house alarm system.

On the way through the dining room, I grabbed my untouched plate of "celebratory" spaghetti and shoved it into the fridge in the kitchen. I was no longer hungry, though I wished I'd had some wine—of either color.

When I returned to the cellar, Lero lay on his side, seemingly asleep. His massive body pressed tight against the cage, he had stretched his right arm between the bars as far as he could, almost up to his elbow. My chest tightened with ache and compassion. It looked as if he was waiting for me even as exhaustion had claimed him.

I quickly swept the glass from the floor, then rolled the ruined rug aside. Arranging my loot of cushions and blankets next to the cage, I made a sleeping pallet for myself. I managed to cover Lero with a blanket too, working my hands between the bars.

All this time, he appeared deep asleep, his chest rising and falling rhythmically. His breath came out with a low rumble in his chest, deadly teeth glistening white between his lips.

Even asleep, he was terrifying, but I wasn't frightened of the beast, only of those who'd done this to him.

Lying down on my side of the bars, I took his hand in mine.

"Good night, Lero," I whispered. "Tomorrow is going to be a busy day."

I now had a goal ahead of me—I had to find out what'd happened to Lero and how I could ease his suffering.

Chapter 15

LERO

Awareness returned to him slowly as the fog of madness cleared. Relief came next. The build-up of the Moon's power had climaxed, releasing him for the next few weeks.

He always felt the energy of the Moon. His people were born with its magic coursing through their veins. Back before Ghata corrupted it in Nerifir, he'd heard that the nights of full moon used to be filled with joy and love.

For him, it had only been pain and madness.

He stretched his legs, sore muscles screaming in protest. His bones ached after the transformation. But his mind cleared, and the pain was quickly receding. All he needed was a hot shower to wash off the blood and soothe his aching body.

The ache seemed to be more pronounced in his right arm, which felt especially stiff. A weight was pressing down on his hand.

He opened his eyes, finding...Stella lying just outside his cage in the cellar. He wondered if he was still asleep and dreaming. Stella had been his constant companion in his dreams. Without ever knowing, she'd been his morning star who led him through darkness. She'd helped him fight the madness and hold on to his sanity through the torture of Ghata's captivity. And now, the dreams of her chased the lingering nightmares away.

Lately, Stella had caused a different kind of insanity in him, however. Over the past weeks, his dreams of her had slowly turned from warm and pleasant to burning hot and filled with things he never could do to her in real life. Desire for her consumed him both while asleep and awake.

Her touch as she'd cut his hair a few days ago ignited an inferno. For a few terrifying moments his control had slipped. She was so soft and delicate, and he burned to ravage her, to fuck her until she screamed his name and prayed to the Moon with him.

Gods, the things he would've done to her had she not run and locked herself in the cottage. A shudder shook his body, jolting his aching muscles.

He'd traced her scent to the front door of the manager's cottage and found it locked. He had the key back at the house. He could have simply broken the door in, too. But the extra effort it would require gave him the moment he needed to regain a modicum of control.

Instead of barging in, which would've surely traumatized and terrified her, he lurked around the building for hours, hoping to catch a glimpse of her through the windows, but she'd never even turned the lights on.

He hadn't gone to bed that night, roaming the island until the bout of madness subsided closer to the morning. Only then had he ventured to unlock the door and check on Stella. She slept on the couch, barefoot, in her shorts and top. Curled up, she looked so small and defenseless.

He'd vowed to protect her. Yet, he had become the biggest threat to her peace and safety. Instead of going down to the basement just for the night of the full moon, he needed to get away from Stella right away. He'd covered her with a blanket and, after making her breakfast, went to his cage, starting his self-confinement early.

The memories of the past three days were a blur of pain and desire—the agony of lust. This had been his first full moon in this world without *womora*, and he'd needed to fuck more than he needed to breathe. But not just anyone. Lately, he'd only wanted Stella, so badly it'd been worse than any torture.

He wanted her still.

Her eyes closed, Stella appeared to be peacefully asleep just outside of his cage. There was so much trust in her placing her head into his hand like that. The heat of her skin warmed his palm. He gently moved his thumb, stroking above the curve of her eyebrow.

Why was she here?

The trashed state of the cellar behind Stella had finally registered with him. The wall that was supposed to conceal the monster the Moon turned him into was gone. The space reeked of spilled wine. The rug shoved aside, Stella slept in a pile of blankets on the floor.

He tried to sift through the fog of his memories from the last night. Shattered and distorted like shards of glass, the fragments of what he remembered shifted and aligned enough to form a picture.

Stella had seen his beast!

Fear shot through him, chasing away the post-transformation drowsiness. Worry pulsed in his chest as he slid his gaze down Stella's sleeping form.

Sleeping?

"Please, gods, let her be asleep, not...dead," he fervently prayed in his mind.

He spotted a rusty smidge of dried blood on her temple. There were a few on her arm, too.

The blinding lust had driven him mad as much as the Moon. It'd spurred his rage when he'd caught a tendril of her sweet scent through the wall of his prison.

What had he done?

Gently pulling his hand free, he scrambled up to his feet and opened a compartment in the wall to the right of the barred entrance. The barrel bolt on the compartment's door had been specifically designed to be opened with the fingers of a man, not the claws of a beast. Only when he turned into his usual, less threatening form, could he release himself.

He took out the key that was hanging there and unlocked his cage.

"Stella," he exhaled, struggling against the suffocating panic. He trailed his shaking fingers along her face and neck, begging the stars she was indeed just asleep.

"Mmm?" she murmured. Her eyelids fluttered open.

For one most amazing moment, a gentle warm smile lit up her peaceful expression as she gazed up at him. If it were a dream, he wouldn't want to wake up. Ever.

"Lero?" Her brows drew together, a frown replaced her smile. Her peaceful expression was gone.

Sadly, last night had not been just a dream.

"You're hurt," he rasped.

"What?" She blinked, sitting up, the blanket clutched to her chest.

"The blood." He gestured at her arm. "Where did I scratch you?"

It must have been his claws. Had it been his teeth, she would no longer be alive.

He shuddered at the thought of what could've happened had it not been for the bars of his cage. He shouldn't have stayed on the island during the full moon while Stella was here. He'd been selfish, stealing every last minute he could still spend with her. He should've let her go the moment he'd come back, but he just couldn't...

The room behind the cellar was secure and sound-proof. He'd had it made during the first weeks of taking the possession of Blue Cay, before he was taken by *bracks* just a month later.

The walls were supposed to conceal him in his beast form. Obviously, he'd failed to take into account the effect Stella's scent would have on his lust-crazy beast.

"Where did I hurt you, Stella? You're bleeding."

"Me?" She tugged down the fabric of her shirt, inspecting the long, rust-colored smears on her side. "It's yours, Lero. I'm not hurt."

He cast a glance at his hands, covered in dried blood, too. Suddenly, he knew where it'd come from. He didn't need to see his bare thighs to know there would be blood there, too.

As a beast, he couldn't make himself come, which didn't mean that driven to delirium by unfulfilled desire he hadn't tried. Over and over again. Clawing at his rock-hard, aching cock, drawing blood, and hurting himself, with no release.

Shame chilled his chest and heated his face. Never had he loathed what the Moon forced him to become as much as he did now. His beast state was uncontrollable, dangerously unpredictable, and...mortifying.

"I'm sorry you had to see...that." He winced but forced his gaze to remain on her, studying her face for any signs of trauma.

She looked confused, still adorably sleepy, shaken... But had she been traumatized? Somehow, she was relatively calm after what she'd seen.

How had she survived the night? And managed to fall asleep?

"How are you?" he asked, as gently as he could muster.

"You turned back." She stared at him. "You were... You had fur." She gestured at her shoulders and chest. "You couldn't speak. What happened, Lero?"

He feared the damage she'd suffered might be deeper than he could see. Maybe if he kept things as normal as possible for her now, she'd get over the terrifying experience more smoothly.

"You know what?" he said. "We both need a bath, a decent breakfast, and some fresh air."

With a deep cleansing breath, he scooped her off the floor and lifted her in his arms.

"A bath? What are you talking about? Dammit, Lero, what happened?" A panicky note rang in her voice, making him dread the worst.

"Shh," he whispered soothingly into her hair as he carried her up the stairs and into his bathroom. "The night is over, and so is the nightmare, Stella. You'll leave this place as soon as possible, I swear. Nothing and no one will ever threaten you again. Not even me."

"You want me to leave?" She clung to his shoulders, her entire body trembling. He prayed to every deity in this world and any other that she would survive this unscathed—body and mind.

He turned the tub faucet on, letting the water rush out. The tub was too big and would take forever to fill. He gently sat her down—her bare feet on the tiled floor. She wouldn't let go of his shoulders, though, holding on to him like a drowning woman to a lifesaver.

He was no lifesaver, though. Quite the opposite...

"Lero." She stared into his eyes. "*What* are you?"

He faltered under her question. Simple and direct, it demanded a straightforward answer. Only nothing about his existence was straightforward, not since he'd left his world. And even then...

"Please," he implored. "Please, Stella. Could you think about all of this as a bad dream? Forget last night, forget me. That's your only chance to go on and be happy—"

She let go of him, taking a step back. The disapproval in her stare cut like a knife.

"For half of my life, I tried to forget you, Lero, and failed. It's not going to happen, now, for as long as I live."

Chapter 16

STELLA

I sat in Lero's massive bathtub, naked. The water swirled around me, rising higher.

Below the tub's marble platform was a rectangular pool that ran along the entire back wall of the bathroom. The glass of the large window separated the indoor portion from the big outdoor pool that took up most of the stone patio at the back of the house.

This was a beautiful water feature that the real estate listing highlighted as one of the property's best selling points.

Only the entire pool was empty, now. Its turquoise and gold mosaic floor and walls remained exposed and dry. The passage to the outdoors had been securely boarded up.

It was so like Lero, to trade joy and beauty for security. I wouldn't be surprised if given enough time, he'd get rid of the island's incredible views by erecting a concrete wall all along its picturesque beaches.

Maybe I failed to fully appreciate his efforts because the threat he worried about had never been fully explained to me. It was hard to feel afraid if I didn't know exactly what the danger was.

The last twelve hours had been an emotional rollercoaster. I'd gone from peace, to terror, to heart-wrenching compassion and anger, to... *"It's all been a dream. Just forget about it."*

His withdrawal this morning hurt more than anything.

Nothing made sense, and I had no one to turn to for explanation. A headache pounded inside my skull the more I tried to make sense of things on my own. Unanswered questions piled up, breeding more questions...

I got out of the soapy water, rinsed off quickly, and drained the tub. Putting on the same shorts and blood-stained top I wore last night, I walked out of Lero's bathroom.

I found him standing at one of the glass doors to the back patio, a closed laptop under his arm. He'd had a shower in one of the guest's bathrooms. His hair still looked damp, though brushed and styled in his usual fashion. Wearing a white shirt with the sleeves rolled up and a pair of light-colored pants, he looked so...normal, as if last night had never happened at all.

He turned to me.

"Are you hungry?" he asked, as calm and distant as ever.

As if I hadn't had my fingers wrapped around his fucking dick just hours ago. As if he hadn't bled in my hand. As if I hadn't wept for him...

I bit my lip and fisted my hands to stop them from trembling.

"So, you can change at will, then?" My voice came out hollow.

His chest rose with a deep breath.

"No. Just during the full moon." His mouth pressed into a stubborn line. "Stella—"

"Do you *remember* things when you're...when you look like you did last night?"

He winced, as if it pained him to remember. And maybe it did. But I needed to know.

"If you're referring to, um..."

He jerked his head aside as if trying to toss away the memories.

"It doesn't matter," he said. "I apologize for *everything* that happened last night. Every single thing that happened from the moment you entered the cellar. You weren't supposed to see any of that."

"I came to get a bottle of red wine," I explained. The evening of my planned spaghetti dinner seemed so far away now, as if it'd been a century ago.

He raked the fingers of his free hand through his hair, glossy from the shower.

"I should've brought some up for you before leaving."

"It's not about the wine," I said, my voice soft but firm.

"It could be!" He snapped, his unshakable composure finally cracking. "It could be all about the damn wine or whatever you want it to be—"

"Just not about the truth, right? As long as I don't ask questions you don't want to answer, isn't it?" I raised my voice, too.

He heaved a breath, the muscles in his jaw flexing as he visibly struggled to compose himself. Sadly, I could almost feel the wall between us grow taller, thicker, and more impenetrable as his composure returned.

Silently, he placed the laptop on the kitchen table and opened it, obviously signaling me the conversation was over.

If I were dirty, he'd run me a bath. If I were hungry, he'd feed me a gourmet meal. If I were cold, he'd bring me a blanket. But if I demanded answers, he wouldn't even spare me a glance.

"You make me miss the beast," I said softly. His shoulders jerked, and he snapped his gaze to mine. "You had no ability to speak last night, yet we understood each other so much better."

His severe expression wavered. His frown softened. The red in his gray eyes remained but a distant echo, glowing faintly like the cooling embers of last night's inferno.

"Tell me, Stella, how were you not repulsed seeing me like that? How were you not terrified of the monster?"

He wouldn't allow me any answers, yet he had his own burning questions.

Unlike him, I wasn't going to deny him the answers. Sliding my gaze aside, I took a moment to collect my thoughts. How could I best explain what I felt?

"I saw the man, silently suffering in the body of the beast, Lero. Not a monster. I knew it was you." I spoke from the heart, "Why do you find it so hard to accept that I care about you, in any shape and form?"

He stared back at me, his expression unreadable. His eyes anxiously flicked between mine, something was happening behind them, but I couldn't say what.

He grabbed my arm.

"Come." He tugged me to his side of the table. "Look."

He ran his fingers over the keyboard of his laptop.

A picture of a smiling young woman came up on the screen. She sat next to a flaxen-blond boy at a table set with dishes. Wearing a pastel-blue dress with a lace collar, she had curly chestnut-colored hair styled into a flirty bob. Her arm was draped around the boy's shoulders.

"You've asked me who Amelie was," Lero said, his voice dark and hollow. "That's her."

"She is...pretty," I said softly, halting my breath. "And happy."

"*Was*," he corrected. "She *was* beautiful, happy, and full of life...until she witnessed me *turn* once."

"Turn?" I kept staring at the smiling woman in the picture.

"She saw me change into the beast one night, and she couldn't handle it." His voice saturated with pain.

"What happened to her? Where is she now?" I asked, afraid to hear the answer.

He hit a button on the keyboard.

"Here."

A picture of a grave with a white headstone came up. A fresh bouquet of lilacs and dark purple roses lay on it.

"Dead?" I could barely whisper.

"For almost five years now," he confirmed, solemnly. "Dead and buried in the cemetery next to the mental institution where she'd spent the last thirty years of her life."

"A mental institution..." I gasped.

"Well, they call it a *villa*," he said with sarcasm. "Like it's just a relaxing place to spend a summer. In reality, it's a long-term care home where people who can no longer function on their own spend their lives dependent on others."

"Did Amelie's family send her there?"

He raised his darkened gaze at me.

"I did."

My knees gave in, and I let myself drop into one of the chairs at the table.

"You? Why?"

"Because Amelie was—always will be—my shame, my guilt, and my responsibility. My mistake that I never want to repeat."

"What happened?" I asked, begging him to keep talking for once.

Propping his arms onto the table, he hung his head between his shoulders, standing over the laptop with the picture of Amelie's grave.

"I met her in the restaurant I owned at the time. She came with her family, celebrating someone's birthday. I liked her laugh..." He paused, closing his eyes. "We started dating. A true bond isn't possible with a human, but I didn't even hope for one. All I wished for was to have a companion, someone in this world to share my life with, even if for a little while. I liked Amelie, a lot. I brought her home. She got along well with Zeph. I truly believed the three of us could be a happy little family one day." A bitter smile crossed his lips.

"I'd given her the key to my place, for emergencies. She wanted to surprise me one night and came over without letting me know she'd be there."

He stared straight at the picture on the screen, now.

"She found me in the basement. I had my cage there, it wasn't hidden. We'd just moved into that place. I hadn't even put the lock on the door of the room yet. It was my fault. She saw me in the cage, watched me change, and...she couldn't take it."

"What happened?" I breathed out.

"She screamed." He flinched, shutting his eyes tightly. "I'll never get that scream out of my mind. It'll cut through my brain forever. She screamed so much, again and again. Then, she fainted. I don't remember clearly what came next. I see the world differently when I'm in that state. My memories are often choppy and distorted. But when I turned back in the morning, Amelie was still there, in the basement room with me."

"Unconscious?"

"No. She'd come to sometime during the night, but she was no longer herself. She'd been disoriented to the point that she couldn't find the door and leave. Instead, she'd crawled into a corner and spent the night watching me rage in my fucking cage." Balling his hands into fists, he slammed them against the table, making me jump in my seat.

"She lost her mind completely during that night. I took her to the hospital. Her family came. She didn't recognize anyone. They put her in a home. It wasn't a good place..." He shook his head.

"Was that the villa?" I asked.

"No. She got transferred to the villa later. It was much better, in terms of staff, quality of care, location, food—everything."

"Did you pay for it?" I guessed.

He nodded.

"Her family had no proof, but they knew that Amelie's condition had something to do with me. I was the one who got her to the hospital. They would never accept the money from me directly. I had to arrange for payments with the management privately, as an anonymous donor."

"The family never knew?"

"If they did, they never let me know. At the end of the day, Amelie got the best care money could buy. It was the least I could do."

"Did you ever get to see her again?"

He went silent, gazing over the laptop out into the sea.

"Once," he finally said.

"Just once?"

He nodded.

"Amelie didn't recognize anyone. She couldn't take care of herself, but she wasn't violent—until she saw me. She flew into a vicious fit of rage at the sight of me. After that, the staff asked me not to visit anymore."

"So, she recognized you?"

He exhaled a bitter laugh.

"As someone from her nightmares. Apparently, she suffered from night terrors. And I starred in all of them."

I glanced at the exquisite flower arrangement on top of the gravestone in the picture.

"Instead of visiting you sent her flowers?"

"Still do. Every year on her birthday. She loved getting them, I was told. Purple was her favorite color."

He fell silent again, and I kept quiet, too.

"How were you not terrified of the monster?" he'd asked me.

The truth was, I had been. I'd just been a little better prepared than Amelie, I believed. I'd seen the same animal before, back in the parking garage. I'd watched him being overpowered, hurt, and restrained. And I felt compassion for him, not just fear.

Unlike Amelie, I hadn't seen Lero actually change. That must have been a traumatic experience on its own.

"Who is the boy in the picture?" I asked.

"Zeph."

"Your friend?" I recognized the name he'd mentioned earlier.

"He is more than a friend. I raised him as my own son, though we're not related by blood."

"How old is Zeph, now?"

He lifted his eyes to mine. "He'll be forty-nine, soon."

It shouldn't have made sense, but it did. For the first time ever, things actually started making sense.

"You're not thirty-one like you've said, then." I held his gaze.

"No." He scrubbed his hand over his face. "I turned ninety-six last month."

"Ha!" Air left my lungs with a sharp, nervous laugh.

As incredible as it sounded, the math added up.

I knew the man I met in Paris years ago didn't look like a seventeen-year-old boy he'd claimed he would've been back then.

The picture of Amelie with Zeph as a little boy wasn't taken digitally. It had the quality of an older paper photograph that had been taken decades ago and scanned more recently.

The cut of her dress, Amelie's hair, and makeup were most suitable for the fashion of about four decades ago, when the forty-nine-year-old Zeph would have been a boy.

"I'm not human, Stella." Lero stepped away from the table.

"I gathered that much," I croaked, my mouth turning too dry to speak.

None of this could be real, yet deep in my heart I knew that it was. I could try to come up with a different maybe a little more believable explanation, but I already knew I'd be wasting my time.

"*What* are you?" I braced myself for his answer.

He crossed his arms over his broad chest, rolling his shoulders back.

"A werewolf." There was a certain pride in his answer. As painful as I understood his existence was at times, he didn't deny his heritage.

And what a heritage that was!

"Like in the movies?" I stared at him. I might have guessed already but hearing him admit it out loud made it sound as extraordinary as it was.

"Movies are based on old legends," he replied. "And no legend is without some truth to it."

I kept staring at him—showered, dressed, well-groomed, and elegant, and so very human, it made me think this whole conversation was an insane dream.

"I don't age," he said. "Not until the very end of my life, which won't be for at least four hundred years. Unless I get killed before that of course."

"Is there still a chance of that?" I asked, thinking about his brother.

"There's always a chance of that as long as the people—the beings—who caught me are alive."

"Are they also..." I paused, before uttering the word out loud, "...werewolves?"

"They're worse." He closed the laptop. "But you don't need to worry about them. The less you know the better. If there is one thing I'll do in this life, it's—"

"To keep me safe by keeping me in the dark," I finished for him. "I know. You've made it abundantly clear by now, Lero. Except that it didn't work. I've been thrust into your world, against your wishes and best intentions. Are there many like you in this world? Where did you come from? Why are you here?"

"Stella." He raised a hand, halting my stream of questions. "No. I've said it before I can't answer everything—"

But I wouldn't give up. I simply couldn't stop, now.

"The least you could do is to explain what I've seen, Lero. You said you change forms on full moon. Why did you go into the basement for *three* days?"

He nodded, conceding.

"My appearance changes at sunset on the night of the full moon. Inside me, however, the beast starts stirring days before that."

"What do you mean?"

"For days before the full moon, I lose control, little by little. Once I turn, the base instincts take over—the need to hunt, fight, and fuck. Nothing else remains. I lose control." Propping his arms on the table again, he leaned over it, staring at me intently. "Stella, I've killed in that form, and I couldn't help the murders."

"What murders?" Now, he was actively trying to scare me away, I believed. "But last night—"

He didn't let me finish.

"Last night, things could've ended tragically..." He groaned, shaking his head. "Gods, Stella. This is my entire life, right here. That's all there is to it. I'm constantly fighting with the Moon over the control of my mind and body. But like I said, you don't have to worry about any of this. This is not your world and not your problem. It's now safer for you out there than it is here, with me."

He straightened, giving me a calm look.

"The airplane is coming for you later this afternoon. You're finally free to go home, Stella."

Home?

My small, empty apartment didn't feel like home to me, right now. Just hours ago, I was almost ready to *swim* back to Miami. Now that he'd made arrangements for me to leave, it didn't feel right anymore, like I'd be leaving things unfinished.

Lero heaved a breath, picking up his laptop off the table.

"You'll have your old life back."

Did I want it back? Just the way it was? I had my place, my job, things I'd achieved and was proud of. But had I really missed my old life while being here?

"What about you, Lero?" I asked softly. "What kind of life are you planning to have once I'm gone?"

He glanced out the glass doors toward the open sea once again, avoiding my eyes.

"I promised to keep you safe," he growled low, not answering my question. "I *cannot* ruin your life."

With the laptop under his arm, he stormed out the back doors to the patio then jogged down the stone steps toward the beach.

Passing a copse of low trees, he furiously tossed the laptop into the brush under them as I watched speechless.

Chapter 17

My bag had been packed for three days now. It was the same bag I'd come here with. Lero had bought me clothes and toiletries during the month I'd spent on the Blue Cay, but it felt wrong to take anything of that with me—they weren't really mine. The only extra things I was taking with me were a couple of polished rocks and a colored piece of glass I'd found in the strait under the bridge.

With more than an hour left before the airplane was supposed to arrive for me, I waited for it on the beach.

I had cleaned the room where I'd stayed, washed the sheets, and changed the bedding. When Lero had returned to the house, I snuck out, not willing to face him. I knew I'd have to come back to say goodbye before I left. Despite everything, he'd been a generous host. It would be extremely rude of me to leave without at least thanking him for everything he'd done for me.

Except that parting from Lero would hurt, I always knew that. And getting nothing but a cold "goodbye" and a handshake would make it so much worse. I longed to see him again, knowing it'd probably be the last time ever. And I dreaded that moment when I had to look at him for the very last time.

I waded into the warm waves, digging my toes into the soft sand below.

If there was anything I'd learned about my host, it was that his calm façade was forced, carefully practiced, and hard-earned. An inferno raged inside that hard, cold shell of control. Lero had been fighting the storm all his life, alone.

It felt horribly wrong leaving him on his own again. Yet what could I do if he'd been so adamantly shoving me away?

The sun dipped past the summit, its rays twinkling in the waves and forming a shimmering path on the surface of the ocean.

Strangely, the shimmer seemed to be moving, shining brighter the closer it got. I admired the dancing lights for a moment, wondering what would cause the effect since I'd never seen anything like it before.

After a while it became apparent the movement wasn't natural. Something was heading through the water to me.

Lero's warnings rose in my mind. I slowly backed out to the beach as the shimmering glow advanced.

Then, a head popped out of the water. A man emerged from the waves, wading onto the sand to me.

I saw no diving equipment on him, no weapons either, unless he hid any in his rather tight, navy-blue swim shorts. In his hand, he held a small net filled with gray shells.

Just in case, I stepped behind a nearby tree, getting out of view. Too late, it seemed, as he had spotted me already.

"Hi there!" he yelled, waving his free hand at me.

I peeked from around the tree trunk, studying him closely as he approached. He was very handsome, beautiful even. Flashing me a toothy smile, he shook the water out of his white hair, cropped close to his head on the sides and longer on top. Against the afternoon sun, the water droplets broke into an iridescent mist around him, making the newcomer look like a mythical being, not merely a man but a vision, like a water spirit.

"Is Lero in the house?" he asked, cheerfully. "I brought oysters!" He lifted the net filled with shells over his head.

I stepped out from my not-so-secret hiding place. The man's behavior was friendly, not at all threatening. Though, I still had no idea how he got here. There was no plane or boat in sight. Also, the island's security system had been armed ever since Lero got home four days ago. Unless he'd turned it off already, in anticipation of the airplane's arrival?

The man took a few steps closer but not too close, keeping a comfortable distance from me, which I appreciated.

"Lero is here," I said, deciding it was best for him to know I wasn't alone. "Who are you?"

"I'm Zeph. Lero's friend."

"Zeph?"

Of course! Now that he'd introduced himself, I recognized the light-blond hair and the dimply smile of the boy from the picture with Amelie.

I knew Zeph wouldn't look his forty-nine years when Lero told me his age. But I didn't expect him to appear this youthful. The boyish smile made him seem even younger.

"I'm very glad to meet you." He stretched his hand my way.

I took it.

"I'm Stella." I studied him now with a new curiosity. Was Zeph a werewolf, too? He didn't seem as stiff and tense as Lero. On the contrary, Zeph appeared as relaxed and happy as could be.

"Stella?" His dark eyebrows shot up in delight. "It means 'star,' doesn't it?"

I nodded. My father had big dreams for me when I was born. All of them revolved around riches and stardom. Hence the name he chose for me, Stella—Star.

"How is Lero doing?" Zeph asked. "I thought I'd check on him since it was a full moon last night. He doesn't feel his best around this time."

"Um...Lero is well," I replied carefully, unsure of how much I should say.

He peered at me from under the wet strands of hair falling over his forehead. His eyes, I noted, were of exactly the same color as the sea behind him.

"Are you a friend of his, too?" he asked.

I tried not to flinch.

A friend? Could I call myself that?

"I'm...just a house guest." I blinked, glancing away from his inquisitive stare.

I felt the light touch of his fingers on my hand.

"Lero could really use a friend, Stella," he said softly, then added, "And more."

More... More than a friend?

My heart skipped and my face felt hot at the thought of how much I actually wanted to get a chance to have *more* with Lero.

"Zeph!" Lero's sharp voice cut through the air like a whip, from the entrance of the house.

"Oh, and there is the old man himself!" Zeph's smile returned. "It was very nice meeting you, Stella." He tipped his head to me, sun twinkling in his sea-blue eyes, then headed up the slope toward Lero who was rushing our way from the house.

"It was nice to meet you, too." I gave Zeph a friendly wave, catching myself smiling back at him. It was impossible not to, his cheerful mood proved highly contagious.

Watching the two men embrace briefly, I wondered what an easy-going man like Zeph could possibly have in common with someone as distant and withdrawn as Lero.

Wrapping one arm around Zeph's shoulders, Lero led his friend into the house. He threw but a glance my way before going inside and shutting the door.

The airplane would be here to pick me up soon. I had less than an hour left on this island. Then, I'd be back in Miami, just like Lero wanted.

Was that what he truly wanted, though?

"Lero could really use a friend...and more."

Lero did want more. I knew it now. He wanted it possibly even more than I did.

I thought back to how desperately he had clung to me through the bars last night. It wasn't just lust, his need had been so much deeper than that.

He'd said he lost control in his beast form. Without the iron grip of his constant composure, his true feelings and emotion got the chance to be seen last night. He'd wanted me and needed me, badly. So much, he'd been reaching for me through the bars even as sleep had claimed him.

He'd held me in his arms, his hands armed with knife-sharp claws. He'd had his teeth near my skin. The violent beast, he thought himself to be, could've torn me to shreds and killed me many times over. Yet he'd never so much as nipped or scratched me.

Lero was not a danger to me as much as his fear made him believe—his fear for me. That was the only thing that stood between us, I realized.

How could I leave here? How could I leave *him*?

I kept pacing the beach, alone, my thoughts barraging my brain. The waves rolled softly over my feet, washing away my footprints in the sand. If only my worries could be washed away like that.

My father had always made me feel like a failure for not delivering on *his* dreams. However, when *I* wanted anything bad enough, I worked hard for it, and I always got it. From that point of view, I was never a failure. I just needed to want something badly enough.

And there was nothing and nobody in this world I'd ever wanted more than Lero.

Because of him, I had now glimpsed into the incredible world I never knew existed. No matter how dangerous Lero said it was, I'd never forget it now. I'd never be able to forget Lero, either. For as long as I lived, he'd be in my mind.

Anger stirred in me, along with hope and desperation. Despite Lero's stubborn insistence that I could simply return to the life he'd plucked me out from, I knew it was no longer possible. I couldn't dismiss my experiences on the island as simply a dream.

I glanced up the path toward the house. There had to be a way for me to make him see it, too. I couldn't leave here without at least trying to make him understand.

Stomping up to the house resolutely, I shoved at the door and barged in.

"Would you stay for dinner?" I heard Lero's voice from the back of the house. "Or for a glass of wine with the oysters?"

If I had to speak to Lero in Zeph's presence, I would. My determination was that strong.

Zeph declined, however, "I need to go. I hate leaving Ivy alone for too long."

I paused in the hallway, unseen by either of the men, waiting for Zeph to leave.

"Bring her over, next time," Lero offered. "Maybe she'll like it here enough to stay."

"To stay?" Zeph exclaimed, with surprise. "Does that mean you're willing to let me keep her?" Even not knowing Zeph well, I could tell he was teasing. He obviously didn't think he needed Lero's permission to "keep" Ivy, whoever she was.

The swishing sound of the back door sliding open came next.

"Ivy is clearly yours already," Lero's voice sounded from the distance now. "All I can do is accept that."

The voices moved away, turning to a distant hum then disappearing completely.

I walked through the formal area into the kitchen. No one was here. Only the net with oysters lay on the counter, dripping sea water on the speckled white granite.

Through the glass of the back doors, I saw Zeph and Lero strolling down toward the water. Both talked animatedly, accompanying their words with hand gestures.

At the water edge, they hugged, then Zeph jogged into the surf. He jumped into the waves, his athletic body arching gracefully. Unless my eyes deceived me, I believed I saw a flash of an iridescent fin open like a fan on his back. The moment I blinked, he was gone.

I watched the surface closely, expecting Zeph's head to bob above the waves any moment, but it didn't. He never came up.

Hands in his pockets, Lero turned back to the house, seemingly unconcerned about his friend's complete disappearance into the waves. Somehow, I knew that Zeph must be fine, too. Whoever Zeph was, he was no ordinary human.

Lero crossed the patio and came into the breakfast room where I stood. He stopped in his tracks, spotting me, then squared his shoulders as if readying himself for disaster to strike.

"Is the plane here?" he asked, his voice low.

He'd thought I'd come to say goodbye.

"Not yet." I cleared my throat. Words that had formed clearly in my mind on the beach scrambled and left me, now. "I...I want to talk first."

"If you have more questions—"

"No. Not those types of questions. Not right now, anyway." I clasped my hands in front of me, gathering my resolve. "What I want to know is... Is it hard for you letting me go?"

He frowned, staring at me for a few moments in complete silence. He obviously hadn't expected that question.

"Because it's impossibly hard for me to leave you," I continued.

"Stella," he breathed out, taking a step my way.

For one incredibly short moment my heart dared hope, then he spoke, crushing it.

"As long as there is a chance for you to have a normal life—"

"What if I didn't want to go back to that life?" I cut him off. "What if I wanted to stay here with you?"

He gripped the back of one of the kitchen chairs, leaning over it and squeezing so hard his knuckles turned white.

"You need to go," he gritted through his teeth.

Lero was worth fighting for, even if *he* was the one I had to fight. "Is that what you really want?"

"I don't want you involved in this mess!" The back of the chair snapped in his hands like a toothpick, sending splinters of wood all over the floor. He didn't seem to notice, his hands fisted tight. "I'm not human, Stella. My life has been nothing but planning for centuries of survival. I move often, change names, hide. And that was before this new threat appeared. Now, it's a true life and death situation."

His mask of composure cracked and blew away, like last year's leaves. He opened his fists, flexing his hands. His fingers trembled slightly.

"Don't you see?" he said a little softer. "I just want you safe, far away from all of this...and from me. My world is like quicksand, Stella. The more you know, the more you sink in. Until there is no more escape, and you're trapped. I want you to run while you still can."

"I'm not scared." I came closer, and he stepped back, as if I were a plague. "I'm not Amelie, Lero. I proved I can handle it. When I saw you in the cage, fear was not the main emotion I had."

"What did you have? Pity?" he scoffed.

"Compassion!" I raised my voice, allowing the words to come straight from my heart. "I care about you, Lero. I've cared for so long. You can't hide from me. I saw *you* in the beast, not a monster. As long as we're together, I can handle anything. Whatever challenges you face in your life, I can help you deal with them. Just let me in. Please."

"Gods help me..." he groaned, closing his eyes, as if he could banish me and my feelings by simply shutting me from view.

"You're pushing me away, because you care about me, too," I insisted. "You believe you're protecting me. But forcing me to go on without you is sentencing me to a lifetime of misery. I can never be truly happy without you ."

"Stella..." His voice was full of sorrow. "If something happens to you because of me, I'd never forgive myself."

"A minute with you is worth a lifetime without you, Lero. Can't you see? I'm in love with you." I opened up my heart, exposing the deepest places of my very soul to let him see all of me. "I've been in love with you for so long, I have no idea how to go on without this feeling. No matter where I am, you're with me, in my heart. And I'm only ever happy when I'm with you. I believe you have feelings for me too, you're just so frustratingly good at hiding them, in *this* form."

He kept backing away from me, shaking his head. Every step he took hurt me, as if he kept stabbing a knife through my chest.

"Prove it," I demanded in desperation. "Kiss me, like you did the day we got here. Then try to tell me it's all just a dream and you'd rather be alone."

"Don't," he croaked, his expression grave, his hands fisted at his side, his eyes of stormy gray. "Please, Stella."

He looked on edge. His control stretched so tight, it'd snap at the slightest provocation. If I touched him, if I kissed him myself, I believed he would let go.

But I couldn't take this last step for him. I needed him to meet me if not half-way than at least one step of the way. One tiny, little step he still wouldn't or couldn't do.

There was nothing else I could do on my own. I'd said everything I'd came here to say and so much more, and still it wasn't enough.

Pain from his continuous rejection suffocated me, making it nearly impossible to breathe. Unshed tears burned my eyes.

"You think you need to protect me from your beast, Lero," I said, willing my voice not to shake. "But you're so much crueler in *this* form. You've hurt me the most when you looked your best."

Pivoting on my heel, I rushed out of the house.

Away from him. Just like he wanted all along.

Chapter 18

I rushed out to the stone patio in front of the main entrance to the house.

The airplane was supposed to arrive any minute now to take me away. But where could I go from here? How far did I have to run to be free from this place and the man who lived here?

He'd rejected me over and over again. I'd tried my best to fight him on it, but maybe I'd made a mistake by believing he could ever let his feelings win.

I tipped my head back, letting the sea breeze cool my face, wishing it could soothe the burning pain in my chest, too.

The door behind me slammed open, the crashing sound startling me.

Two strong arms wrapped around me tightly from behind before I had a chance to look back.

"Don't turn around," Lero rasped in my ear.

One arm just above my breasts, he pressed my shoulders to his chest and leaned the side of his face against mine to stop me from turning to see him.

"Stay just like this." His hot breath fanned across my cheek, sending a flock of goosebumps down my bare arms. "Let me say what I have to say without seeing the hurt in your eyes, or the hope..."

"God, please, speak, Lero," I begged in my mind silently, afraid to say a word out loud. *"Please talk to me."*

"You want to know what my life will be without you? It'll be hell. But I'll endure, knowing that you're happy—"

"I can't *possibly* be happy!"

202

He covered my mouth with his hand, cutting off my protests.

"Shh." He rubbed the side of his face against mine, his lips almost touching my cheek. "Your words have the power to strip me of my last resolve, and I need you to hear what I have to say first."

I held still, focusing on my breathing and his words.

"I could never forget you, Stella," he said softly, pressing his nose against my skin. "The memories of you kept me sane in the hell I went through for the past year and a half. You're my morning star. Nothing will ever change that. Against my best efforts and best intentions, you've made it so deep under my skin, I'd have to claw out my own heart to get rid of you."

I trembled. It suddenly got even harder to breathe. Maybe because he held me so tight.

"I *know* that being with me would expose you to danger," he continued, his heart thundering wildly against my back. "If any harm came to you, it'd kill me. Yet I selfishly want you, come what may. I want you so much it burns my body and mind, driving me mad without the full moon."

His embrace no longer felt like a restraint but a caress. The heat of his body coursed through mine. Leaning back against him, I felt the fire he was speaking about burn inside me.

"Because of you I've learned what real fear is, Stella." He brought his head lower, growling against the side of my neck. "I'm scared that because of me they may get to you still. I'm terrified that I can hurt you myself. I can't stand the thought of being your ruin. Yet I just don't know how to live without you anymore. I kept you here, for your protection. But I just as much kept you here for me. I don't want you to go home. Ever."

Wrapping my arms around myself, I gripped his hands with mine.

"Lero," I squeezed through my tightened throat. "I only ever feel *home* when I'm with you."

His chest pushed against my back with a long breath.

"I have no means to manage what I am, Stella," he warned. This was said for his sake, not mine—I'd accepted who he was the minute I knew. "I will *turn* every full moon night. I'll rage, and snarl, and rampage for days before that."

"And I'll be there for you, to soothe you." I leaned my head to the side, inviting more of his caresses to my neck. His heated breathing spread ripples of pleasure through my skin.

"What if I hurt you?" He pressed his mouth to my neck, trailing his lips down and breathing me in.

"You won't. Not on *purpose*," I replied confidently. "We'll think about how to prevent anything from happening by *accident*."

"I won't age," he kept going in his desperate attempt to warn me away. "Not during your lifetime."

"It doesn't bother me if it doesn't bother you."

A moment with him was better than a lifetime without.

Raising his mouth to my temple, his lips moved above my ear, as he said the words that felt like a vow, "Once you're mine, you're mine forever. If you're not afraid of me, I'll protect you from any other danger. If you spend the rest of your life with me, I'll live to make you happy. I'll give you my heart, my soul, and my body. All I want is yours in return. Always."

The way he spoke, with reverence and obvious respect for each word, it really sounded like a vow. My skin prickled as I sensed the significance of this moment.

Slowly, he released me, stepping back. I swayed on my feet, feeling bereft of his strength and warmth.

"Your last chance to run, Stella." His voice sounded strained, and I sensed the avalanche of emotions he fought to contain. "Run without looking back, because if you turn around, I *will* kiss you, and I won't stop."

My next step felt more profound than saying "I do" on a wedding day. He demanded a commitment larger than life, one that would ruin us both if broken. Only there was no longer parting from him for me.

I drew in a shaky breath, turning to face him.

He stood but a foot away from me, yet it appeared to cost him a huge effort even keeping that small distance between us. His hands fisted at his sides, his hair messy and wild, his eyes burning with passion.

He may have the appearance of a man right now, but the beast was clearly inside him.

"Kiss me then." I stepped into his arms.

It felt like jumping off a cliff. But he caught me. Gathering me in his arms, he claimed my mouth, claiming me. His kiss was punishing, fervent, and frantic, with bruising passion and scraping of teeth. He parted my lips with his, sliding his tongue in, searching for mine. And I met him, sinking my hands into his thick, silky hair that felt so much like his fur.

He held me so tight, my feet lifted off the patio stones.

"I want you," he growled against my mouth. "Madly."

He slid his hands under my shirt, gripping my sides.

"Take me, Lero," I panted, wrapping my legs around his middle. "Please, please, take me," I begged.

He swung us around, pressing my back to the wall next to the front door of the house.

I frantically tugged at his shirt, ripping the buttons open, needing to feel his skin.

He reached behind me, getting hold of the waistband of my shorts. Holding on to it with both hands, he yanked hard, ripping the shorts in two along the seam and the zipper. The thick material of my denim shorts tore like tissue paper in his fingers.

A frost of trepidation sprinkled through my chest from the demonstration of the inhuman physical strength this man possessed. The feeling quickly turned to tingling anticipation as he promptly tore down the front of my t-shirt and got rid of my bra.

His large, warm hand cupped my breast, leaving me breathless. He groaned, rocking his hips into me. The hard ridge of his erection pressed against my panties through his pants. The layers of fabric now felt like maddening barriers. I fumbled with his belt buckle then tugged his zipper down. He ripped off my panties.

"Stella," he breathed out my name as I slid my hand into his underwear, wrapping my hand around his hard, pulsing length.

"That part of you doesn't change much." I gasped at the familiar sensation of holding him in my hand.

"Gods, I need you." He sounded almost delirious, thrusting into my hand.

I needed him too, so much it hurt.

One arm around my waist, he slid a hand between us, slipping a finger inside me. My inner muscles clenched around his finger, desire spreading through me like wildfire.

With a moan, I arched my back, riding his hand.

"More..." I panted. "More of you, Lero."

All of you.

I'd wanted him for so long, his touch still felt like a dream.

In one firm, smooth movement he slid inside me, his length replacing his finger. I sucked in a breath as my body stretched around his sizable girth, my need for him growing stronger.

"Mine," he growled, nuzzling my neck.

I clung to his shoulders as he moved faster, pumping his hips.

For the first time ever, I witnessed Lero lose control completely. Even as the beast, I'd sensed he was holding back. Now, he truly let it go, fucking me ferociously against the wall.

I'd never had anyone take me this passionately and completely before. The world ceased to exist. My entire existence narrowed to where our bodies connected—to that hot, smooth glide of him inside me.

The pressure built between my legs with each fierce thrust of his. I flexed my legs around him, grinding against him in desperate need for release.

"Oh God, yes..." I moaned when it reached me, the white-hot wave of pleasure crested, rolling over me.

My legs trembled, too weak to hold on. I wrapped my arms tighter around Lero's shoulders, holding him close as I rode my orgasm.

Growling against my neck, he came hard, frantically pumping his hips into me. His mouth at my neck opened. Then, I felt a sharp sting of his teeth.

I cried out in pain as he gritted again, "Mine."

My hand pressed to the wound on my neck, I felt the blood trickle warm between my fingers. This wasn't a gentle nibble or a love bite. He'd broken skin.

Jerking my head back, I stared at him in a silent question.

He met my eyes, the red glow in his burning bright. Blood stained his lips—my blood.

His wild expression reminded me of the ferocious beast once again, though he retained the appearance of a man.

The red glow dissipated eventually, giving space to the gray.

I unwrapped my legs from around him.

He took my face between his hands. The wild expression was slowly replaced by the warm affection I'd only ever briefly glimpsed in him before.

"Your blood is in me now. We're one and the same," he said softly. The reverence in his voice made his words sound especially poignant. "Always."

The time seemed to stand still. I felt exceptionally connected to him right now—no longer in body but in spirit and soul.

"We're one and the same."

I understood these words with my entire being. I sensed Lero's presence in me. His pain, his sorrow, his loneliness, and his current bliss were now my own. I *felt* what he felt.

"It's the mating vow of my people." He stroked my cheeks with his thumbs, our gazes locked. "I said you'd be mine, now you are."

He gently moved my hand away from the bite wound he'd in-flicted.

"For as long as I shall live." He bent his head down and licked the blood off my neck.

The brush of his tongue soothed the sting of the bite. The pain was gone. The tingles that followed felt rather pleasurable.

"For as long as *I* shall live, honey," I corrected him. "Remember, I'll die before you."

"No." He pressed his forehead to mine. "Werewolves mate for life. There'll be no other for me but you, whether you're dead or alive."

Sorrow squeezed my heart. I didn't want to think about death right now. I refused to let anything spoil this moment between us.

"I'm yours, Lero." The words came easily, their meaning clear and true. "And you're mine, now. Always."

The sound of the airplane engine didn't register with me until it was right above us. The pilot was taking the aircraft in for the landing on the water in the lagoon.

From the air, he wouldn't be able to see us on the covered front patio. Once he'd landed, however...

"The plane is here." I tried to wiggle out of Lero's arms. "He's come for me."

"He can fuck right off." Lero grinned, giving me a quick kiss, before finally letting me run inside to hide my bare bottom from

the view of the unsuspecting pilot. "You're not going anywhere anymore."

Chapter 19

Lero set a large plate with shucked oysters on a bed of ice in front of me.

"How do you like your oysters?" he asked, arranging an array of small dishes filled with sauces and garnish next to it.

"Oh, I don't eat them nearly often enough to have a preference." I smiled, trying to remember when I'd had oysters at all. Probably at one of Javier's business parties. "I don't even know what half of these are." I gestured at the dishes.

The plane had dropped off some supplies and left without me. My bag was still packed, sitting on the bed in Lero's room. He'd informed me I'd be moving into it with him. I'd be spending every night in his bed from now on.

I had a new pair of shorts on, but my body still hummed faintly with the thrill from Lero's touch. Glass of white wine in hand, I had yet to take a sip from it. However, my head was swimming already, drunk on happiness.

Instead of the nervous energy that had tended to hang in the room when Lero and I had been here before, the atmosphere was warm, tender, and with a new kind of tension gently buzzing between us.

"This is the best hot sauce for these." Lero pointed at a small bottle on the table between us. "And this is Mignonette. Dill and coriander right here. Horseradish and seafood sauce... You know what?" He leaned on one arm at my side, tilting his head to catch my eye. "How about I do one for you to try?"

"That'd be great." I smiled, relieved I didn't have to make any decisions at the moment.

The last decision I'd made had been so overwhelming, it'd drained me. Though, of course I didn't regret it a bit. I'd never traveled anywhere today, yet it felt like I'd finally arrived in my one true home.

Lero gently took a shell off the platter.

"A little of Mignonette." He scooped some of the finely chopped shallots with red-wine vinegar on top of the contents of the oyster shell. "A drop of the hot sauce, not too spicy. Have you ever tried whiskey on oysters?"

"You mean drinking whiskey with them? How about the wine?" I glanced at my glass. The almost full bottle of chilled wine was sweating with condensation on the table to my right.

"No, you *eat* oysters with whiskey." He raised a shot glass filled with amber liquid. "Would you like to try?"

I nodded. "Why not?"

He drizzled whiskey from the shot glass onto the all-dressed oyster then placed it on a small plate for me.

"Voila!" He grinned. "For you, *mademoiselle.*"

"Thank you."

Our fingers touched when I took the plate from him. He paused before letting go of it. I looked up at him, catching his smile waver and a bright spark flash through his gaze.

The heat in his eyes hadn't been quite extinguished after our sex on the front patio. It seemed more intense now, charged with the knowledge of what we had and what we could have more of.

I lifted the oyster shell off the plate and quickly sucked in its contents. The array of amazing flavors hit my palate. The slight burn of the hot sauce and the whiskey, combined with the crisp texture of shallots made for a delightful combination. I closed my eyes, savoring it.

"And?" Lero's raspy voice reached me. "How do you find it?"

"Simply delicious," I said slowly, opening my eyes.

Sitting in a chair next to me, he watched me closely as I licked my lips, then handed me my glass of wine.

"To us." He lifted his glass.

I clinked against it with mine and echoed, "To us."

I'd never had "us" before. It'd always been just "me." Until Lero. This realization made today feel like a wedding day.

Pleasantly cool, the refreshing taste of wine was welcome after the oyster. I set the glass down, then touched my neck, the spot where he'd bit me, needing a reminder that all of this was actually happening.

The bite mark was no longer detectable by touch. The scar might still be visible, but I couldn't feel it with my fingers.

"You can heal." I'd long suspected it but refused to accept as a fact even having the evidence since I was fourteen.

"Yes. I can heal if I lick and kill if I bite."

"Well, you've bitten me," I stroked my neck, and he followed my movement with his gaze. "But I'm still alive."

He leaned close, taking my hand in his.

"My teeth only have poison when I'm in my beast form. I would've never bitten you if there was any threat to you, sweetheart." The word of endearment rolled off his tongue, slightly accented and smooth as butter. He brought my hand to his lips, gently kissing my knuckles.

I breathed harder, faced with this new Lero, unrestrained in his tenderness to me. I didn't think I could take it without melting into a puddle at his feet.

"Why bite me at all?" I asked.

"A bite to the neck is a part of the mating ritual of my people, to taste each other's blood."

This wasn't the first time he'd tasted my blood.

"When you licked my leg, back in Paris. I couldn't stop thinking about you ever since. Why? Did it have something to do with my blood, too?"

"No, Stella." He shifted back. "The mating bond is only possible between the same kind—a werewolf with a werewolf. Even then, though, the bond can't form with a child. That night, I simply saw a hurt little girl. You asked for a band-aid, and I happened to have something more effective than that for your pain."

I couldn't blame my early infatuation with him on anything but myself, then. A lonely, socially awkward teenager, I'd responded to the random act of kindness by a stranger. The fact that he also happened to be movie-star gorgeous surely played its role too.

Or maybe, my heart had recognized my soul mate, even then. I didn't care about any magic bonds, but I always felt a connection with Lero—whether it was years ago or now.

"I'd licked plenty of bruises, and scratches for Zeph while he was growing up." Lero chuckled. "The boy was a menace to himself, still is." He shook his head.

"Is Zeph coming back?" I asked, remembering the bit of their conversation I'd overheard.

"I hope so."

"Is he also a werewolf?"

"No. Zeph is a siren, a water fae. Wait until you hear him sing." He smiled. "Humans love Zeph's voice."

Humans.

"Where did you and Zeph come from? Are there more like you here? How come no one knows?" I'd been collecting questions for weeks, and the more I learned, the more I wanted to know.

He took a sip of his wine, silently regarding me over the rim of his glass.

"You have me for life, Lero," I reminded. "There can't be any secrets between us now, no half-truths either. You have to tell me everything."

He set his glass down on the table and ran his hand through his hair. After keeping secrets for decades, I imagined it would be hard to put them into words now.

"Zeph and I are fae," he started. "We may look like humans, but unlike them we have access to magic that humans do not."

"How did you...come to be?"

"We were born." He shrugged. "Like humans, fae mate, have babies, and die. Except that we live longer."

"How many of you are there?"

"Millions, but we live in a different world, called Nerifir. It's a beautiful but dangerous place, connected to your world by the River of Mists, a strong current of magic that flows between dimensions and connects realms."

"There're more worlds out there? With sentient beings? How come people, *humans*, don't know about it?" This all sounded like a fairy tale.

"They used to know. Long ago, humans knew about many of these things until they started to explain their knowledge away, using science."

"So, you don't believe in science?" I asked, with a skeptical smile.

"Science is hard facts. It doesn't require belief but understanding. Magic is unexplainable. People believe in it and feel it. Magic and science are two different things, but they aren't mutually exclusive. They can co-exist. That's what humans have forgotten. My kind live and breathe magic. We're born with it. It's a big part of our existence, though not all can wield it. For werewolves, Moon magic is a source of power. Other fae have other powers derived from different kinds of magic."

"And does everyone in Nerifir speak French?" I asked with a teasing smile.

"No!" He laughed. "French was the first language I heard when I came to this world."

"Is that how it works?"

"Yes. The first language you hear becomes yours. French is now what you call my *mother tongue*. I had to learn to speak English just like any non-English speaking human would. I can't get rid of the accent, either."

"Well, thank God for that!" I genuinely meant that. I loved his soft, purring accent. It'd be a shame if he'd ever lost it for any reason. "Do you ever go back to Nerifir?"

"No. It's not simple to travel between worlds. If I go back, I won't arrive to the same time and place I've left. And if I try to come back to this world again, I will never come back to *here* exactly." He planted a hand on top of the table as if marking the spot. "I may find myself on another continent, hundreds or thousands of years in the past or in the future. Though, it could be just a day or a month from now. There's no way to predict."

"Does it mean you're staying here forever, then?"

He nodded.

"But do you miss your home at all?" I sked. "How long have you been here?"

"For over forty years now. Enough to get used to this world. I'll always miss some things from back home, but my life is here now. This world is the only home I'll ever have. I'm not going anywhere, especially now that I have you."

I reached out and placed my hand on top of his, vowing in my heart to make this world a happier place for him.

My fingers brushed by his wrist, bringing to mind the wounds he'd had there and how fast they'd healed.

"You can heal yourself, too, can't you?" I gently brushed around his wrist with the tips of my fingers.

"Yes." He smiled. "Only it happens on its own. I don't have to lick myself to heal."

"Well, that's good," I said with a soft giggle. "Some places are hard to reach for licking."

My mind then went to the last time I'd seen him injured. The gruesome memory of his blood-covered hands and blood-soaked fur on his thighs quickly dimmed my merry mood. The wounds had been self-inflicted.

"What is it?" Lero stroked the side of my face with his knuckles. "Where did your smile go? It's the most amazing sight in the world, but it never stays long enough for me to fully enjoy it."

I couldn't deny him, could I? I smiled again, my face heating under his attention.

"I thought about last night," I clarified, sadness gripping my heart despite the smile. "You hurt yourself."

The tanned skin on his cheekbones flushed. He grabbed his glass, taking a large gulp from it.

"I really wish you hadn't seen that." Lero looked uncharacteristically flustered.

"Are you...embarrassed?"

He set his glass down and admitted, "Mortified."

"Why would you be?"

He cleared his throat.

"Well, I don't usually, um...touch myself in front of others." An elbow on the table, he rubbed his eyes with his hand. "On the night of the full moon, the restraints of culture, civilization and any other kind fall off me, Stella. The wild nature takes over. The legend says my people came from animals, *voukalaks,* and back into the animals we turn every full-moon night. The beasts know only hunt, hunger, and lust. Those are the things I feel the most on those nights."

"Lero," I shifted closer to him, taking his hand in mine again. "There is nothing to be ashamed of here. I don't mind your 'wild nature.' I rather enjoy it, actually."

"Enjoy?" Lacing his fingers with mine, he peered at me from under his long eyelashes, studying my face carefully. "To my knowledge, human women like their men to make love to them. What I did to you there..." He tipped his head in the direction of the front door. "Wasn't it."

I leaned even closer.

"I'm afraid your knowledge about human women is severely outdated, *old man*," I teased, remembering what Zeph had called Lero. I then added quietly, as if sharing a secret, "Making love is lovely of course, but some of us don't mind some good, hard *fucking* once in a while."

I took a drink from my wine glass but kept my gaze on him. The blush thickened on his hard, chiseled cheekbones. With all the men before him, there had been so much unfulfilled desire on my part. I hated for Lero to think he'd been inadequate in any way when in fact, he'd been the best for me.

Heat smoldered in his eyes, and I couldn't resist stoking the flames.

"Do you think I should be embarrassed, too, if I touched myself while you watched?" I asked innocently.

He groaned, then slid off his chair, sinking to his knees in front of me.

"Don't say things like that if you want to have dinner made on time."

I cupped his face with my hands.

"You don't ever have to feel embarrassed about who you are with me. Okay? And I'm not hungry for dinner right now." I slid my hands to the back of his head, threading my fingers into his hair.

"Fuck dinner then," he growled, taking my mouth in a kiss.

I slid forward in my chair, opening my knees wide to let him closer.

He hiked my shirt up to my shoulders, breaking the kiss only to take my top off over my head. His hands then went around me, finding the closure of my bra. Quick and urgent, his movements were more controlled now as compared to the last time. Deftly unclipping the bra, he slid it off my shoulders then leaned back, sliding his gaze down my body.

My chest heaved, my lips hot and tingling after his kiss.

He reached for my left breast with his hand. Cupping it, he gently glided his thumb over my nipple, watching it grow hard under his touch.

"I do both, Stella," he said in a low, rough voice. "Fuck *and* make love. Which one would you prefer right now?"

He gently kneaded my breast, rolling the nipple between his thumb and his finger. I squirmed in the chair, feeling suddenly hot all over.

"I—" I gasped as he put his mouth on my right breast, sucking the tip in.

I wrapped my legs around him. Fisting my hands in his hair, I arched my back, pressing my breast into his caress. Desire throbbed hot between my legs, making me moan in need.

"Both it is," he rasped.

Scooping me out of the chair, he got up and pivoted toward his bedroom, carrying me in his arms.

"Dinner will have to be postponed." He nibbled on my lips in quick, hot kisses while taking me to his room.

Tossing me on his bed, he crawled over me. Air rushed out of my lungs as he leaned closer.

"I don't think I'll ever get used to being able to have you any time I want," I whispered, wrapping my arms around his neck.

"I don't think you'll ever want me as often as I want *you*," he said before kissing me again.

He slid his hands down my body, and I quickly unbuttoned my shorts.

"Don't ruin this pair." I smiled when he moved his kisses down my neck. "I don't have many more left."

He kissed the spot where he'd bit me earlier.

"I'll buy you more shorts," he groaned into my shoulder when my fingers brushed against the bulge in his pants.

I lifted my hips, and he slid my shorts and underwear off, carefully this time.

"Or maybe you'd like to start wearing more skirts?" He traced a line down my inner thigh with his finger. "And no underwear at all." The tip of his finger touched between my legs.

I exhaled sharply as he lazily circled my most sensitive spot.

Leaning over me, he took my nipple in his mouth again, playing with it with his tongue.

'Healing unless it's deadly,' rushed through my brain when I thought about his mouth.

Nothing about Lero was normal. He was further from my world than any person I knew. Yet I felt closer to him than to anyone else.

Arousal coursed through me. Gripping his shoulders with my fingers, I lifted my hips into his touch.

Letting go of my breast, he shifted his body down mine.

"I want to know how you taste," he murmured, kissing a trail down my belly. "Everywhere."

The brush of his tongue between my legs made me whimper with need. I jerked my hips, and he held my thighs to keep me in place.

Moaning, I raked my fingers through his hair. The silk of it tickled the insides of my thighs, spreading hot tingles through my body.

"Oh, it's so good..." I breathed out.

He dipped his tongue inside me then swirled it around, ripping a sharp gasp of pleasure from me.

"Exquisite," he whispered, his breath cool against my heated flesh.

He put his mouth on me again, licking, sucking, and nibbling until I couldn't take it anymore.

"Lero..." I moaned his name before the climax hit me, rendering me speechless.

His touch turned gentle as he helped me ride my pleasure with tender kisses.

The moment I stilled, he pulled himself back up my body.

"You taste delicious," he stated with satisfaction, kissing my neck, then my mouth again. "Everywhere."

"You would know about delicious, the gourmet that you are." I smiled, as the post orgasmic warmth lazily took over my body.

He unzipped his pants, fitting himself between my legs.

"Take this off, Lero." I fumbled with the buttons of his shirt. "I need to feel your skin.

Not bothering to open it all the way, he tore his shirt off over his head, tossing it aside.

I splayed my hands along the firm planes of his torso. My fingers slid through the dusting of dark hair on his chest. I cherished the sensations of his bulging muscles underneath, the warmth of his skin, and the weight of his body over mine.

He pushed inside me, slowly, as if savoring every inch. Rising over me on his arms, he gazed at me, his eyes flickering between mine.

With a soft groan, he bent his elbows, lowering over me while moving faster. "Pure pleasure," he breathed out.

At this angle, the pressure of his body on me teased with another orgasm. I quickly reached between us, needing just a little help.

"No. Mine." He swatted my hand away, placing his finger on me instead.

I gasped, tossing my head back, as the tingling pleasure spiked.

"Yesss," he hissed through his teeth, thrusting harder.

"Oh, Lero!" Tossing my head back, I dug my fingers in his shoulders, riding through my climax as he pumped his release into me.

"I've waited decades for this." He buried his face in my shoulder, catching his breath.

"For decades? For me?"

"For someone I'd feel about the way I feel for you." He lifted his head to meet my eyes.

"Decades are an awfully long time, honey." I stroked the side of his face, and he leaned into my touch. There was so much unguarded tenderness in his expression, the question slipped off my tongue, "Do you love me, Lero?"

He drew in a breath, shifting off me. My heart dropped into the hollow of my stomach. He'd pledged a lifetime of loyalty to me but couldn't say he loved me? The longer the pause grew, the more I dreaded his answer.

He rose on his elbow over me and cupped my face with his other hand, turning me to him.

"I enjoy you, Stella. You are my dearest treasure, my heart's deepest desire. Here, on this island, I've been the happiest ever—because of you. I will die to defend you."

I bit my lip. It sounded very much like love. Why wouldn't he say the word then?

"I've lived enough in this world to know how much love means to humans. But I don't know if I can feel it myself. The fae bond takes the guesswork out of that for my people. The physical attraction comes first, then the bond happens."

"What exactly is this bond?"

His gaze slid by me. He stared at the rising disk of the moon outside the glass door. Still perfectly round to the naked eye, the moon shone bright, reflecting with silver in his eyes.

"It's the strongest connection between two beings," he said slowly. "Your blood, your body, and your soul long for that one person in the world. When you find them, the true magic happens. The power of the Moon flows through both of you. You become each other's strengths and each other's weaknesses. When you're together, nothing is impossible. And when you're apart, nothing can stand in your way back to each other."

It did sound like magic, the most wonderful kind.

"Have you ever been mated, Lero?"

"No." He lifted a strand of my hair away from my face then gently placed it behind my ear. "I was just over fifty when I left. A good age to start looking for a mate, but it can take decades to find one."

"Do fae... um, remain celibate while they search?"

"Gods, no!" He laughed. "Why? Sex is too enjoyable. And my people are, well, too virile to stay celibate, anyway."

"But *you* did. For decades you said."

"There are no females of my kind here. And after Amelie... I didn't want to destroy another life."

"Was it easier to stay alone?"

"It was necessary."

We remained silent for a few moments, while I pondered his words.

"Why do you think this connection wouldn't be possible with a human?" I challenged. "We're capable of feelings that even you would call *magical*."

Propped on an elbow at my side, he trailed his finger down my neck, between my breasts, then cupped the curve of my hip.

"A mating bond doesn't happen between species. A werewolf cannot create one with a water fae, or a sky fae or a gorgonian. Only with another werewolf."

He lowered his head to place a kiss on my temple, then nuzzled my hair.

"I chose to be alone because my being with someone from this world could destroy them." His hand slid from my hip to around my waist. "The poison of a bonded pair of werewolves no longer harms either of them. But a nick of my teeth on a full-moon night would kill you in seconds." He drew me closer to him. "Giving in to keeping you was a weakness, a selfish one, too. But I can't give you up anymore. I'll have to find a way to make sure you're safe while living with someone like me. For one, you'll have to promise me not to go down in the cellar next full moon."

Pain stabbed through my heart when I thought about Lero spending the night alone, locked in his cage. Compassion squeezed my chest.

"There's a few weeks until the next full moon still," I offered, not promising anything. "Maybe we'll come up with a better solution by then?"

"Stella," he warned. "I won't let you play with your life."

I gently stroked his chest, enjoying the soft tickle of hair over his hard muscles.

"I'm not going to take any unnecessary risks." I worded my promise carefully. "Now that I finally have you, I love my life way too much to risk it."

He caught my hand and brought it to his lips for a kiss.

"I don't know how to love without the bond, Stella, but I promise I'll do everything to make you *feel* loved. Whatever it takes."

I'd never been loved, but Lero had already made me feel cherished and cared for.

"You definitely make me feel special," I confessed, then added with a smile, "Of course all those fancy homemade dinners with lobster, oysters, and wine, don't hurt, either."

He shifted, and my fingers slid from his chest to the side of his ribcage.

"Good food is necessary for survival, in my opinion." He squirmed under my touch with a chuckle.

I trailed my fingers along the side of his ribs then over to his belly. The only hair here was the dark trail running from his belly button to the nest of curls that surrounded his renewed erection. It bobbed as I stroked the hard squares of his abs.

"I'm not complaining," I said softly. "If you continue to cook the way you do..."

He huffed a strangled half-laugh, half-moan as I increased the pressure, dragging the tips of my fingers along the hard ridges of his abdominal muscles. He bent his legs, slightly arching his back.

"Don't tell me you like belly rubs!" I exhaled a giggle, scratching his rippling muscles a little harder.

His hard-on jerked higher, a shudder ran down his large body as he groaned.

"You really like that, huh?" I murmured, sliding my hand down, until my fingers sank into the dark hair around his shaft.

"Come here now." He grabbed me under my arms and rolled me over on my back. "I'll show you exactly what I like." He crawled over me and swallowed my laugh with a kiss.

I welcomed him, wrapping my arms around him and opening my legs wider.

"*I love you*," rushed through my mind, but I didn't let it out, not even when he slid inside me again, whispering how wonderful I felt and how happy I made him feel.

These three little words required a reply if said out loud. I now knew I wouldn't get one from him.

Chapter 20

STELLA

A phone ringtone shrilled from Lero's closet. It was loud enough to startle me in the lounger on the back patio where I sat, reading.

Could it be Lero again?

He'd been away for the past three days. It wasn't the only time he'd been gone during the three weeks since the last full moon. As much as we loved our quiet life here on the Blue Cay, there were matters on the mainland that required his personal attention.

Lero had already called me this morning, to check on me. Our phone calls now were very different from before. No longer holding back his affection, he was so much more generous with words.

"I miss you," he'd added before we'd said our goodbyes. The longing in his voice was so intense, it sent shivers down my arms.

"I miss you, too," I'd barely whispered—the emotions had almost taken my voice away. "Come home soon."

"Tomorrow."

Home.

This was what the island had become for both of us. Without Lero, however, our home felt empty.

The phone rang again. Leaving the book on the lounger, I ran into the bedroom through the back doors.

"Hello?" I managed to pick up before the phone stopped ringing.

"Stella?" Zeph's voice sounded excited as if I were his long-lost friend. But maybe this man treated all people like friends. The image of his easy smile rose in my mind, making me grin back even though he couldn't see me.

"Yes, it's me. Lero is not around at the moment," I added carefully.

I knew Lero trusted Zeph. I also knew he'd told me not to discuss his whereabouts with anyone. Always cautious, he didn't want anyone to know when I was left on the island alone.

"I'm calling to invite myself for dinner," Zeph announced cheerfully. "When would be the best time to come over?"

"Dinner?" The prospect of having company on Blue Cay was new and thrilling. We had more than enough space, plenty of food, and fine wine for a real party. "Oh, it'd be fun. Please come. Any time this week would work. How about the day after tomorrow?"

The following week was a full moon again. I sensed Lero's anxiety increasing with it approaching. Having people over while he had to deal with it would be too difficult for him, I believed. The sooner the dinner happened the better it would be.

"Sounds great!" Zeph replied. "I'll bring a guest if you don't mind."

"A guest?"

"My fiancée. Her name is Ivy. She's a sweetheart. You'll love her," he added with optimistic confidence.

"Is she...a fae?" I asked, intrigued. "Like you?"

"A fae? No." He laughed. "She's human."

He spoke so easily about it. There was none of Lero's reservations. Zeph seemed to enjoy having someone to speak freely about what he was, too.

"I'll talk to Ivy and call back to confirm," he said.

"I'm looking forward to seeing both of you soon," I replied sincerely. Seeing Zeph again presented an exciting opportunity to learn more about the world he and Lero had come from.

During the past weeks, Lero had been telling me more about Nerifir. It indeed sounded like a magical place, where villagers turned into mythical creatures every full moon. He told me about the dangers of his world that had come to ours. He told me about Ghata and her *bracks*, one of whom happened to be his own brother.

His stories often sounded like fantasy tales.

But Zeph was a real person, whom I'd met. He had a fiancée, which meant he was engaged—such a normal, human thing. I was looking forward to meeting Ivy and to see them interact with each other. Would they be like a normal human couple, too?

Or was their relationship more like the sweaty, needy, desperate, undefined mess that Lero and I had? I doubted anyone could have a relationship similar to ours. Somehow our mess seemed to be uniquely us.

———◆———

HE WAS HERE!

I'd been straining my hearing all morning, listening for the sound of the sea plane engines, and still somehow, I'd missed it. I saw the plane land in the lagoon visible from the front entrance of the house only when worn out by the anxiety of anticipation, I'd decided to go for a walk.

Lero jumped off a float onto the wet sand and rushed to the house, carrying a crate in his hands.

I met him on the front patio.

"You're here..." was all I managed to say before he dropped the crate at my feet and grabbed me in his arms.

He caught my mouth in a hot, messy kiss while walking me backwards into the house.

"The pilot..." I protested when he broke the kiss for a moment to kick the door closed behind us. "The supplies..."

"They can wait. But I can't," he rasped.

The eerie red flashed bright in his eyes. I noted the perspiration beading on his temples and the way his fingers trembled when he tugged at my clothes.

"Shorts," he muttered, grumpily, tearing the hem of my sleeveless top out from the waistband of my cotton shorts. "I've *got* to buy you some skirts."

Only when his hands finally connected with the bare skin on my back did he relax a little. He slowed my frantic disrobing for a second, pausing like a drowning man who suddenly got a long breath of air.

"I need you, Stella," he groaned, with a shudder across his back. "So badly."

I quickly unbuttoned and unzipped my shorts.

"I missed you," I whispered in his ear.

His need fueled mine. It was thrilling to be wanted this desperately, as if I were the vital part to his very survival.

I shoved my shorts down past my hips, taking the underwear with them.

My gesture seemed to snap the restraints Lero had been trying to hold himself in. He pushed me against the wall right there, next to the front door in the hallway. Hooking his arm under my knee, he lifted my leg, opening me for him. With another biting kiss, he shoved inside me, groaning against my mouth.

I fisted my hand in his hair, halting my breath at the sting of his rough invasion. He growled, moving faster. The sleek heat of my intense desire for him soothed the pressure of his massive girth inside me. The tingling pleasure quickly spread through my belly and along my inner thighs, building up where our bodies connected.

My leg draped over his arm, he grabbed my backside with both hands, shoving my lower body closer to his, as he rutted into me.

Sudden and violent, the orgasm rocked through me in blinding shudders of intense pleasure. I gulped in the air in broken, desperate gasps, my fingers gripping Lero's hair. Still, it wasn't enough. I craved more of him. I needed to become a part of him.

I pressed my mouth to his neck, just above the collar of his shirt. The scent of him was stronger here, and I greedily breathed it in.

Growling through his clenched teeth, he threw his head back, chasing his climax in hard, brutal thrusts. Wild and animalistic, this was not "making love," it was something else. And my body responded to it in inexplicable but delightful way. Every hard thrust brought on another rocking wave of my never-ending orgasm as he came into me, over and over again.

I flexed my jaw, my teeth piercing his skin. The salty taste of his blood coated my tongue, making me dizzy and drunk with pleasure.

He sank to the floor, sliding my back against the wall, as if his knees suddenly gave out.

Weak and trembling, my muscles quivering, I untangled my fingers from his hair, watching in horror as quite a few strands remained in my hands. The collar of his white shirt was stained with bright red. I wiped my lips with the back of my hand. It came smeared red as well.

"Lero?" I whispered, horrified by what I'd done.

He didn't seem to notice, panting wildly, his head on my shoulder.

"I'm so, so sorry." I hovered my hand over the wound I'd inflicted.

He rubbed his neck, smearing the blood over his skin.

"Did you just mark me?" he glanced up, an amused smile dancing in his eyes.

"I'm sorry?" I repeated, tentatively this time as he seemed rather pleased about having been bitten.

He'd done the same thing to me before, but that was a part of his people's ancient mating tradition, which I understood and accepted. For the life of me, I couldn't explain what had come over me to bite him back, now.

"You're sorry you've claimed me as yours?" he asked, tilting his head.

"Well, if you put it that way..." With my finger, I lightly circled the couple of small puncture wounds my teeth left on his neck. The blood had stopped seeping from them already as the healing process began. "If that's what it means, I'm glad I did it, then. Because you are mine."

He had been mine and only mine from the moment I met him. It just had taken him over fifteen years to figure it out.

I smiled as he kissed me.

"Thank you," he murmured. "Thank you for being there."

His hair was mussed, his skin flushed when he looked at me, but his eyes were back to their normal color—the wild, unhealthy glimmer in them gone.

"Are you feeling better?" I asked, thinking about the feverish state he'd arrived in and the frenzy with which he'd taken me.

He stared at me for a long moment, searching my eyes with his.

"It'll get worse in the next few days, with the last two nights before the full moon being the most excruciating."

I cupped his face with one hand, gently stroking his cheek.

"How does it feel, Lero? Tell me."

He drew in a long, shuddered breath.

"Like slowly losing myself. I'm surrendering my body and mind to another entity, little by little every day."

"To the moon?"

"Yes. I'm losing control, handing it over to it. And there is nothing I can do to stop it."

I couldn't stop it either, but maybe I could slow it down, or at least help him cope.

"You're feeling better right now, aren't you?" I ran my fingers through his hair, smoothing it down.

"I am. As temporary as the relief may be, it feels good."

He caught my hand and placed a tender kiss on the inside of my wrist.

"Can you bear this, Stella? Month after month?" He wouldn't meet my eyes, keeping my wrist pressed to the corner of his mouth.

"Bear what? Being the one you make love to?" I smiled, caressing the back of his neck with the fingers of my other hand.

He huffed a sad laugh.

"This wasn't 'making love,' and you know it."

I shifted in his lap. After the wild sex and the mind-blowing orgasm, I'd just now realized that we both remained mostly clothed. Only my shorts and underwear were off. Lero's pants were undone but he'd somehow managed to keep them on his hips. It all had happened so suddenly.

"Sex with you is no burden, honey. There's nothing wrong with being thoroughly fucked once in a while." I laughed softly, nuzzling his cheek. "Isn't that how ferocious werewolves do it?" I wiggled my eyebrows, keeping my tone light.

"But you're not a werewolf." He glanced at me, still clutching my wrist.

"No. I'm not." I stifled a sigh.

I'm just deeply in love with one.

Chapter 21

STELLA

"That was my last trip for a while," Lero told me as we took a leisurely early afternoon stroll the day after his return. We had some time before Zeph and Ivy would arrive for dinner tonight. Excitement bubbled in me at the thought of having company on Blue Cay.

I brushed by Lero's fingers with mine, and he quickly caught my hand in his—large and warm. I loved the physical connection with him. No matter how much sex we'd had last night and this morning, I still welcomed every touch of his throughout the day.

"Are you confident Ghata will leave you alone now?"

"It's impossible to be confident on anything as far as Ghata is concerned. I'd trusted her once, I'll never make that mistake again. As long as we share the same world with her, we'll always have to be careful."

He'd been teaching me caution, by fae rules—never make deals with them unless you think through every word very carefully, never eat anything unless you trust where the food came from. Apparently, there were many magical substances in his world that would alter one's perception or even the personality if consumed. Only a few worked on fae, but many were effective on humans. Through *bracks*, Ghata had been able to gain access to some of those substances, and no one knew when and how she might decide to use them.

"I'd love to go back to my job again, at some point," I ventured. "Full-time."

We'd talked about this a little. Despite it being quiet lately, Lero was reluctant to let me go anywhere on my own, and I didn't know if I wanted to do all my viewings accompanied by him as my body-guard.

"Maybe soon." He heaved a sigh.

I knew he blamed himself for "dragging" me into his life of magic and mayhem, and I didn't want it to make harder on him. After all, I'd never stopped working. I'd just been sharing my commissions with the agent who did that part of the job that required me to be physically present, which was a lot. But it also allowed me to spend all this time with Lero, which I was grateful for.

"With Ghata moving her show to Asia soon, we'll have less to worry about, right?" I asked.

He nodded, though his expression remained pensive.

"It looks like Ghata is wrapping up her show," he said. "She's not advertising it past the upcoming performance in Singapore."

Lero had put a price on the last sentient fae in Ghata's possession, a gargoyle she'd kept as a statue in her collection. We'd gotten a report recently that the gargoyle had been stolen from her and freed.

"Did the gorgonian and the gargoyle return to Nerifir?"

"Yes."

"So, they're safe, then." Their safety was the most important, though deep inside I wished I'd had a chance to meet them before they left our world.

"As safe as one can hope to be in Nerifir. It can be a dangerous place, no matter what time one lands in there."

"That didn't stop the two from returning," I pointed out. "You said you wouldn't go back, but have you ever considered it?"

He rolled his shoulders uneasily. "Unlike the two fae who went back, the worst for me would be if I returned close to the time and place I left."

"Why?"

His fingers flexed over mine. For a moment, I wondered if he'd brush this question aside.

"No more secrets, right?" he muttered softly as if to himself.

"No more secrets," I echoed.

He drew in a long breath as if about to jump off a cliff.

"I didn't simply cross over to this world one day, Stella. I fled," he finally said.

"You ran away? From whom?"

"Not who, *what*," he corrected. "An arrest and prosecution. A possible execution, too."

"For what?" I gasped in disbelief.

He stopped abruptly, facing me. His gaze, open and imploring, rested on mine, making him look uncharacteristically vulnerable. He cared about what I thought of him, and he knew what he was about to say would test my opinion of him.

"For murder," he confessed grimly. "Multiple murders, possibly."

A chilling sensation trickled through my chest, but I didn't yank my hand from his.

"Possibly?" I repeated numbly. "You aren't even sure how many people you've killed?"

He winced, hanging his head between his shoulders. "I... I don't remember."

"How could you forget?"

"It was the night of the full moon."

"You were the beast?"

He nodded.

"You keep some memories in that form, though, right?" I asked.

"Not much. Back in Nerifir, the Moon's magic was under Ghata's power. Full moon nights turned wild, unhinged, and especially violent there. Instead of hunting in couples and making love under the moonlight, my kind turned into a raging army, roaming the Sarnala Plains with our only purpose to fuck and kill."

"So, you killed..."

My fingers trembled, and he squeezed my hand tighter.

"Yes.

"Did you rape, too?"

He sucked in some air through his teeth. A grimace of agony crossed his face.

"I hope not."

"You *hope*?"

"The idea of violating someone like that terrifies and sickens me possibly even more than murder. I desperately hope my inherent aversion to the act of forcing myself on someone kept me from committing it. From the few shreds of distorted memories I retained, there're none of rape."

I exhaled slowly. My heart beat wildly.

"What *is* in those shreds of memories?"

He stared straight ahead, but his gaze turned unseeing. His pupils grew wider, darker, as if the things passing through his mind's eye terrified him anew.

"Blood," he said somberly. "So much blood, I felt drunk on its smell and dizzy with violence. The savage need for more blood... Running so fast, my lungs burned. Hitting, smashing, and ripping apart flesh so ferociously, my muscles hurt..."

He drew in a shaky breath, unsteady on his feet from the weight of the memories he'd carried for decades. He might not remember the details, but he'd obviously never forgot the horror of that night. He might've escaped the punishment, but he hadn't been spared the torture of guilt.

"It was the madness," I whispered, frozen in horror with him. "It wasn't you, Lero. That's *not* who you are. It was the madness of that night."

"Moon Madness," he whispered, closing his eyes.

It wasn't the fear of an arrest and prosecution that had tortured him.

"You told me you surrender all control on those nights. To a magical entity. That is what's to blame, Lero." Letting go of his hand, I cupped his face, forcing him to look at me. "Whatever happened that night wasn't you fault. If you had no control over your mind or your body, you cannot hold yourself responsible for what happened."

He stared at me for a long moment. Slowly, I believed, he started seeing *me* again instead of the past.

"It wasn't you," I repeated as he pressed his forehead to mine.

"You are my morning star, Stella," he said softly. "You're the light that always guides me out of my nightmares."

Wrapping his arms around me, he drew me closer for a kiss. Deep and long with a hint of lingering sadness, it was not like any of the kisses we'd shared before.

"I love you, Lero," I murmured.

"Why? How can you love me?"

"You have been a part of me for such a long time." I hugged his neck, running my fingers through the short hair on the back of his head. "I honestly couldn't tell you when exactly I first fell in love. But you've been in my dreams ever since that night in Paris."

"It was so long ago," he said with a hint of a smile. "And all I did was just bring you home that night, not much."

"Maybe, but I didn't get much attention growing up. Finding kindness in a stranger impressed me as a kid." I felt a bit foolish admitting that. But I wanted to be completely honest with him. "When I said I was hurt, you *heard* me and made it better. Of course, helping me didn't mean much to you. But for me, it was special. It didn't hurt that you were...well, still are, drop-dead gorgeous, either." I exhaled a soft laugh. "I'd never seen anyone like you before—or after, for that matter. Your eyes... The memory of them was enough to get my imagination going for years to come."

"My eyes?" He squinted at me, with a curious expression on his face.

"Don't tell me you don't know how good-looking you are." I shook my head.

"Well." He shrugged. "Human women tend to find me attractive."

"Do they, now?" I squinted at him.

"In *this* form only, though. But you..." He stared at me in wonder, as if *I* were a magical being from another world, not he.

My feelings for him went past an adolescent infatuation based on looks long ago. I loved the man he was inside, no matter what he looked like on the outside, whether the handsome fae or the terrifying beast.

"I don't know what lucky star to thank for sending you to me." He hugged me tighter, kissing my hair.

"Despite what you may think, it's not hard to love you," I said, snuggling against his wide chest. "When you're with me, I feel at home. When you're gone, it's like something in the world is missing. No one has ever touched me the way you do. You use me, greedily, like a man dying from thirst would drink water. And at the same time, you give my life a new meaning, filling me to the brim with the love of living. I have something you need, and it thrills me to be needed by you. On the other hand, you fulfill all my desires, even those I wasn't aware of myself." I lifted my face up to his. "I love being with you, talking to you, having sex with you. I love everything about you. I love you, Lero. That's the only way I know how to love—giving my whole to you."

"So much of what you've just said I feel for you, too, Stella." His expression was thoughtful. "Does it mean I love you, too?"

Suddenly, it wasn't that important to hear those three little words from him anymore. What he *did* for me meant so much more.

I smiled wide.

"You most certainly make me feel *loved,* honey."

I held his face in my hands, losing myself in the stormy gray of his eyes. The lightnings of red showed up in them again, but they didn't scare me. They excited me.

"Next full moon, stay with me," I begged. "Don't lock yourself in that basement cell ever again."

His chest rose with a deep breath. "Stella—"

The peaceful afternoon shattered with an explosion.

The island's security system blared an alarm, its splitting sound hurting my ears. The ground shook under my feet. And a humongous cloud of water mist rose in the air, breaking the sunlight into bursts of color.

"Lero!" I dug my fingers onto his biceps. His arms went rigid around me. "What's happening?"

Another explosion thundered through the air. A fountain of sea water blasted up into the sky, flipping a black boat in the distance upside down. Another boat bobbed upturned in the wake of the first explosion. At least three more were sneaking into the lagoon from around the bend in the shore and past the reef. All the boats were laden with men.

It was an invasion!

My head pounded from the noise of the blasts. The echo of them was ringing in my ears.

"Stella!" Lero's voice reached me like through a cotton wall.

He shook me so hard my teeth clanked.

"Run!" he shouted, gripping my shoulders. "Run to the house. Lock the doors. Arm the system. Get in the basement. Lock yourself inside."

He gave me another firm shake, forcing me to meet his eyes.

"Do you hear me?"

His words registered with my brain.

House...

System...

Basement...

I nodded.

The men from the upturned boats waded toward the beach. Some held knives in their hands, swords. One had a bow with a quiver of arrows over his shoulder. I saw no guns.

"Run!" Lero shoved me toward the path to the house.

My feet tripping over themselves, I made it through the sand of the beach to the packed-dirt path, then over to the house, running as fast as I could.

My mind went blank, shock clouding any coherent thought. The racket of the explosions ringing in my head. The noise of new blasts sending violent shudders through my body, again and again.

Lero's orders kept spinning through my mind on a loop, *"House, system, basement..."*

I dashed into the house, shutting the door behind me, then made it to our bedroom and the walk-in closet. My hands hovering over the buttons of the control pannel, I paused, not arming the system yet. The fog of shock had finally cleared somewhat, allowing me to think.

If I locked and armed the house, I'd be shutting Lero out along with the men from the boats. He'd ordered me here, trying to save me. But if they harmed him, nothing would stop them from attacking the house and finding me here.

Or maybe they wouldn't come to the house at all. He'd told me before that they would use me to get to him. They didn't need me. They'd come for him. It was Lero who was in danger, not me.

I darted back to the front entrance and peeked out of the main hall window.

Some of the men from the boats had reached Lero. He met them on the beach, two short swords in his hands. Their blades glimmered red as he wielded them. Lunging forward, he stabbed the first man through his chest.

The man threw his head back, falling to his knees. Lero yanked his sword out, sparks of red running along its blade and fanning across the man's chest clad in a black t-shirt. The man dropped to his side and stilled.

Lero got no rest, though, as more invaders emerged from the water, rushing him. All bald-headed, with elaborate tattoos circling their necks and covering their right arms. They looked the same as the men I'd witnessed capturing the beast—who I now knew had been Lero—back in the parking garage.

Bracks.

They'd come to get him again.

I couldn't just hide here and let them take him. But how could I possibly stop them?

There were no weapons in the house that I knew of. I had no idea where Lero got the swords he was using now. Maybe he'd kept them hidden on the beach all this time. Or maybe he'd snatched them from a *brack* when I wasn't looking.

Dashing to the kitchen, I grabbed the two biggest knives from the knife block on the counter. If he could stab someone protecting me, so could I, to stop him from being taken.

With a knife in each hand, I ran out the door, heading for the path to the beach.

"Not so fast!" a deep voice snarled behind me. Then, a thick tattooed arm grabbed me across my chest from behind and lifted me off the ground as if I weighed nothing.

The *bracks'* strength was clearly inhuman.

Fear seized my heart, and I fought against it. I couldn't allow fear to paralyze my mind or my body. Twisting in his grip, I stuck one of my knives into his side.

Held from behind, I couldn't see the blade sink into his flesh, but I *felt* it. I sensed through the handle gripped in my hand as the blade cut through the muscle and scraped the bone of his rib on its way in.

The sickening feeling made my stomach roil.

He growled in pain, his grip on me slacking. I twisted out of his hold and jumped away, leaving the knife in his side. Eyes wide open, I stared in shock as he slowly pulled the knife out of the wound.

The *brack* staggered on his feet. Dark blood trickled out of the cut in a steady flow, but he didn't fall. Holding the bloodied knife in his hand, he stomped toward me.

Over his shoulder, I caught the sight of two more *bracks* rushing in our direction from around the house. They must've landed on the beach behind the house or any other small beaches around the island. Blasts of distant explosions, coming from other directions, confirmed my guess. There were so many more of them than when they took Lero the last time.

With a strangled gasp, I pivoted on my heel and ran down the path to Lero.

He'd been busy. Several bodies lay on the sand around him. The slash wounds in them sparkling red.

There must be something in his swords that made the *bracks* go down and stay down for good—something that my knives didn't have. The *brack* I'd wounded was now running after me, as alive and fit as ever.

"Stella!" Lero growled, burying his right sword in the shoulder of one of the *bracks* attacking him while deflecting a blow of a long sword held by another with his left.

Several more *bracks* hurried from the water edge, dragging the dreadfully familiar black net behind them. It crackled and sparked, scorching black the golden sand of the beach.

"Get the net here!" One of them yelled.

Dez.

I recognized him.

Despite all *bracks* looking almost identical in their appearance, I could not have mistaken this man for anyone else. The glimmer of intense hate in his gaze directed at Lero set him apart.

"You! Get over here." Another *brack* yanked me by my right arm, dragging me aside. I swung my left hand with the knife his way, stabbing him in the neck.

This time, bringing harm to someone came easier to me. The blade went in smoothly, right under his jaw. Blood gushed out of the wound when I yanked the knife back. The *brack's* eyes opened wide in shock and pain. He obviously hadn't expected me to act. His hand went up to his neck, in a futile attempt to block the blood from leaving his body in a pulsing flow.

With a gurgling sound, he crashed to the ground. Though I had a feeling he wouldn't stay there for long—my knife was not Lero's sword. There were no red sparks from the *brack's* wound, which meant it didn't kill him.

More *bracks* rushed us from all directions. More showed up from behind the house, heading to the beach down the path, too. There were so many...

Lero stabbed, sliced, and cut, the pile of dead bodies growing higher around him. But many more kept coming.

"Get him!" Dez ordered to those with the net. "I want him alive. For now, anyway."

The *bracks* tossed the black net over Lero. One of his blades connected with it, setting off an explosion of red sparkling fireworks. Knocked out of his grip, the blade fell to the sand at his feet. The net slid away too, but first it grazed his elbow. He hissed in pain as the sleeve of his shirt smoldered.

I dropped to all fours. Evading the hands of another *brack* grasping for me, I crawled toward Lero.

The *bracks* surrounded him, circling him with the net again.

I climbed over the bodies on the ground, reaching for the sword Lero had dropped. If I got it, I'd be able to fight these men so much more effectively.

A heavy boot stomped on my wrist, stopping me from grabbing the blade.

"Where do you think you're going, human?" A *brack* grabbed me by my ponytail, dragging me away. I screamed in pain, anger, and disappointment.

The net descended on Lero, trapping him. The black ropes of it glowed bright red, burning through his clothes and searing his flesh underneath.

Baring his teeth, he roared in pain.

"Lero!" I screamed, agony wrenching my heart.

"Stella, run!" he yelled.

His eyes glowed red. The veins on his neck bulged. Smoke and red sparks rose from his hands as he gripped the net, straining to rip it apart.

Despite his incredible strength, I knew he wouldn't be able to break free from it. I'd seen it trap him before, hopelessly and securely.

Only this time, I was no mere observer. I *felt* his pain and anguish in my soul and flesh.

The agonizing fire of the net.

The crushing devastation of the impending defeat.

His excruciating worry for me.

His rage.

All of that rushed me, as if they were my own feelings and emotions. As if I were him. I strained my muscles, struggling against the fiery net along with him, even as I was being dragged away from him.

An approaching *brack*, still knee-deep in the sea water, yanked the bow off his shoulder and nocked an arrow. He aimed and shot it in Lero's direction, piercing his upper arm. A bright red spot bloomed on Lero's white shirt that soaked up his blood from the wound. The ominous red lights sparked, running up the arrow embedded in his flesh.

"Lero!" I yelled. My scream mixed with his roar of pain.

I felt his agony, grabbing on to my own arm with my hand. The pain spread through me like a wildfire, melting the chill of fear away and igniting anger. The fury grew, until it was a weapon on its own.

"Get them, Lero!" I screamed at the top of my lungs.

Despite being dragged through the sand, my skull burning from the pull on my hair, I no longer felt weak or powerless. The vicious, unstoppable need to crush, rip, and kill those who wronged us coursed hot through my veins.

"Be the beast that you are. Get them all!" With my entire being, I wished him to be bigger, stronger. Ruthless. I pushed my rage to him, like a blast of power.

His roar grew louder and deeper as his lungs increased in size. He grew taller, his figure hulking, his muscles rippling with strength. His shoulders hunched over, widening and tearing through his shirt.

The shape of his body distorted its outline, turning from that of a man to...something else—unnatural and grotesque.

Black fur burst through the tears in his clothing, immediately smoldering where it touched the net. The sea breeze saturated with the pungent smell of the burnt fur.

With another deafening roar, the beast yanked at the net, knocking the astonished *bracks* who were holding it off their feet.

"Free yourself..." I whispered the command he couldn't possibly hear, but I was certain it reached him somehow.

Shaking the murderous net off his shoulders, he reached for those who kept clinging to it with their glove-protected hands.

My beast growled, closing his needle-sharp teeth over the head of a *brack* and cracking his skull. He bit the other one on his shoulder, ripping his chest open with his long claws. The third one turned to run, and Lero jerked to follow.

Saliva dripped from his fangs and down the back of the escaping *brack*. A thin tendril of smoke rose from the spot where the few drops landed on the *brack's* t-shirt. The material immediately burned through. The poison turned from clear to crimson against the man's bare skin. It glistened, thick like hot lava.

The *brack* howled in agony, arching his back, then crashed to the ground. Dead.

Dez whipped his head my way.

"You!" he gritted through his teeth.

His eyes narrowed to slits, he stomped my way. Grabbing my arm, he yanked me from the hold of the *brack* who'd been dragging me by my hair.

"*You* did this?" Dez growled.

"How?" The other *brack* stared at me in utter bewilderment. "No one can turn a werewolf without the full moon. Not even the most powerful hag. And she doesn't even look like a hag."

Dez brought his face to mine. Red streaks sparked through his dark-brown eyes. The red brought out some eerie similarities, making Dez look momentarily more familiar. The shape of his face, the sharp rise of his cheekbones, and the sensual curve of his mouth, all brought Lero's face to mind.

Even if I didn't know it already, it became obvious Dez was Lero's brother. And his torturer. Despite the physical similarities, however, these two were so different. I couldn't imagine in Lero the pure hatred I saw in Dez's eyes.

"How could you be the sons of the same mother?" I asked in disbelief.

"I have no mother!" Dez snarled. "No family. I belong to the Goddess and her alone. And soon, I'll have no brother, either."

He dragged me back to the part of the beach where Lero fought against the ever-increasing crowd of *bracks*. More of them kept coming from all over the island, swarming the place like rats.

"You started this. You'll end this." Dez spat the words in my face. "Feed the beast!" he yelled, tossing me to Lero.

Propelled by his powerful shove, I fell, hitting the beast's flank with my shoulder. His back to me, Lero turned quickly, snapping his teeth at me.

A spark of recognition flashed in his red eyes, at the last moment. He held back, his teeth clacking shut a hairbreadth away from my bare upper arm. A few drops of poison dripped from them on my skin, burning me like hot lava.

I screamed in pain, rolling on the ground. The poison spread through my body like liquid fire, the burn eating my flesh alive.

The beast's roar shuddered the air, full of anguish. He crouched at my side, turning his back to his enemies.

They used the moment to toss the damn net back on him, yanking him away from me.

I had given him strength. Now, I proved to be his weakness.

"Lero," I wanted to call to him, but my mouth wouldn't open to form the word.

My body seemed paralyzed by fire. The muscles felt as if burnt to a crisp, the joints locked up. I lay on the beach, my head propped on a raised tussock of long grass.

Helplessly, I watched the *bracks* wrap the net over Lero as he thrashed against it to get to me. And I was powerless to help him in any way.

Lifting one of Lero's swords off the sand, Dez moved on to the beast.

"Do you know why I'm here, *voukalak?* Because Madame granted me a wish for my service to her. You know what I asked her for? The chance to murder you. That is my only wish, to see you dead. Madame doesn't need you anymore. No one does."

Far in the distance behind him, I saw the sea swell and rise. The water rolled back from the land, as if a sudden low tide had rapidly come in. Or a tsunami was approaching.

Unable to move, I could only watch.

Dez came closer to Lero, lifting the sword ready to strike.

"You should've accepted Madame's offer when she granted you the honor of becoming one of us. She is taking over this world as we speak, and you could be by her side, ruling it with us. Instead, you're going to die here. Useless as you've always been. *Brother*," he spat the last word out like a curse.

The swell behind him rose higher, moving into the lagoon. The sea water crested, foaming white, with...a man on the very top of it, riding the giant wave.

Zeph!

I recognized his silvery white hair, but there was no smile on his beautiful face this time. His dark eyebrows furrowed. Steely concentration settled in his blue eyes.

Submerged up to his waist in the foamy water, he remained upright. His arms spread wide, Zeph appeared to direct the water toward the beach with his hands. He wasn't simply carried by the wave. He commanded it.

He wasn't alone. A young woman in a yellow sundress was at his side, her arms wrapped around his bare torso. This must be Ivy.

The wave paused, the movement of the water unnaturally suspended behind the tideline. Zeph slid from the crest, bringing Ivy down with him. He gently set her into the knee-high water at the edge of the beach.

Without saying a word, he moved his hand out toward Dez. A stream of sea water shot from the giant wave, like from a water cannon, knocking Dez off his feet. Unlike a blast from a cannon, the mass of water didn't flow away. Instead, it remained, pressing Dez down with a powerful deluge.

"Fucking *bracks*." Disgust distorted Zeph's handsome features.

With another wave of his hand, the mass of water arched in the air then crashed onto the *bracks* on the beach, washing them away in every direction.

Zeph stepped to me. Lowering himself into a crouch at my side.

"Stella, are you okay? What happened?"

My eyes remained open. I saw everything but could say nothing. It was as if the burn of the poison on my arm pressed me into the ground, sucking the warmth and life out of me.

Or maybe I was dead already? And it was my spirit, watching the devastation on the beach—a silent, passive witness.

With no one holding the net, Lero growled loudly, shrugging the thing off him once again.

Zeph squinted at him, cautiously.

"Is that...Lero? I've never seen him changed..." He rose to his feet slowly, his focus on the massive, black beast who was shedding the last of the net that had burned deep lines in his fur and flesh.

While Zeph's attention focused on his friend, Lero's turned to me. He stumbled my way as fast as his injuries allowed.

Neither of the fae noticed the *bracks* climb out of the shrubs and patches of tall grass around the beach. The massive amount of water hadn't killed them. I believed nothing would, unless it sparked red when it hit them.

A scream of warning bubbled in my chest, growing painfully strong, but nothing came out, no matter how hard I tried to scream to warn them.

Dez gestured to another *brack*, who swung a thin, black rope over his head. Made from the same material as the net, the rope crackled with red sparks when the *brack* threw it at Zeph like a lasso, catching his head in the noose.

Yanked back, Zeph lost his footing, his hands flying up to the rope that burned his neck. The *brack* pulled on the rope, tightening the noose around Zeph's throat, choking him.

"Are you willing to die for the *voukalak*, water man?" Dez taunted. "Will you give your life for the monster who killed your family?"

Lero halted on the way to me, then turned to lunge at Zeph's tormentors. More *bracks* jumped from the hills to the beach. Apparently, not all of them had been washed away, or maybe some had hidden elsewhere on the island before Zeph showed up.

"Drag the siren off the beach!" Dez ordered to the two *bracks* who held the rope with the noose around Zeph's neck. "Get him farther away from the water. Then end him. He killed Trez. Madame will be happy to have him dead."

Welding Lero's sword, Dez attacked the beast to keep him from helping Zeph.

"Zeph!" The high-pitched, feminine scream cut through the air like a blade.

Ivy stood in the water where Zeph had left her. Her clear voice rung high above the island and the sea.

Her arms down her sides, she appeared to vibrate with strain. Her fingers curled. The water under her hands bubbled and boiled, churning around her legs in a whirlpool, faster and faster.

The water rose in a spiral, using Ivy's body to climb up like a vine climbed a pillar.

"Zeph!" Ivy screamed again, throwing her arms up toward him.

The waterspout rose over her head, slid up her arms and arched toward Zeph. The stream sparkled in the afternoon sun, stretching and twisting through the air like a brilliant crystal rope—a lifeline.

It showered over Zeph. Uncontrolled at first, but only for a fraction of a second. The moment the stream connected with his skin, it took shape. Instead of sliding off his body, the water gathered over him, then exploded out in a powerful blast that scattered the *bracks* away from Zeph and the rope. Burning his fingers, Zeph ripped the rope off his neck and climbed to his feet.

"That's it!" he growled, his voice low and grave.

Lifting his arms into the air like the wings of an angel bringing justice, he wielded the water like a terrifying weapon.

It slid up and off Ivy's body, forming a massive bridge from her to Zeph. He directed all of its power against the *bracks*.

This time, they didn't simply get washed off. The current spun and turned them like twigs in a drain during a torrential rain. The weapons they'd brought with them were ripped from their hands then plunged into their chests. The rope and the net tangled some of them into a bundle. The flood of seawater then washed over the island, taking them all far into the sea.

"What are you going to do with that one?" Zeph asked Lero, who held Dez down with his knee pressed into the *brack's* chest.

Tossing his great head back, the beast howled to the sky.

Rage vibrated in that sound, devastating and deadly. But I also heard a long sorrowful note woven through. Dez had claimed to have no family, but for Lero it wasn't that simple or straightforward.

"Get your paws off me, you filthy *voukalak*." Dez struggled against Lero's hold.

The beast pressed Dez's head down with one hand, then leaned over and closed his teeth over the *brack's* neck. Dez's body jerked once as the poison-soaked fangs pierced his skin, then stilled.

My eyes closed, shutting off the death and devastation.

Chapter 22

LERO

From the corner of his eye, he saw Zeph directing the stream of water to sweep Ivy off her feet and carry her into his arms. Once Zeph had her, the water dropped to the ground and flowed back to sea.

"Zeph, baby, how are you?" Ivy hovered her fingers over the red angry scar on Zeph's neck.

His own injuries burned and ached. The one from the arrowhead hurt the most. The iron from Nerifir didn't just stop the wounds from healing, it could kill a fae. Had the arrow pierced any of his vital organs, he'd be dead.

Stella...

He staggered to his feet, leaving the body of his dead brother for Zeph's water power to deal with. It proved easier to walk on all fours after all, as he crawled toward a motionless Stella.

He'd killed her. He had no other entity to blame for this. Unlike any other time he'd been in his beast form, today was no full moon. It wasn't even night yet, the sun hadn't touched the horizon in its descend.

His transformation had been triggered by another power, the one that did not demand the control of his mind. Even as the beast, he retained the clear thinking of a man. And he'd been careless, endangering the only woman in this world who meant the world to him.

With a pained groan, he dropped to his knees at her side.

She remained still, her lovely face pale and cold as the wet sand she lay on. The three drops of poison glistened red on her upper arm.

His poison.

He'd been granted the greatest gift by gods when they'd sent her to him. And he'd killed her.

Agony twisted his soul, burning more than any of the wounds on his flesh. He faced the sky and released the pain with a long howl. There was no moon to receive his sorrow. It crashed back down on him, crushing and suffocating.

He gathered her into his arms and pressed his nose to that spot where her neck met her shoulder, nuzzling the tender skin he'd loved to kiss when making love to her.

His tenderness for her, the intense longing, the excruciating pain of loss all rolled into one, growing and encompassing every strong wholesome emotion he'd ever had. The sensation threatened to overwhelm him, yet also strangely uplifted him, making him feel one with her.

"Lero?" Zeph's hand landed heavily on his shoulder. "We should take Stella...her body to the house."

He didn't move. There was no place for death between Stella and him. If she went, he'd be gone too. Why was he still here?

With his nose pressed to the base of her neck, he felt the faintest pulsing sensation. It came again, then again, like a gentle flutter of butterfly wings under her skin.

Stella's pulse!

Her heart kept pumping blood through her body.

He moved his nose to hers, afraid to hope yet desperately wishing to believe. The gentlest puff of breath tickled his sensitive nostrils.

She was breathing!

He grabbed her face in his large, furry hands. His claws pierced through her hair, but he flexed his fingers, keeping his claws away from her skin.

As the beast, he couldn't speak, couldn't even call her name. So, he howled again, softly this time, to coax her awareness to the surface, back to him.

Her eyelids quivered, and he dared to let the hope blossom in his heart, stroking her cheeks with his thumbs.

She opened her most amazing eyes, of no particular color and of all colors at once. Her gaze focused on his scruffy animal face. Instead of fear or repulsion, a brilliant smile curved her lips.

His chest tightened with so much emotion, he wished he could let it all go and cry, but the beast had no tears. He held her instead, rocking on his haunches with her in his arms.

"Lero..." She twined her arms around his neck. The burns left by the nasty iron net from Nerifir protested at her touch, but he didn't care. Her caress soothed his soul.

Zeph and Ivy crowded them.

"She's alive," Zeph said, gaping at Stella in wonder.

"Stella. How are you feeling?" Ivy placed her hand on Lero's woman's shoulder.

He growled softly, the rumble reverberating through his chest. He loved Zeph as his own blood. And lately, he'd been looking forward to seeing Ivy again. But this very moment, he needed Stella all to himself.

"We'd better go," Zeph said, his voice unusually distant.

Dez calling him the monster who killed Zeph's family rose in his mind unbidden. He'd never spoken to Zeph about his true reasons for leaving Nerifir. The conversation was long overdue.

Right now, though, he only wanted Stella.

"We have to make sure they're both all right," Ivy argued with Zeph. "We can't just leave them."

Stella shifted in his lap, her bottom rubbing against his cock hidden in the thick fur between his thighs. She snuggled against his chest.

He released a soft rumble, brushing strands of her hair away from her face. More than anything in the world he wished to keep hearing her voice as the reassurance that she was all right.

"How is she?" Ivy crouched in front of them.

Stella closed her eyes tight then opened them again, moving her gaze from him to Ivy then to Zeph.

"Everyone is safe..." she said softly, the smile lingering on her face.

She was right. For now, all four of them were safe and alive.

Stella rubbed her face with a slight wince.

"I'm fine," she replied to Ivy's question. "My head is a little fuzzy, but it's getting better..."

He tightened his arm around her shoulders, helping her to sit up in his lap. Her bum pressed against his cock again as she adjusted her position. Blood rushed to his groin. She cast him a furtive glance, obviously feeling him grow harder against her.

"Um..." she started, rather breathy, then turned to face Zeph and Ivy. "Glad to see you here, guys."

"Well, if you're feeling better, Zeph is right, we should go," Ivy suggested, a little hesitantly.

"No," Stella protested, rubbing her upper arm, the spot where his poison left three red, tear-shaped scars.

He couldn't explain how she was still alive, he was just insanely grateful that she was.

"Stay, please" Stella said to Ivy. "You've come for dinner. Let's have it."

Ivy glanced at Zeph, who cast Lero a reproachful glance.

"Please." Stella tried to convince them both. "We need to talk."

Ivy wrapped her arms around herself. The breeze must be chilly for her in her wet dress. The sea mist lingered in the air after Zeph's impressive waterworks show.

"We could stay, couldn't we?" she asked the siren. "For a little while?"

Dressed only in swim shorts, Zeph looked as comfortable as ever. He put an arm around Ivy's shoulders, drawing her into his side to shield her from the breeze. Sliding a hand down her dress, he made the water drip out of the material of her dress onto the ground, making her clothes dry in seconds.

"We'll need to warm you up," he said in a clipped voice, avoiding looking at Lero.

"Let's go to the house then. Are you coming?" Ivy asked Stella.

"Um... I'll have to help Lero shift back." She gave him a quick look.

"How?" Ivy asked, gazing at him with curiosity and obvious trepidation.

Stella blew out a breath. Her face momentarily turned a lovely shade of pink, the blush spreading to her neck and shoulders.

"I'm not entirely sure." She rubbed her forehead, hiding her gaze. "But I believe it may need to be something...um, of a sexual nature."

"Oh." Ivy straightened, grabbing Zeph's hand. "We'll wait at the house, then." She tugged the siren toward the path.

"Make yourselves at home," Stella called after them. "Have some tea."

"Thanks! Will do." Ivy waved at her, with Zeph glaring in Lero's direction as both headed up the path.

Lero paid little attention to their departure. His focus had zoomed in on Stella's words "sexual nature" and stayed there. No longer muffled by rage or grief, lust spread through his body, warming his skin under his fur and straining his cock. Pulsing hot, his erection throbbed right beneath Stella's ass. She wiggled it, her eyelids dropping. A wisp of the tantalizing scent of her arousal reached his nostrils, heating his blood.

"Let's hope this works," she said softly, the moment Zeph and Ivy disappeared into the house. "Since I made you shift into the beast, I should be able to reverse it, too, right?"

She turned to face him, spreading her legs wide, one on each side of his hips.

"I'm not even sure if that's what I'm supposed to do." She brushed her hand over the three red marks on her arm again, then slid a strap of her top down her shoulder. "But I want it, so badly." Her breathing turned hot and heavy as her lips parted. "I want you, Lero. So much, I ache..." Slipping her hand inside her bra, she squeezed her breast while grinding against him. "Please... I feel like I'll die again unless you touch me."

His existence narrowed to the present moment. His body vibrated with need. Tossing his head back, he howled with the pain of anticipation.

"No?" She misunderstood him, anxiously searching his eyes.

Yes! He wanted to shout. So much yes! Instead of words, however, only growls came out.

He couldn't speak, but he could *show* her.

Cupping her other breast through her shirt, careful not to pierce her skin with his claws, he circled the hard pebble of her nipple with his thumb. She exhaled a soft moan as he rubbed and pinched it through the thin material.

His cock grew impossibly hard, throbbing with heat. But he shifted away from her, laying her on her back on the warm sand higher up the beach, away from the waves. He slid his fingers along the waistband of her shorts, ready to rip them. He had no patience to deal with buttons and zippers, his claws getting in the way.

"Here." She guessed his intentions, hurriedly unbuttoning her shorts and sliding them down her legs, along with the white lacy underwear underneath.

Her warm scent teased his nostrils, spurring his desire. His mouth watered, craving her taste. Lust blinded his mind, depriving him of reason. She spread her thighs wide in invitation, raising her hips to him. And he dove in, lapping between her legs like the starving beast that he was.

She gasped and hissed, arching her back as his teeth grazed her tender flesh.

A spear of horror chilled his heart. He'd nearly killed her with his poison. And now...

"Oh, it burns... So hot," Stella moaned. Getting hold of his pointy ears, she shoved his head closer to her. "More!" she demanded.

His poison had failed to kill her. Now, it excited her.

Eager to give her everything she desired, he dove in again, lapping along her heated folds, sucking on the hot little bud at their apex, and swirling his long, thick tongue inside her.

Drunk on her taste, he rose to his knees and grabbed her hips. Leaning back, he yanked her to him, impaling her on his cock. He roared from the intense pleasure of sinking into her slick, tight heat.

Her shoulders and head on the sand, her back arched, she threw her arms over her head, moaning loudly.

The lust took over, and the world fell away. Stella and he were all that remained, suspended in the bliss of mating.

He thrust wildly, chasing the climax that teased him with licks of heat running up his inner thighs and pressure squeezing his groin.

Stella released a shuddering groan, her inner muscles spasmed around his cock as her hips jerked, sending him over the edge. He pumped his release into her, tension draining with every drop. His knot grew inside her, anchoring him to her.

Only when the orgasm stopped rocking his body did the cloud of lust finally clear.

Stella lay beneath him, her arms thrown wide, her hair wild, her shirt hiked up to her armpits. A huge, satisfied smile graced her lips. She looked thoroughly ravaged, but...happy.

He released a breath of relief.

Chapter 23

STELLA

The aftershock of the most violent orgasm still quivered through my inner muscles. Now, I understood completely the meaning of "being ravaged by a beast," or by *my* beast, at least.

Heat pulsed in my veins, spreading through my body. The pulsing resonated with the one on my upper arm where the poison from his fangs glistened in three red drops embedded in my skin.

I no longer felt even a hint of weakness. Energy buzzed through me, making me feel stronger and more alive than I'd ever been.

Something had happened between Lero and I, something more than the eye could see.

He let go of my hips, sinking down over me. The warmth of his large, furry body enveloped me like a blanket, so pleasant against my chilled skin. Sliding his arms under me, he rolled onto his back, taking me with him. My body felt boneless, allowing him to move me like a rag doll.

For a moment, I just lay there on top of him. My face pressed to his chest, I listened to his heartbeat slow down and his breathing calm.

Then I rose on my arm over him.

"Do you think it worked?" I watched his face for any signs of Lero's human features. Aside for the calming gray of his eyes, he remained the beast.

"Well, I guess we should wait until the sunrise?" My voice carried the uncertainty I felt. The sunrise was far away. The sun hadn't even set yet, with dinnertime just approaching.

Oddly, the pressure of him inside me didn't ease. I wiggled my hips, trying to make him slide out of me. With a soft, soothing rumble, he placed his large warm hand on my buttocks, keeping me in place.

"What is that?" I asked, as something clearly kept him inside me. Then it dawned on me as the memory of the swelling at the base of the beast's penis I saw in the basement came to me. Swollen inside me, it would act like an anchor, keeping us connected.

"Well, this is...um, new." I relaxed against him again. "How long do you think it will last? We have guests waiting for us in the house." I released a mortified giggle, thinking about Zeph and Ivy.

I knew Lero couldn't answer me. Instead, he stroked my back gently and nuzzled the hair over my temple. I didn't mind staying like that for a while, just cuddling and enjoying his closeness. Wrapped in his arms I felt safe and warm.

"It forces you to cuddle whether you like it or not, doesn't it?" I laughed quietly, raking my fingers through the long, thick fur on his chest. "Good thing I know you like cuddles."

He snorted softly, which I took as him agreeing with me.

Gradually, his fur thinned under my fingers. My hand connected with his skin.

"Lero?" I raised my head again, to see his face.

Unlike his transformation into a beast, which had been brutal and grotesque. Lero's turning back into a man proved to be smooth and gradual.

The fur slowly disappeared, as if melting off his skin. His pointy ears and long snout flattened. His teeth shortened. Within a minute or two, the beast was gone, and I lay on top of the man I knew and loved.

"I love you," he said suddenly.

The shock at finally hearing these words from him dissolved with warmth through my chest.

"You don't have to—" I started, but he wouldn't let me finish.

"I still don't know exactly what love means for others, but I know what it means to me. What *you* mean to me, Stella." He sat upright, sliding me into his lap and finally disconnecting our bodies. "Everything. You mean absolutely everything to me, in this world and any other. I love you."

I blinked at him, happiness spreading through me like sunshine and melting into a wide smile on my face.

"I love you too, my beastly man." I stroked his cheek, the short stubble of his five-o'clock shadow pricking my skin. "Kiss me, Lero," I whispered. "Kiss me like you always do. Like only *you* can do."

Chapter 24

STELLA

"This is a beautiful house," Ivy said politely, both hands tightly wrapped around her cup of tea.

All four of us sat in the family room, having tea after a dinner of pasta with tomato sauce—Lero's homemade tomato sauce, not mine from the jar.

After I'd snuck the naked Lero into the house through the back-patio door to the master bathroom, we'd gotten changed. Then the three of us had helped Lero make dinner and had eaten in relative silence.

I had so many things I wanted to talk about, but the atmosphere was far from easy at the moment. Zeph's friendly disposition would liven up the conversation, I was sure. But even he seemed unusually gloomy and subdued, his contagious smile had yet to make an appearance.

"I hope you don't mind, but we took a little tour of the formal area of the house," Ivy added, sitting next to Zeph on one of the two white couches in the room. Having arrived wearing nothing but his swim shorts, Zeph had reluctantly accepted one of Lero's shirts and a pair of pants before dinner.

Lero and I occupied the couch across from them, with a long magazine table carved from a single piece of wood between us. A tray with a porcelain tea pot and a cheese platter stood on the table.

"Oh, I can give you a proper tour of the entire property." I stirred.

"Later," Zeph bit off.

Lero shot a glance his way.

"So," I turned to Ivy, giving up on the men for the time being. "You're human, aren't you?"

"I think so." She didn't sound very convinced.

"Have you always been able to...well, do that thing you did with the water back on the beach?"

"Me? Noooo." She turned her head side to side slowly, her eyes growing big with wonder at her own abilities. "That was the only time, ever. I still don't know what exactly happened there or how I did it. Zeph, what the heck was that?"

He finally smiled, gazing at her.

"You tell me. How did you do it, my love?"

She frowned in visible concentration.

"I-I just remember being very angry—angry at them for hurting you. I was so scared for you."

Angry and scared.

That was exactly how I felt when I ordered Lero to take his beast form—angry at them and scared for him.

"Can you do it again, sweetheart?" Zeph asked, pointing at the cup in her hands.

"Well, I'm not feeling the same at the moment..." Ivy took one hand off the cup and held it over her tea.

She moved her fingers above the cup in a circle, huffing a laugh.

"I really have no idea what I'm doing."

The four of us stared at her tea intently. I even rose in my seat for a better look. The surface of the liquid remained still, with only a subtle ripple from the slight trembling of Ivy's hand holding the cup.

"I need to touch the water to manipulate it," Zeph offered.

"Okay. Maybe I need too." Ivy dipped the tip of her pointer finger into her tea, swirling it around.

Without stopping the swirling motion, she lifted her finger out of the cup, and the tea followed.

"Wow!" I breathed out, mesmerized.

A human woman was bending water to her will, right in front of my eyes. Back in the heat of the fight and the dread of mortal danger, I had no chance to fully appreciate the miracle of it.

"It works!" she whispered, in awe herself.

She lifted her hand a few inches higher, and the contact was broken. The spiral of the tea collapsed and fell back in her cup with a splash.

"Well, that's not that impressive." Ivy laughed.

"Hold on." Zeph shifted all the way to the other end of the couch from her. "Try to toss it to me, like you did with the seawater at the beach."

"All right."

Ivy stirred the tea in her cup again. Making the spiral rise a couple of inches over the rim of her cup, she flicked her finger Zeph's way. The tea stretched in a long arc from her cup, forming a bridge between her and Zeph, curved like an amber rainbow.

He met it with his hand open, palm up. The end of the "rainbow" barely touched his skin, then the whole thing looped, landing back into Ivy's cup.

She laughed, and I giggled, too. It turned into a fun show.

Ivy then took a small sip from her cup.

"That's one way to cool off your tea!" She laughed again.

"Fascinating," Lero observed, obviously impressed. "And you're absolutely positive you couldn't do it before?"

"No, I could not." She shook her head. "Of course, I've never tried, either."

Clearly, Ivy's new-found abilities had something to do with Zeph's powers.

"Why do you think it happened?" I asked the entire room, inviting any explanation.

Zeph inhaled deeply, but Ivy replied first.

"I *feel* him," she said simply. "The connection between us, I feel it. It's like..." she waved her hand between her and Zeph. "Like that bridge that the tea made. No matter where he is, I'm always..."

"...*aware* of him," I finished for her.

Goosebumps rushed down my arms when she stared at me, the understanding shining in her eyes. She knew what I knew. I felt the same connection with Lero as she did with Zeph.

Lero gently rubbed the three red drop shapes on the skin of my upper arm.

"That's why my poison didn't kill you," he said softly. "What can't harm me can't hurt you, either. You're a part of me now, Stella."

Ivy's large eyes flew open even wider as she twisted her torso to Zeph. "I bet your spikes wouldn't harm me, either!"

He lifted an eyebrow. "You may be right."

"Oh, and how about guns, then?" Ivy continued. "Earth's weapons can't kill you. Does it mean I'm invincible to them now, too?"

Lero stopped her by lifting a hand.

"I wouldn't bet on that. You are of *this* world, after all."

"Let's *not* try to find out, okay?" Zeph got hold of Ivy's hand and kissed her knuckles. "Stay away from all gun shots."

Lero stared straight ahead for a long moment.

"What is it, honey?" I touched his knee.

"The fae mating bond implies shared power. In Nerifir, both partners have similar magic and abilities to begin with, so it's not as apparent. Here..." He moved his gaze to me. "You got access to my magic, and Ivy did to Zeph's. When mated, if the couple live long enough to die of natural causes, they die together, on the same day."

"What are you saying, Lero?"

"That I'll live as long as Zeph!" Ivy gasped.

"And you, as long as me," Lero added, not taking his eyes off me.

"Are you sure?" I pressed both hands to my chest as my heart started beating so fast, I worried it'd jump out. Living for hundreds of years sounded great. Spending all of those years with Lero was truly magical.

"I have no proof, of course," Lero added. "But we'll find out for sure in a decade or so, when you stop aging."

"Tell me, please, how does the water fae mating bond happen in Nerifir?" Ivy asked Lero with eager curiosity. "Zeph was too little when he left your world, he doesn't know."

Lero smiled.

"Sorry, Ivy, but I don't know the details, either. In Nerifir, water fae mate on the bottom of the ocean."

"Oh." Ivy glanced at the cup in her hand. "Well, I've learned to swim pretty good by now, but I still can't breathe under water."

"I'm more than happy to keep mating on the surface with you," Zeph cheerfully announced, shifting closer to her and wrapping his arm around her shoulders.

His words made Ivy blush.

"So, the fae bond you told me about actually happened between us?" I asked Lero, still trying to wrap my mind around all of it.

"The power of human love created it where I didn't think it was possible." He nodded. "Somehow, you managed to harvest the magic of the Moon to *turn* me at will."

I just stared back at him, silently. He already knew all about my feelings, and I had no other explanation to add to that.

"You have power over me now, Stella," he said. "Use it wisely."

"Are you worried?"

"Worried? No." He leaned over, placing a tender kiss on my lips. "Your hold is so much gentler than that of the Moon. It was a pleasure to surrender to you."

Air rushed out of me with a breath of overwhelming relief. I cupped his face. "Are you saying you weren't hurting this time?"

"No, my star. For once, there was no pain and no madness. I changed how I looked but not the way I felt or thought. With you, I remained myself, even in the beast form. Some emotions I felt more strongly, the desire—" he cut himself short, casting a glance in the direction of our guests. Bringing my hand to his mouth, he brushed his lips over my knuckles adding in a softer voice, "The desire is always there, with you around. No matter what form I'm in."

Smiling, I gave him a peck on the tip of his nose.

"I have to say, Lero," Ivy chimed in. "Your other form is amazing. When I first saw you on the beach..." A tremble ran across her shoulders. "It was impressive."

"Um, thank you?" Lero smiled.

"I can't look at you without a certain trepidation, now." She gazed at him with awe. "Though, you've always had that air of intimidation about you, even when we first met."

"You've met before?" I asked.

"Briefly," Lero confirmed. "Outside of my cabaret, back in Paris."

"I had a feeling he didn't like me much," Ivy shared with me, casting a glance Lero's way.

"It wasn't you, personally," Lero said apologetically, looking ashamed as if he'd been called out on lack of good manners. "I worried about the dangers that being with a fae would mean for a human." He squeezed my hand in his, giving me an adorable little smile. "Obviously, I was wrong. There are dangers, but I now believe *some* humans can handle them."

I beamed at him, wishing I could kiss him, thoroughly and completely. But we had company tonight.

"You can stay the night. Or as long as you want, really," I told Ivy. "There's plenty of space. You know it's actually twin islands, with two houses?"

"Well, we..." She glanced at Zeph.

Zeph's expression turned even more serious, his lips pressed together tightly.

Letting go of my hand, Lero drew in a long breath and rose to his feet.

"We need to talk, Zeph. Come with me."

Chapter 25

LERO

He walked through the back door out to the patio. From the corner of his eye, he saw Zeph get up from the couch to follow him out. Lero exhaled in relief. He'd used his authoritative voice of a parent when he'd told Zeph to come with him. However, Zeph hadn't been a child for a long time, now. He was a grown man who very well could tell him go fuck himself. The fact that Zeph actually listened and came out to the patio with him gave him hope.

Zeph didn't go far, however. Closing the door behind him, he silently leaned with his back against it.

"I've never really told you why we left Nerifir," Lero said, wondering where to even begin his explanation. Some things could never be explained. He just hoped that whatever connection he'd managed to build with Zeph over the past decades would hold even after what he had to say.

"You said we came with Ghata," Zepf replied, evenly. "She was escaping prosecution."

"I was escaping, too."

Zeph gave him a heavy look from under his brow.

"After killing my parents?"

Lero'd come out here, ready to talk about that night. However, Zeph's deliberately direct question felt like a punch to his gut. It knocked the air out of him, rendering him speechless.

"That's what that *brack* said," Zeph muttered, obviously expecting an explanation. Or maybe he was hoping for Lero to deny it.

He couldn't deny it, though. He couldn't even keep it a secret anymore.

"The *brack*'s name was Dez. He was my brother."

Zeph paused, staring at him.

"My older brother," Lero explained. "For many generations, Ghata demanded the eldest son from each family be given to her to serve as her priest. The *bracks* are former werewolves that she'd changed into her slaves."

"And the families did that? They gave up their children, willingly?" Zeph stared at him in obvious disbelief.

"It was considered an honor for the boy to be Ghata's priest, to worship her daily, and to live in her grand, luxurious temple. The families were given many blessings in return."

Zeph's gaze turned heavy with accusation.

"You killed your own brother today."

Lero straightened under the siren's judgement. As true as that statement was, Zeph didn't entirely understand what had happened.

"I lost my brother almost nine decades ago," Lero said. "When my parents brought him to Ghata's temple, he stopped resembling my brother in every way. Today, I killed a *brack*, Ghata's slave, who had no will of his own and thrived on murder and torture. Hate was the strongest emotion he'd retained. He hated me because I am what he once was."

"It wasn't easy for you to kill him." A soft note slipped into Zeph's voice. "I could tell."

"Murder is never easy," he agreed. "Unlike *bracks*, neither you nor I seek it or enjoy it."

Zeph dropped his gaze, without arguing. H'd killed his share of *bracks* and knew murder too well.

"Tell me about that night," he demanded, somberly.

Lero drew in a long breath, bracing himself.

"It was a full moon—"

"Of course it was," Zeph scoffed. "Isn't that a great excuse for everything?"

His derisive tone scraped against Lero's nerves with a flare of irritation. He forced it down. Zeph meant too much to him to give up, enough to tell the whole truth and bare himself to his judgement, no matter how condemnatory it might be.

"I'm not using the full moon as an excuse. I'm telling you how it was." He paused for a moment, giving Zeph a chance to reply with anything he had to say.

Zeph remained quiet this time, so he continued.

"As a child, I heard from the elders that the full moon nights used to be spent by couples hunting together and making love. That was not my experience, however. Full moon nights always brought pain, raging lust, and violence. My people call it Moon Madness, and that's exactly how I feel when the Moon takes over—mad. I dread watching the moon grow, every month."

"Smoking *womora* helps?" Zeph asked, with a glint of compassion in his sea-blue eyes.

"It did. But I lost the access to *womora* the moment I escaped Ghata's freakshow. It doesn't matter now at all. Having Stella in my life is the best help. Her presence is better than *womora*, better than anything." He smiled, his heart flipping with excitement and tenderness at the thought of her. "But in Nerifir, it was only *womora* that helped manage the signs of the approaching madness. *Womora* has always been scarce, however. It can only be harvested during the full moon, and none of us was ever functioning enough on those nights to do the harvesting. Ghata organized it for us by employing other fae, sirens included. She paid them generously. They would gather *womora* and bring it to her temple 'for safekeeping.' Now I know of course that hoarding it was just another way of her keeping control over us."

His thoughts went back in time, to the place he'd long left, but which would never leave him.

"That night was no different. As the Moon rose, I *turned*, along with all the people in my village. Then, there was nothing but madness and...blood. So much blood. We were supposed to hunt meat for the village for the month ahead, but the Moon deprived us of any reason, leaving only bloodthirst. In that state, I never cared what or *whom* we hunted."

He paused, overwhelmed by the images of bloody carnage attacking his brain once again—torn flesh, broken bones, and blood, so much of it, it flowed in red, glistening rivers.

The pull of the approaching full moon tugged at something deep and carnal inside him, teasing his nostrils with the phantom smell of warm blood. He forced it down. The calming presence of Stella in his heart made it so much easier to control.

"At some point during that night, we came close to the seashore. The water fae had gone deep into the forest to collect *womora* leaves, too far from the water to escape us."

He stopped. The words lodged in his throat, and he could not push them out.

"You attacked them?" Zeph prompted.

"That's what it looked like the next morning. When I woke up... There were dead bodies everywhere. Pieces of sirens, ripped apart by the werewolves' claws, were scattered around. People from my village, no longer in their animal form, were lying dead. Deep, bloodied grooves from the water fae's fin spikes oozed poison on the werewolves' naked bodies. I have no idea how I'd survived. I had scratches all over my body, but none of them came from the poisonous spikes. The true miracle, however, was you."

He lifted his gaze to Zeph, seeing the little boy in the grown man again.

"A little siren boy was sitting in the waves on the beach, playing with seashells among all that death and blood. I don't know if you'd been left on the bottom of the sea while your folks went to the surface, and you came up in the morning looking for them. But there you were—innocent, defenseless, and completely alone."

"So, you took me?"

"I saw no other choice." He ran his fingers through his hair. The memories pounded inside his skull with a mounting headache. "Ghata came upon us. The patience of my people for her atrocities had been wearing thin for some time. That morning, overwhelmed by her crimes, the entire kingdom of the Sarnala Plains went to her temple to overthrow and prosecute her. She escaped, but barely. They were on her heels, furious in their search for justice. She knew she wouldn't be safe from their wrath anywhere in Nerifir, but she was scared to flee to another world alone."

"You went with her," Zeph muttered under his breath.

"Yes. I'm not claiming that was the right decision or that it was the only solution at that point. I wasn't much older back then than you are now, Zeph. Faced with the evidence of all the murders I must have committed that night, I believed myself no better than Ghata. She offered me an escape, and I took it. Like me, you had no one left alive from your clan. So, I took you with me. Back then, I truly believed you needed me. Later, I realized how much *I* needed *you*. Ever since, you've been my one true family—"

"Stop it!" Zeph bit out.

Raking his fingers through his silvery hair, Zeph peeled his back from the glass door he'd been leaning against and hurried past him down to the beach.

For a moment, Lero thought he might jump into the waves and be gone, never to return. But Zeph stopped at the water line, pacing the beach instead. Ivy was in the house, Lero realized. As much as Zeph might want to flee Lero with his confessions, he wouldn't leave Ivy behind. Right now, she was his anchor to this place.

Instead, Zeph paced, trapped between water and land, between past and present, between love and hate. The Moon shone down on the beach, her chipped disk bloated but not yet perfectly round.

The moonlight tangled in Zeph's blond hair and bounced off his skin with a shimmer, making him look like the true siren he was— a water spirit, almost an apparition.

When Zeph was growing up, Lero had often been afraid that the little water fae's ethereal appearance would make humans question how the boy came to be. So often he'd worried that someone would recognize a being from another world in his silver-haired child.

It was only the humans' general ignorance and their inability to accept the existence of someone other than themselves that saved the two of them from being discovered.

His heart ached seeing Zeph in pain, now. His confession had just flipped Zeph's entire world upside down. All his life, he'd thought Lero the one person he could trust, and he'd just learned that Lero was the one responsible for him being an orphan in the first place.

Led by compassion, Lero headed down the path to the beach. Zeph might not want to see him right now—or ever—but Lero could never give up on him.

With a glance in his direction, Zeph stopped pacing and slowly lowered himself to the ground. Lero sat on the wet sand next to him.

His knees bent, Zeph placed his elbows on them.

"It's hard to mourn those I never knew," he said staring straight ahead.

Lero kept silent, letting him speak.

"I don't remember anything. I've tried so many times to remember something from Nerifir, and I can't. I thought you telling me all of this would trigger a memory of that night or the morning after. And I still have nothing..."

"You were so young," Lero offered. "If you witnessed any of the massacre of that night, your mind might've blocked those memories, sparing you any further trauma."

For that he was grateful. He shuddered to think what the boy might've seen that night. The lack of memories would be a blessing in Zeph's case.

"Why did you never tell me before, though?" Zeph frowned.

Because he always dreaded this very moment right now, this accusing, reproachful look in Zeph's eyes.

"You...weren't old enough," he said instead.

"I'm almost forty-nine, Lero. I've been 'old enough' for over three decades, at least."

"Because I didn't want to see you hurt," he confessed. "And I didn't want you to hate me for it."

Zeph shook his head.

"Do you realize you're my only source of information about the place where I come from, Lero? There is no way for me to ask anyone else, no chance for me to ever go back and find out on my own. I need you to talk freely and truthfully to me. There can never be any lies between us."

"I've never lied to you," he objected firmly.

"You can't withhold information from me, either," Zeph replied. "For any reason whatsoever. Not even if you think it's in my best interests not to know. You have no right to make my decisions for me. Only I can make them."

In his heart, Lero screamed, *"It's my job as a parent to protect you!"*

In his mind, however, he understood Zeph perfectly, so he said nothing like that out loud. Whether he liked it or not, his little boy had grown. Lero tended to forget that.

Finally turning to face him fully, Zeph met his gaze. "I can't hate or even resent you. Even if I tried."

Lero drew in a slow breath, not relaxing yet.

"Zeph." He shifted uneasily. "I don't remember much of that night. I have no clear memories of it. I'll never be able to confirm that I was the one who killed your parents. However, I can never say with any certainty that I did not."

"Living with the weight of what you've done—of what you think you might have done—must be a punishment of its own."

Lero just sighed in reply. It had not been easy, but he always believed he deserved the constant feeling of guilt he'd lived with, the guilt that got even more punishing after Amelie.

"I've seen what it did to you," Zeph continued. "I don't recall you ever laughing out loud, while I was growing up, not even once. You barely even smiled."

Lero winced. For so long, his focus had been on keeping Zeph and himself fed and safe. He forgot children paid attention to the state of mind of the adults around them.

Zeph heaved a breath.

"Yet you're the only parent I ever knew. You gave me shit for what I did wrong and praised me for things I got right. When I was hurt, you licked my wounds, often literally." He smiled. "You've been my safe place since I was little. And you're still the only family I have."

"Zeph..." He stirred. Something ached so much in his chest, it rose up to his throat and prickled his eyes behind his eyelids.

He'd felt so many new, strong emotions today, it made him dizzy.

Zeph squeezed his shoulder in a gesture that felt both grounding and supporting.

"You're my only family, too," Lero croaked.

"May not be for long!" Zeph laughed. "I can't believe you found yourself a woman. After trying so hard to talk *me* out of a relationship with one."

"Stella," he whispered her name, loving the way the sound resonated in his heart.

"You really like her, don't you?"

"I love her," he said. The confession came easily. He simply stated the truth.

"Listen..." Zeph rubbed the back of his neck, asking hesitantly, "Do you know anything about fae reproducing with humans?"

He didn't. How could he? To his knowledge, there hadn't been any human-fae couples before them.

"You tell me," he exclaimed. "You're the one with a fiancée."

"Ivy is on a pill, for now anyway. We decided to wait a little before thinking about starting a family. I just hope it'll be possible when we're ready to start."

"I don't see why not. We know now that humans can bond with us." The power of human love proved to be stronger than magic, after all. He now firmly believed it knew no boundaries.

He took a long look at Zeph. His little boy sounded so grown up—he was settling down, making plans. Lero on the other hand hadn't thought about any of that yet. The past weeks had been a mixture of pain and worry, with the blur of pure bliss and pleasure blended in. All he had felt and thought about was Stella.

He made a mental note to talk to her about the practical things, like birth control and if she wanted to use any, or about their future living arrangements, her job, and her condo in Miami.

Dez might be gone, but Ghata remained. He sensed she'd be furious to learn that a huge chunk of her *brack* army had been decimated. To replenish their numbers, she'd have to bring more *bracks* from Nerifir, which would take time.

For now, the four of them were safe. The future, however remained murky.

"We should go back." Zeph stirred to get up. "I don't like leaving Ivy alone for too long. Even if Stella is there."

"Move here with us," he said and added, not giving Zeph a chance to decline right away, "With Ivy, of course. It'd be easier to keep the women safe if the four of us are together."

Zeph fell quiet, and Lero asked, "What does Ivy do for a living?"

"She is a graphic designer. She works from home."

"She can work from Blue Cay, then?"

"Well, she likes it here. What she's seen anyway." Zeph sounded contemplative.

"Did she like the house? Take it. Stella and I will move to the other one."

"But isn't the other one smaller? That's what Stella said when you were making dinner."

"With four bedrooms, it's still more than enough for the two of us." Even if they had children one day, they'd have enough space for a family, too.

Zeph slid him a glance.

"Where do you keep your cage?"

The cage. He'd been tied to it for decades. When he first arrived in this world, he had one made, refusing to let his beast roam free on the full moon nights and wreak havoc. Since Stella came along, however, things have been changing. Even the past full moon, he realized, he'd been able to control himself better. His mind found a way to her calming presence, even in his beast form.

"I may not need a cage anymore, now that Stella is with me. She's been trying to convince me not to use it the next full moon."

"But what do *you* think?"

"I'd love to be free from the fucking cage," he voiced his deepest desire. "For good."

Zeph nodded. Hiding his own true nature his entire life, Zeph knew well enough what restraints meant.

"You can fill in the pool again," Lero suggested, still trying to sell Zeph the idea of moving to the island. It would bring his heart peace, having him here, close by. "You'll love the pool. It goes right into the master bathroom."

Zeph huffed a laugh. "You hate tubs and pools. Did you buy this place with me in mind?"

He didn't deny it—he always made his decisions with Zeph in mind. Lero himself preferred showers to baths. Water running down his body soothed him. Being submerged in it made him uncomfortable. As a siren, Zeph thrived in any pool of water. He even had an enormous tub installed in his small studio apartment in Paris.

"I'll talk to Ivy about moving," Zeph promised.

A weight dropped from Lero's chest at his words. They were a family, after all. Living close by would be the most natural thing to do.

"Let's go back, then." Lero got off the sand and gave Zeph a hand, helping him up as well.

Through the glass of the patio doors, he saw Stella. She was sitting on the couch next to Ivy, talking and laughing. Their expressions were light and carefree.

She turned her head as he stepped into the light on the patio, and their gazes met through the glass.

'I feel you,' she'd said.

He felt her, too. Deep, warm, comforting, and thrilling at the same time—he now had the name for this feeling.

Love.

EPILOGUE

STELLA

The sun, large and rusty-red, was sinking behind the horizon. The crimson ribbon of reflected light stretched from it across the sea, like a river of blood.

I felt Lero's fingers twitch in my hand as we walked along the path to the bridge between the two parts of the island.

"How are you feeling?" I asked, tightening my grip on his hand, as if I could stop him from slipping away from me and into the realm of the full moon.

He drew in a long breath, still looking like the man I loved, despite the already wildly disheveled hair and the steady red glow in his eyes.

"Soon," he said.

We stopped on the bridge. The low tide had drained the water under it.

A magically sensual voice reached us. It was coming from the main house where Ivy and Zeph had moved to a day earlier. The song was in a foreign language I didn't speak. Italian, I believed.

"Beautiful," I whispered, hardly realizing I was taking a few steps into the direction of the voice, led by it to the singer.

Lero laughed softly, tugging me back to him.

"Zeph is serenading Ivy."

"It's so...wonderful," I murmured, mesmerized by the sound which I could only describe as silver and velvet, and pure magic. "Enthralling."

"It's supposed to be," Lero chuckled. "Zeph sings for entertainment, but in Nerifir, a siren's song is often used as a lure during hunting."

"They sing while hunting?"

He nodded. "Water fae sing often. It's one of the ways they express their emotions. But they also sing to attract prey—birds and other animals, mostly. If another sentient being hears it, however, they'd better watch out, too."

"Do water fae hunt and eat other people?" I gasped.

"No, they don't eat them when they catch them. At least I don't think they do." The slight uncertainty in his voice was worrisome. "But they can do a lot of other things just as unpleasant." He shrugged.

The song ended, and a new one started. This one had a popular dance rhythm, which sounded familiar, but I couldn't remember its name.

"A pop song?" Lero winced. "Really. Zeph could do so much better in his choice of music for romance."

"What's wrong with pop music?"

"It's just so..." He waved his hand in the air. "Light and fast. And the lyrics? No substance at all."

"Now you really sound like an *old man!*" I laughed, and he smiled at me.

The angry-red disk of the sun dipped lower, only a narrow sliver of light still peeked over the horizon, awash in the orange and burgundy of the sunset.

"You should go," Lero rasped.

Letting go of my hand, he gripped the railing of the bridge instead. The knuckles on his hands already looked sharper, more prominent than normal.

I had talked Lero into not locking himself in the cage in the cellar tonight. He'd agreed, but I knew he was worried. He always worried about me.

Unlike him, I remained calm. I didn't believe Lero could ever hurt me again, not intentionally, not otherwise. Instead, the anticipation of his letting go sent a shiver of thrill down my bare arms. I *felt* his lust taking over him. It warmed my blood, too.

I took but a tiny step back and tilted my head.

"I won't go, honey, but I will run," I said, teasing. "And when I run, will you chase me?"

"Stella, my star," he growled. His hands flexed on the railing, the angles of his knuckles growing even sharper with a soft cracking noise. "You're playing with fire—"

His voice broke off, ending the sentence in a snarling, animalistic sound.

My body buzzed with excitement. I loved this part of him. I loved all the pieces of this man.

I shook my head, smiling. "I can't wait to play with your beast, my love."

His shoulders widened, bulging out of the ripping shirt. Lero, being Lero, had insisted on getting fully dressed tonight, even knowing perfectly well what would happen to his clean, pressed clothes when he shifted forms. Now, they were ripped to shreds as the bulk of the beast emerged from the body of the man.

Turning his great head my way, he snarled.

Backing away from him, I smoothed my hands down my white cotton sundress.

"I'm wearing a skirt tonight, honey," I challenged, adding. "And *nothing* under it."

His eyes flashed wild.

I whipped around and ran.

Off the bridge. Down the dirt packed path. Then, along the beach.

A long, loud howl cut through the air. It rose to the sky, drowning out Zeph's upbeat singing.

The beast had completely taken over my man.

I ran faster, arms pumping, air rushing through my lungs, burning as if setting them on fire. I was not going to make it easy on him. I wanted to be chased in earnest, and I ran as if my life depended on it.

The sound of his footfalls came from behind me. Not feet. Paws. They hit the wet sand with thuds that reverberated through the ground, coming closer and closer.

I almost made it to the end of the beach. There'd be another path after that, leading to the back of our house, the manager's cottage, and then another beach on the opposite side of the island.

No matter how fast or how long I ran, there was nowhere for me to hide. Yet I tried to run even faster. My heart thundered in my chest, its sound echoing in my head. Unable to keep up, my feet tripped over themselves. A heavy hand gripped my shoulder, sending me down to the ground.

The beast rolled under me, taking the impact of my fall on his shoulder. Instead of slamming into the wet sand of the beach, my body tangled with his, large and furry.

We rolled once more, together. Then, he gripped my hips, flipping me over on my back. Hiking up my skirt, he shoved his head between my thighs, thrusting his tongue inside me.

I arched my back under the onslaught of pleasure, digging my heels into the sand. The tingle of his poison felt invigorating, not dangerous. It spread through my veins, setting my body on fire with intense desire.

"Oh God, yes...Lero," I moaned his name as he devoured me in the most savage way. His sharp teeth grazed my sensitive flesh. His mouth sucked and nibbled. His fingers dug into my hips, not letting me escape. His claws scraped my skin without breaking it.

My orgasm blinded me, rocking though my body.

He wouldn't wait for the tremors to subside. Flipping me over, he slammed into me from behind. That long, thick cock of his stretched me to the limit. His heat pulsed through me.

He growled, thrusting wildly, and I echoed his sounds with my moans. My inner muscles still trembled with the first climax when the second one started building up.

I clawed at the wet sand as he had his way with me, ravaging me in the most delightful way. A wild growl left my throat when another orgasm hit me. I was no longer sure if the primal passion that coursed through me was even human. It felt base and animalistic—wild and free.

My beast roared to the sky through his release. His frantic thrusts stopped, and he collapsed over me. Connected, we fell to the ground, spooning, side by side—his arms around me, his legs intertwined with mine.

He nuzzled the side of my neck softly, the spot I knew he loved to touch and kiss. I whimpered when I felt a sting of his razor-sharp fangs. He quickly dragged his tongue over the bite, replacing the sting with a tingle of healing.

"That will leave a mark, you know?" I said, remembering the three drop-shaped spots that remained burnt into the skin of my upper arm.

Other than those three spots, his poison left no marks or scars anywhere on me anymore. However, he'd broken my skin this time.

A deep rumble rolled through his chest, and I understood him perfectly.

"That's what you want, isn't it? To mark me?" I stretched in his arms, snuggling deeper into his fur, unable and unwilling to part from him in any way.

The mark from when he bit me in his human form, the first time we had sex, had healed after he'd licked it. He obviously wanted to leave something more permanent.

I raked my fingers through the fur on the side of his neck, over the spot where I had bitten him weeks ago. Unlike every other scar that disappeared within hours from his skin, the two little dots from my teeth had paled but never went away completely. I couldn't see them through the fur, but I knew they were there.

"As if I'm not yours already, silly." I chuckled as he kept nuzzling the spot on my neck he'd just marked.

He held me tightly from behind, and I raked my fingers through the long fur on his forearms.

"I'm yours, Lero. Always will be."

Power of Rage

BOOK 3
Unedited and subject to change
Chapter 1
Heike

"Ten thousand dollars? Is she insane?" I scoffed, waving my hand in a circle next to my temple.

"No clue. Maybe." Omkar shrugged, gesturing to the passing waiter for another round of drinks—whisky on the rocks for him and a mango juice for me.

I didn't come to his bar to drink. I'd come here to hear what he found out for me about Madame Tan's and her show. If I were to decide to spend that much money on a single ticket, I'd better be completely sober before making that decision.

"That's crazy!" I shook my head sending the end of a long strand of my black-brown hair into my juice glass. "Oops." I fished it out and dried it with a napkin.

The price had been quoted in the US dollars, too, not the Singapore, which made it even more expensive. No person in their own mind would demand that amount of money for a one-hour show of...something. That was the craziest thing—no one could tell me exactly *what* Madame Tan offered for the money.

I personally knew a few people who'd seen her show. They'd shelled out ten grand each, some in the United States and a couple in Europe.

"Out of this world!"
"Incredible, magical, and simply fantastic!"
"I've never seen anything like it!"

That was all I'd been able to get from them when I asked about it, however. Those of my acquaintances who'd seen the show, highly recommended it. However, no one would tell me exactly what they'd seen.

Omkar took a drink from the glass that the waiter had just deposited in front of him.

"Apparently, that's the reduced rate." He leaned back, his trendy leather jacket creaking against the back of the booth seat. "This being her last show, some of the tickets went for as high as fifty grand."

"What? You're kidding me, right?"

Not that I didn't have the money to spend. I came from a family who believed in hard work. My mom was Chinese and my dad German. They met here, in Singapore, when both of them worked for the same financial company. Dad's contract ended shortly after they got married, and they moved to Munich, Germany. I was born and grew up there until my parents divorced when I finished the German secondary school. Then, I moved to the States with my dad.

I'd been earning my own money since I was two, first by appearing in commercials then fashion magazines. My mom signed me up with a modeling agency when I was a baby. By the time I was twelve, I'd earned enough to pay for any college in Europe or North America. By then, however, I'd had enough of modeling and of working for others. I'd figured I could do something for myself.

Social media seemed interesting, and I'd tried a few things, some of which stuck. Whatever had worked I'd expanded and grew, constantly trying new things of course.

Now, by my current ripe age of twenty-nine, I was running several video channels, had a couple of older but still very successful blogs, and maintained several websites. I ran a podcast, traded domain names, managed a number of interest groups. I still did some modeling, but for my own social media accounts, as well as for my travel and lifestyle blogs. My revenue came from selling ads, indorsements, and publicity services. And my expenses were low.

I was also a part of a network of people like myself. We helped boost ratings, expand each other's reach, and maximize exposure.

Omkar was a part of it, too. Originally from India, he owned a few businesses in Singapore. The bar where we were sitting in was one of them.

"Have you seen the show?" I asked, casually swirling the ice cubes in my glass of juice.

"No." He shook his head.

"Are you getting a cut of the ticket price?"

"No. I don't know Madame Tan personally. I've heard about it from a friend of a friend. It sounded like something you'd like to do. So, here we are."

"Do you think she'd do a barter?" I hated spending my hard-earned cash if there were so many other ways to get what I wanted. Barter was my preferred form of tender in many cases.

"For what?"

I shrugged. "For publicity."

I had millions of followers on some of my accounts. The power wasn't in numbers, however. I often had better results with some of the smaller, but highly targeted groups. If Madame Tan let me, I could blow her show up in popularity in no time.

"I could do an interview, record—"

Omkar stopped me with a hand gesture, leaning in across the table.

"Absolutely no recordings of any kind. That's the main condition of purchasing the ticket."

I narrowed my eyes at him, as if he were Madame Tan reincarnate.

'We'll see about that,' flashed through my mind.

"Would you like to go?" I asked, keeping that thought to myself instead of arguing.

"Me?" Omkar winced, furrowing his thick, ink-black eyebrows. "I'd rather spend the money on other things."

So would I. Except that curiosity nagged at me, now. With it being the last show, I'd never have another chance to find out what this was all about.

"Tell your *friend of a friend* that we'll pay fifteen thousand," I offered.

Omkar sputtered his sip of whiskey.

"We what?"

"We'll pay fifteen for two tickets" I said. "You're coming with me."

I was curious but not stupid. There were some places a woman shouldn't be going alone, especially to some underground nightclub on the East Side of Singapore, where this show was rumored to be held at midnight.

"Heike..." Omkar racked his hair through the glossy mass of his thick wavy hair. He obviously didn't want to come but couldn't think of a polite way to decline. I was fully intending to take advantage of that.

"Come on. This could be phenomenal. Everyone says it is." I pressed.

He blew out a breath.

"You need to get yourself a man. Someone who would take you to all those places you always want to go but shouldn't."

I knew Omkar was not hinting in any way for him to be my man. I wasn't his type. Besides, he had a fiancée. A demure girl next door from the village where his parents lived in India. It would be an arranged marriage, but Omkar really cared about his future bride. To my knowledge, he was faithful to her, too.

I found Omkar attractive and intelligent. He'd been a great friend, and were he available, I might possibly consider to have something more with him. Though, with my track record, it would be best for him to stay away from me, single or not. The last and only meaningful relationship I had was when I was eighteen.

Omkar's leather jacket screaked against the pleather of the bench seat again.

"Heike, I'm really not that interested to see the show."

"Don't you want to know what it's all about?" I leaned over the table to him.

"I'd love that. But I could just as well live without ever knowing."

"Listen, fifteen thousand for two." I wouldn't give up. "I'll pay ten grand, you'll just have to pay five."

"I don't think she'd sell you two tickets for that price. Besides, I told you there is only one ticket left anyway. Heike..." He shook his head. "She won't go for it."

"But it's worth a try, isn't it?"

If I had to spend this amount of money, I'd better made it an investment. Madame Tan might not be interested in publicity, but a video of her show might end up being very valuable one day, especially if it was indeed the very last show ever.

———◆———

THE TWO TICKETS ENDED up costing twenty thousand dollars after all. Madame Tan refused to budge on the price, though she agreed to sell two instead of one. I paid for Omkar's ticket, too, since the poor guy didn't even want to be here in the first place.

I was extremely grateful that he came, though.

The place ended up being deep in the basement of a tall skyscraper. Two levels under the underground garage. There wasn't even a button on the elevator for that floor. We had to take a set of concrete stairs to get there.

A massive bald man with neck and arm tattoos met us as we exited the stairs. Tall and muscular, he could be a bouncer.

"Names?" he asked, hardly sparing us a glance.

"Heike Schneider," I said.

"Heike?" he lifted his dark-brown eyes at me. "What kind of a name is it?"

"German." I took in the empty hallway—a wide space with concrete walls and a red runner on the floor.

"You don't look German," the man observed, marking something on the tablet in his hands.

I glared at him. If I got a dollar for every time I'd heard a comment like that, I would've possibly made close enough to any of my other revenues by now.

"Sorry. Left my *lederhosen* at home," I quipped one of the many responses I'd stored in my memory for this kind of situations.

He smirked, giving me a once-over, then moved on to Omkar who stood at my side.

"Follow me," the bouncer said after verifying our identities.

I shifted the strap of my purse on my shoulder to make sure the camera in the flower pin on my jacket wasn't abstracted in any way. I'd turned it on still back in the elevator. Madame Tan might have her rules, but I had to get my money's worth, too.

We passed by the entrance to the nightclub. Red light pulsed inside in the rhythm to techno music blasting through the doors.

"This way." The bouncer gestured to us to proceed down the corridor.

After a turn, another set of doors came in the view, with velvet burgundy curtains opened in front of them, each half was held back by a twisted, golden rope with tassels.

The bouncer opened the doors, and we were greeted by another man, who looked nearly identical to the first. Of similar built and wearing the same dark clothes, he was also bald and had the identical tattoo on his right arm and neck.

"A drink." The man handed each of us a tall glass with shimmering blue and pink liquid. The way he said it, it didn't sound like an offer or an invitation, but an order.

I sniffed at the liquid as Omkar took a tentative sip.

"It's good." He nodded.

It smelled very good, too.

"Does it have alcohol in it?" I asked the man at the door.

"Do you want it to have?" he replied.

That was an odd question.

"No," I said.

"Then it doesn't," he said flatly.

His reply did nothing to assuage my suspicion. I moved my gaze to Omkar, who kept gulping his drink, making it half-way through his glass already.

"What?" He lifted an eyebrow at my stare, his lips shimmering from the liquid. "It's really good. Try it."

His happy expression and the glossy sheen in his eyes made me pause, however. Omkar could relax and enjoy himself, by all means, tonight. But I was here for work. With the camera rolling, I was breaking the rules, and I couldn't afford to be inebriated in any way.

We followed the two bouncers toward another door. This one was roped with the glowing *VIP* letters attached to the rope.

"Here." I discreetly traded the glasses with Omkar as soon as his was empty. "Have this, I'm not thirsty."

He didn't argue, immediately taking a huge drink from my glass.

"Good evening, my darlings," a melodious feminine voice thrilled from inside the room.

The bouncers removed the rope and a tall beautiful woman invited us to enter.

The room was lavishly decorated with colorful rugs and soft, multi-colored lights. A large round object stood in the middle, covered by silver silk. But it was the woman who attracted my attention the most.

Dressed in a long red garment of an unusual cut, her fiery red hair coiffed into a voluminous up-do with a long, elaborate braid draped over her shoulder, she appeared like a vision of fire and beauty.

"Welcome," she cooed. "My name is Madame Tan. I'm so happy you joined us." She gestured at the long table set next to the large, silk-covered object. Seven people sat in the chairs on one side of the table, the glasses in front of them shimmered pink and blue in the dim lighting of the room.

The long sleeves of Madame's dress draped all the way to the floor, with the cut-out slits for her hands. Leaving her shoulders exposed, the robe cascaded in soft silk faults down her hips and legs, streaming in a wide train behind her as she moved. The gold-embroidered ends of the wide, black sash tied around her waist draped down her skirt at the back.

"Please enjoy the refreshments." She pointedly paused her gaze on the half-full glass in Omkar's hand, and he hurriedly gulped down the rest of the liquid.

We took our seats at the end of the table. One of the bouncers appeared, with a pitcher to refill our glasses. Another one came, bringing out a tray with small round dishes. He placed a dish in front of each of us.

"That's great!" Omkar happily popped the appetizingly looking roll from the dish into his mouth.

The middle-aged Asian lady on his right gave him a smile.

"Simply delightful," she said in a slightly accented English, daintily lifting the roll between her fingers and taking a small bite. "Truly out of this world."

Their eager praise felt a bit off to my ear. Their giddy expressions didn't seem natural. I decided to leave my food on the plate, no matter how "delightful" they claimed it was.

Madame Tan slid her gaze along the table, pausing it on my glass. I lifted it in my hand as if ready to take a sip.

"This is...um, delightful cocktail," I gushed, trying to imitate Omkar's enthusiasm. "What's in it?"

A wide smile spread on Madame Tan's beautiful face, her dark eyes narrowed with cunning glee.

"Magic," she purred.

"Oh, I can't wait to see what's behind the curtain!" The lady next to Omkar clapped her hands, like an excited little girl at a carnival.

Madame glanced back at the silk-covered object, and I quickly traded my plate with Omkar. He eagerly swiped the roll off the plate and shoved it in his mouth.

Whatever was in the food and drink Madame had been serving made him happy. I knew for a fact spectators of Madame's show didn't get sick or died from it. If anything, Omkar would have double-good time tonight. While I had work to do.

I straightened my back, sticking out my breasts, to give the camera in my pocket the best angle as it kept rolling.

Madame dramatically waved her hand in the air. Three red spotlights fell on the silk, merging into one—crimson bright.

"Ladies and gentlemen! One show only! Behold, the most amazing transformation never before seen by a human eye."

I had to give it to her, she was a true show woman, not stingy on dramatics.

The silk flew away as if with a blast of wind, revealing a huge, spherical cage. I'd seen this type before at fairs and carnivals. It was about fifteen to seventeen feet in diameter. Usually, there was a motorbike inside, and someone would ride it in circles up and down inside the cage.

The bars of this cage, however were too thick and too far apart for a bike. There wasn't one inside the cage, either. Instead, a man stood in the middle of it.

Tall and muscular, he had the identical tattoo to the bouncer who'd greeted us. Unlike the bouncer, he sported a full beard and was completely naked.

I blinked, unsure what to think. The man certainly was a sight to behold. He wasn't just well-built, he seemed like he worked hard on it, too, probably spending his days and nights in the gym and living on a steady diet of protein shakes and steroids. Was the "amazing" show supposed to be all about nudity, to show off his hard work?

He didn't appear to be here for the attention, though. In fact, he didn't appear to want to be here at all.

Ominous music flowed from the speakers somewhere. Trepidation scraped unpleasantly inside my chest at the sinister sound.

"Allow me to introduce the species I created myself—the rage shifter. A fine specimen, isn't he?" Madame cooed, sauntering in front of the cage. "I'm proud of my creation, rightfully so. Look at him. Handsome, strong, immortal, but most importantly..." she slid a finger up one of the bars, leveling the man inside a glare with so much hatred it made my skin crawl with dread.

Could a person be proud of someone and hate them this much?

"Most importantly, my rage shifters are *loyal* to a fault. They were designed with one purpose—to serve me. Sadly, no design is without its flows. This one is what you would call 'an older model.' She sneered, lifting a corner of her mouth to display a perfect white canine.

The man inside the cage stared straight ahead over our heads, either not seeing us or purposely trying to ignore us. He appeared calm, but when I looked closely, I noticed that his chest rose and fell rapidly, his hands were fisted at his sides, and the bulky muscles in his arms twitched flexing. Did he know what was about to happen? Did he dread it, too?

"Normally," Madame Tan continued. "I don't let my darlings reach the level of rage that would trigger their transformation. But this one needs to be punished. Lucky for you, you're the only people on Earth who get to see my creation in all his glory."

She raised her hand, directing the palm to the man in the cage.

His strong features crumbled in a grimace of pain as red sparks ran up the tattoo lines on his arm to his neck. Yet he made no sound. The sparks merged into streaks, lighting up the intricate design of his body art.

He threw his head back, baring his teeth, which started to grow, canines lengthening into fangs. His entire body expanded, bulging out of proportions.

The people at the table gasped in awe.

The lines of the man's tattoo swelled and rose like fresh burn scars, changing the colour from black to inflamed red. The man finally released a sound—a blood-curdling roar of agony and rage. His body shook. Much taller and larger than an average to begin with, he grew two or three times his size. The cage was not tall enough for him anymore. He had to curl his shoulders in and drop his head down to fit inside it.

In addition to the dramatic change in size, his proportions changed, too. His neck grew so thick, it nearly merged with his hulking shoulders. His arms stretched longer as his torso got wider. His beard disappeared, the bald head flattening and widening. The veins on his arms and chest bulged, throbbing along with his tattoo, which now looked like one raw inflamed wound.

The sight of him was monstrous and grotesque, no longer resembling a man at all.

He roared again, throwing himself against the cage with so much force, I thought it would break the chains and wrench it off the platform. Snapping tight, the chains held, however, keeping the cage in place.

Madame laughed. The sound was sweet and melodious, like the thrill of silver bells, and I truly hated her at that moment.

"And that's why I call them the rage shifters," she cooed. "You can literally watch his temper grow. Isn't he magnificent?"

The people at the table murmured in agreement. Their expressions were those of delight and awe, with none of my concern for the tortured man. They certainly seemed like they were getting their money's worth in entertainment.

Omkar winked at me.

"Not something you'd see every day, right?" he said with a happy smile.

"Right..." I moved my gaze from him back to the cage.

The scarlet spotlights slid down the man's naked body, making it look like streams of blood. He growled twisting his torso in obvious pain. His mangled arm dangled at his side, the wounds on it pulsing with light. The wound on his neck seemed just as bad. He avoided moving his head, probably as not to aggravate the pain. But it appeared his massive erection tortured him the most. Engorged, it turned bluish in colour, pulsing and bobbing in the air while pointing straight up. He hovered his hand over it, his fingers curled and rigid like claws, yet he wouldn't touch it.

"Turn around, sweetie," Madame ordered. "Let us see more of you."

With a wave of her hand, he jerked as if punched in the tattooed shoulder, pivoting on his heel. His back came into view, covered in long red slashes crusted over with dried blood. These must've been inflicted earlier.

What had been done to this man? And for how long had he been enduring the torture?

The deafening roar of pain ripped from his throat. He clawed at his neck with both hands, tearing at his mangled flesh, as if trying to rip the tattoo off his skin.

"Is he okay?" the lady next to Omkar inquired.

I whipped my head in her direction. Did she share my horror at seeing this?

"Oh no, he isn't okay at all, far from it" Madame said in a sing-song voice.

The lady giggled, as if she'd just heart a witty joke.

"Will he turn back?" someone else asked. The question was filled with curiosity, but not the outrage that I felt.

"Maybe," Madame replied with a lazy smile. "When and if I feel like it."

While the man twisted and rolled in agony inside the cage, Madame spoke, "His name is Radax. He is my first creation. And despite his many misdemeanours, I still have a soft spot for him. Sometimes I think he keeps misbehaving because he craves the extra attention from me, like a petulant child. I have so many children, and they all vie for my attention. Well, here you go, Radax, sweetie. This night is all about you. Time to shine!"

She flicked her fingers and Radax's tattoo wounds on his arm and neck caught on fire. His roars of pain twisted my insides, bringing bile to my throat.

"Wow! How did she do it?" Omkar gasped in awe.

His distorted perception of the "show" made the anger flare high inside me, but it wasn't directed at Omkar. I saw him as just another victim of Madame's tricks. Obviously, his feelings and reactions were no longer his own. The Omkar I knew wouldn't delight in the suffering of another being.

Madame spun back to face her audience, and our gazes crossed. I couldn't fake the delightful indifference of the others. I couldn't even muster a neutral expression fast enough. She saw it all—my horror and compassion for the tortured man in the cage. And my severe dislike of her.

Her eyes flicked to my still-very-full glass. The cheerful mask of lighthearted fun slipped off her face, revealing a smirk.

"I see you aren't thirsty," she prowled my way, menacingly but with some eager anticipation, like a cat about to play with a mouse.

I shoved the glass aside. There was no point in pretending to drink it now. Someone had to do something to stop the suffering of the man in the cage. I didn't care what he'd done to deserve a punishment. This was not a way to treat a living being.

"Let him go," I said softly but firmly.

Fear dampened my anger. The cold menace in Madame's eyes promised nothing good, and I'd seen the level of cruelty she was capable of. But I had to say it, if only to put on the record that she'd been told—this was not okay.

"This is not entertainment. It's sick." I fisted my hands on the table, holding her glare.

She tilted her head.

"Sorry, you don't see it my way. *Our* way." She gestured at the rest of the spectators at the table. All of them were watching us with the same excited anticipation as they'd watched her torment Radax—as if I was the second act of the show.

Madam came flash with the table, opposite to my seat. Every muscle in my body flexed under her stare, getting ready for me to run, but I forced myself to remain seated. I wasn't some "creation" of hers. I was a free human being. I had rights. She wouldn't dare...

"Bring her over here." She gestured to the two bouncers by the entrance.

"No!" I sprang to my feet and dashed for the exit.

Ducking, I tried to evade the hands of the bouncers reaching for me. Surprisingly agile for his size, one of them lunched for me, quickly catching me around my middle.

"The show is over, ladies and gentlemen," Madame cooed in her saccharine-sweet voice she reserved for the public. "Thank you for coming, everyone. Nerkan will escort you to the exit, now."

She ushered everyone from the table to the door where another burly, tattooed man led them out.

"Omkar!" I yelled in desperation, struggling against the hold of the bouncer.

The serene expression on my friend's face wavered. His brows twitched, moving closer together.

"This way, please." Madame stroked his cheek, bringing his attention to her and renewing his smile.

One by one, everybody left. Omkar did, too. Now, it was but the bouncer holding me, Madame, and the man rolling in pain in the cage.

"Are you local or a tourist?" Madame asked me sternly, any hint of the friendly sweetness was gone from her voice and expression.

"She is German, living in the United States," the bouncer said. "Visiting here for two weeks. Traveling alone."

When did he manage to get my background check done?

Madame nodded. "She doesn't really look German."

Despite my dire situation, I couldn't help an eyeroll.

"Half-Chinese," the bouncer explained.

"I'm well-known in this country," I bit back. It wasn't entirely a lie. Some of my followers did come from Singapore. "If any harm comes to me—"

Madame waved her hand, her expression growing bored.

"You know what, it really doesn't matter who you are or where you come from. No one can stop me from doing whatever I want with you."

"There'd be consequences." I made an effort to sound strong and threatening.

"None of which I couldn't deal with." She shrugged, glancing back at the cage. "You want me to let Radax go? That'd do more harm than good with him in this state. He needs to be calmed down to shift back before I can release him. The only way to calm a raging *brack* is sex." She settled her heavy stare on me. "I am the only one in this world who can fuck a rage shifter in this form and stay alive. For me, sex with a *brack* gone berserk is fun. For someone like you..."

A playful smile curved her lips, and a spark of amusement flashed in her kohl-black eyes.

Her pause was pregnant with meaning that filled me with dread, cold and heavy like lead.

"What? No..." I stared at her, my dread turning to pure horror at the realization of what she implied.

"Did you feel sorry for the poor Radax over there?" Madame formed her full, cherry-red lips into a pout. "Then why don't *you* help him instead of me? You see that cock?" She jerked her head at the man's raging erection the size of my freaking thigh, and murmured, "I love riding it. But what do you think will happen to you when he shoves it in you? Do you think you can take it?" She laughed, the beautiful sound sent a spear of panic through me.

"No...please," I begged, clawing at the burly arm that held me as tight as a vise.

She smirked and tossed the order to the man holding me.

"Throw her in the cage!"

Power of Rage is coming Fall 2021
To follow the updates, please subscribe to the author's newsletter
here:

More by Marina Simcoe

PARANORMAL and FANTASY
ROMANCE

Madame Tan's Freakshow Trilogy
Call of Water
Madness of the Moon
Power of Rage

Demons, Complete Series
Demon Mine
The Forgotten
Grand Master
The Last Unforgiven - Cursed
The Last Unforgiven - Freed

Stand Alone Novels
The Real Thing
To Love A Monster

Midnight Coven Author Group
Wicked Warlock (Cursed Coven)

More by Marina Simcoe

SCIENCE-FICTION ROMANCE

Dark Anomaly Trilogy
Gravity
Power
Explosion

Stand Alone Novels
Experiment
Enduring (Valos Of Sonhadra)

My Holiday Tails
Married to Krampus
My Tiny Giant

About the Author

MARINA SIMCOE LIKES to write love stories with human heroines and non-human heroes who just can't live without them. She firmly believes that our contemporary world could always use a little bit of the extraordinary.

She has lots of fun exploring how her out-of-this-world characters with their own beliefs, values, and aspirations fit into our everyday life.

She lives in Canada with her very own extraordinary hero, their three little cubs, and a cat who is definitely out of this world.

Please Stay in Touch

Newsletter signup: http://eepurl.com/c__RGn
Facebook Readers' Group:
Marina's Reading Cave
www.instagram.com/marinasimcoeauthor
www.marinasimcoe.com
www.facebook.com/MarinaSimcoeAuthor/
www.amazon.com/author/marinasimcoe
www.bookbub.com/profile/marina-simcoe
www.goodreads.com/MarinaSimcoe

Made in the USA
Columbia, SC
17 May 2021